ISLE of MAN

Book Two of The Park Service Trilogy

By Ryan Winfield

D1444508

Isle of Man
Book Two of The Park Service Trilogy
By Ryan Winfield

ISBN-13: 978-0-9883482-3-3
ISBN-10: 0988348233

Summary: After learning the horrific truth behind the Park Service and
overthrowing its leader, fifteen-year-old Aubrey Van Houten sets out with
his best friend Jimmy and his girlfriend Hannah on a quest to take control
of the drones and free his people from Holocene II.

Printed in the United States of America.

BIRCH PAPER PRESS
Post Office Box 4252
Seattle, Washington 98194

Also by **Ryan Winfield**

The Park Service
Book One of The Park Service Trilogy

State of Nature
Book Three of The Park Service Trilogy

South of Bixby Bridge

Jane's Melody: A Novel

For Smudgeface
Because you were never alone

ISLE OF MAN

Book Two of The Park Service Trilogy

Part One

CHAPTER I
Picking up the Pieces

I never meant to kill Hannah's family.

Or Jimmy's either. And although I didn't kill them myself, at least not directly, I can't help but think that if I'd never left Holocene II, they'd still be alive.

I'm standing on the bluff looking down on Hannah as she picks through what's left of her childhood home. It isn't much. I watch her run a hand along the jagged stones that outline the remains of the foundation. She turns toward the water, pressing her palms against the air, as if miming where the living room window had been, the window where her mother would sit and watch the lake from the family rocking chair.

Farther out, along the debris-littered shore, I can just make out Jimmy walking the beach in front of Gloria's bungalow. Or what was Gloria's bungalow before the wave came and dragged it out into the lake. Jimmy's head is bent in mourning. Junior, his fox pup, trails at his heels.

I have no idea where any of us go from here.

By the time I climb down off the bluff, Hannah is standing in the exposed, flooded basement, looking like some exotic red-topped flower with her green dress floating around her waist. She's lost in her thoughts and doesn't even notice me wading toward her until I wrap my arms around her from behind.

"I'm sorry, Hannah."

She leans into me and sighs. "You did the right thing."

I'm tempted to tell her that it wasn't me. That I couldn't do it. That her mother had been awake, and that she came down and triggered the wave herself, then saved me by locking me away in the safe room. But if I tell her, she'll know that her mother let the wave take her—that she committed suicide. I won't risk spoiling Hannah's memory of her mother.

Hannah moves through the water toward the open door of the safe room. I slosh after her and watch as she peers inside, searching the shadows of the room. Her eyes land on the open safe where her father kept the vials of longevity serum, the genetic elixir that would grant us each a thousand years of life. She sees that it's empty and frowns. I reach in my pocket and pull out the case of loaded syringes, and Hannah smiles for the first time since seeing that I was alive yesterday. She grabs the clear-plastic case of syringes and holds it up to the light.

"Oh, Aubrey!" she exclaims. "You've saved us!" Her voice sounds like an angelic harmony, echoing off the water.

"You sure you wanna do it?"

"Of course," she says, as if there should be no doubt about it at all. "Why wouldn't we?"

"I don't know. Your mom seemed to have some regrets."

"She was sick."

"What happens when we get sick?"

"I would have fixed it for her if I'd had more time."

"But she had lots of time, Hannah, and she couldn't fix it. And you're just sixteen."

Hannah waves the syringes at me and says, "Yes, but my mother taught me well. Plus, I only have to pick up where she left off. Science is a relay race, Aubrey, not a marathon."

"Even so. What will we do with a thousand years?"

"Everything," she says, leaning in to brush her lips against mine. "And why settle for a thousand? That's just the start."

"Just the start?"

"Sure," she says. "There are three doses here. One for you, one for me, and one left over to study. We can recover the lab at the Foundation and with as much time as we'll have, I'll find a way to extend our lives longer. Let's live forever, Aubrey."

"But that third dose has to be for Jimmy."

"Jimmy?" she asks, sounding disappointed.

"Yeah, Jimmy."

"Of course, you're right," she says, frowning and handing me back the syringes. "I'm sorry."

"Did someone say my name?"

I look back and see Jimmy standing on the steps, holding a stick strung with fish. Junior is crouched at his feet, lapping water from the flooded basement.

We gather wood to the edge of the lake and Jimmy strikes a fire lit. He wraps the gutted trout in strips of green bark and buries them in a shallow trench beside the fire. Then we wait, sitting in a semi-circle looking at the lake, and listening to the popping wood as Jimmy uses a stick to push coals over the fish. It's only late morning, but clouds have descended like theatre props in windless skies, bringing an evening gray and the bite of winter's cold with them.

"I figured the lake would be too stirred up yet to fish," I say, feeling the need to break our long silence.

"Junior caught 'em," Jimmy says.

I look over at Junior, gnawing on a fish head. "Junior?"

Jimmy nods. "He found 'em anyways. They's swimming circles in a puddle back there left by the wave. Easiest fishin' I ever done."

Hannah tosses a pebble into the water, shaking her head and huffing. "You could have set them free."

"Fat chance," Jimmy says, uncovering the steaming bark with his stick. "I dun' plan on starvin'."

"Just try some, Hannah," I plead with her. "Please. You need to eat. We all need to eat."

"I'll eat the bark before I'll eat the fish."

Jimmy holds out a blackened strip of tree bark to Hannah, and she turns away. Jimmy winks at me and reaches into his pouch, producing a collection of nuts and roots, leafy greens, and a few mushrooms. He drops them in Hannah's lap.

"What's this?" she asks, surprised.

"Pro'lly won't taste none too good," Jimmy says, "but it'll keep ya goin' for now."

Hannah picks up a mushroom and smells it, eyeing Jimmy. She bites a corner and chews. Her face goes red, and her eyes bulge as she drops the mushroom and clutches at her throat.

I leap to my feet. "Hannah!"

She bursts out laughing, and so does Jimmy.

"Ha ha," I mutter, sitting back down. "Real cute."

A moment ago I was worried about upsetting Hannah by eating fish, but after that performance I grab a plank and dig in with Jimmy. We finish eating and lean back on our elbows and watch the glowing coals, passing Jimmy's canteen back and forth. The lake is still as glass. I steal glances at Hannah as she stares across the water, lost in thought, as if she's seeing some scene play out on its mirror surface. Soon, her eyes well up.

Then, almost to herself, she says: "It's just so strange. One minute they're here, the next they're gone."

"I'm so sorry, Hannah."

"I know you are," she says. "But you lost your dad, too. And I'm sorry for that." Then after a pause she says: "Jimmy?"

"Yeah."

"I'm sorry about your family also."

Jimmy nods, looking down and petting Junior.

"Where do you suppose they go?" I ask, addressing no one in particular. "When they die."

"Nowhere," Hannah says.

Jimmy shrugs. "I 'spose we'll find out when it's our turn."

His comment reminds me about the serum. I reach in my pocket and hand Jimmy the case of syringes. He inspects them.

"Might make a good sewing needle," he says. "But what's it really for?"

I tap the case. "It's a syringe. To inject the serum."

"Inject what?"

"To put that red stuff in your arm."

"Yeah, but what for?"

"Well, it's kind of hard to explain."

"I ain't stupid."

"I know it," I say, nudging him with my elbow. "I'm just trying to figure out how to explain it."

Hannah clears her throat. "It's a longevity serum, Jimmy. It tells your body how to outsmart its aging process. It means you'll live for a very, very long time."

"Am I dyin' or somethin'?" he asks.

"Well," Hannah laughs, "we're all dying. It's just a matter of how fast, really."

"What she means," I interject, "is that if we take the serum now, instead of dying at, say 60, or 70, or even 90, we could live to be 900 or even 1,000 years old."

"Who'd wanna do that?" Jimmy asks.

"Well, I don't know," I say. "Who wouldn't? Hannah and I want to. And you should too."

"Why?"

"Why not?"

"Why not ain't a reason."

"Don't you like life, Jimmy?" Hannah asks.

"There's times I do," he says.

"Well, don't you want to experience as much of life as you can then? Don't you want to keep from getting old and tired?"

Jimmy thinks about it for a moment, then he says, "Guess I jus' want the normal amount of life. Same as ever-body."

"Then what?" Hannah asks.

"Then whatever."

"Then you die."

"Sure," he says.

"You're not afraid to die?" I ask.

Jimmy looks at me and cocks his head, as if he's just now considering his future death for the first time. "Seems to me I was dead before I was born, and that wasn't no trouble."

"But you believe in something after?" I ask. "Don't you?"

"After?"

"You know—after you die?"

"I dunno. Sure. I guess. There must be somethin'."

"What if you're wrong?" Hannah jumps in.

"Then I guess that'd be jus' fine too."

Hannah rolls her eyes. "You're impossible. Let's just do ours, Aubrey. Jimmy can change his mind later if he wants."

I look from Hannah to Jimmy, then to the case of syringes

in my hand. "No," I shake my head. "It's all of us or nothing."

"That's not fair, Aubrey!"

I stuff the case of syringes back in my pocket. "Let's talk about it later then."

"And what if it doesn't keep?" Hannah asks.

"It'll keep," I answer.

"Might not."

"If it doesn't, it doesn't."

"Oh, that's brilliant," she says, sarcastically.

Not wanting to argue, I leave the fire and walk to the edge of the lake and rinse my hands in the water. When I stand up again, I see something dark floating in the distance—a hump cutting above the water like a rock.

"Can you guys see that?" I ask.

"See what?"

"Out there. On the water."

Jimmy appears at my elbow. "Yeah, I seen it earlier," he says. "But it's closer now."

"Are you thinking what I'm thinking?"

"I dunno," he says. "Hard to believe it survived the wave."

"Only one way to be sure," I say, unbuttoning my shirt.

Jimmy smiles and peels off his clothes, too.

I step out of my pants and toss them with my shirt in a pile next to Hannah. "You coming?"

She shakes her head. "I'll watch. Be careful."

Jimmy and I rush into the cold water and dive in. It feels just like old times swimming beside Jimmy. Feeling competitive with Hannah watching, I kick up my speed and pull ahead. But Jimmy easily catches up and smirks at me. I take a deep breath and drop my head and give it all I have, racing through the cold water, my strokes strong, my kicks quick. When I come up for air, Jimmy is five body lengths ahead of me, treading water and laughing. I remember him teaching me to swim in the cove, and how patient he was with me then. I can't help but grin as I paddle toward him. We look back. Our little race brought us farther out than I thought, and Hannah is just a speck on the beach now, the fire sparking up as she adds wood.

"Think we're almost there?" I ask.

Jimmy kicks himself out of the water like a dancing seal, trying to get a view. "Not far now."

Another few minutes breast stroking, and the black hump rises in the still water before us. Jimmy touches it first, stopping and smiling back at me, his hot breath steaming.

"Damn if it ain't afloat," he says.

"Maybe we can tow it back and right it."

"You pull, I'll push," Jimmy says, before disappearing to the other side.

It's slow progress swimming the turtled boat in. I keep a decent grip on a bow edge and kick wildly and paddle with my free arm, but the beach seems a long way off. I can see the fire, its light periodically interrupted by Junior's shadow as he paces the shore, waiting for us to return.

"Keep her pointed true," Jimmy calls from the other side.

I remember seeing this carbon-fiber boat for the first time when I snuck into Dr. Radcliffe's boathouse on my way to visit my dad at Eden. Hard to believe it was only a few days ago now—the day he died, my dad. A horror grips me when I think about it, so I push the thought away. It's too late for my dad, but this boat might just hold the key to setting my people free. It drives me mad to think of them working away five kilometers underground and not knowing the world is up here, waiting. That they could be breathing fresh air, gazing at the actual stars. Maybe after I free them they'll call me a hero or something, and I can give the credit to my dad.

The boat scrapes on gravel when we hit shallow water. After catching our breath, Jimmy and I each take a side and get our feet on the bottom. We rock the boat, seesawing it back and forth, trying to right it. As momentum builds, we work our way toward the bow to stay clear of the enclosed cabin. Just as the boat rocks onto its side, with me stretched tall and pushing, Jimmy leaps and grabs the upper wall, hanging for a moment with only his feet left in the water; then the boat flips over on top of him, throwing me back toward shore. Jimmy comes up coughing, takes my offered hand, and we stand in waist deep water and look at the righted boat.

"Good work," Jimmy says.

"We're just lucky the cockpit's sealed," I say. "Otherwise it never would have flipped."

The lake is dead calm, the ripples created by our efforts rushing in arcs away from the boat to be swallowed in the still water. We drag the boat several feet onto the shore, then we scamper up to the fire to get warm. Hannah sits where we left her with her arms wrapped around her knees and her head down. Before I can ask her what's wrong, I hear Jimmy ask, "What the hell happened here?"

I turn to see Jimmy holding his canteen by its neck and inspecting its underside. The canteen is blackened by fire and Jimmy's hand is smeared with charcoal where he picked it up.

"Must've rolled in the fire," I suggest.

"I used it to boil water," Hannah says, behind me.

"Shit," Jimmy says. "There's better ways to do it than burnin' up my canteen."

"Why'd you boil water?" I ask her.

Hannah doesn't look up. Her hands are still wrapping her knees, her red hair spilling over her arms. Something's wrong.

"Why did you boil water, Hannah?"

Without lifting her head, she holds out her right arm for us to see. Her freckled skin is pale, and the bruise in the crook of her arm is impossible to miss.

I stride to my clothes pile beside Hannah and fish the case of syringes from my pants pocket. Sure enough, there are two syringes filled with serum and one empty. "How could you?"

"I'm sorry," she says.

"No, you're not!"

"Well, one was mine anyway."

"We agreed to wait."

"No, you said we'd wait. I didn't agree."

"I can't believe you, Hannah."

"I said I'm sorry," she says, again. Then her eyes harden, and she juts her chin at me. "Besides, I could claim them all if I wanted to. Since you took them from my father's safe."

I stand there shivering, and I can't tell if it's because I'm half naked and wet, or because I'm furious with her. I don't know what to feel. I'm tempted to tell her that I didn't take them. That her mother gave them to me just before she killed herself because she couldn't live another day after the same serum tortured her for almost a thousand years. But as mad as I am, I won't use her mother's memory against her. I just won't. I storm off with my clothes to dry and dress in private.

We spend the afternoon working separately. Jimmy heads

off to hunt up some food. Hannah collects wood for the fire. I climb the bluff and break pine branches and build a lean-to shelter in the exposed root cavity of a tree stripped from the ground by the wave. It's a perfect spot, halfway up the slope, protected from the wind, where we can look down and keep the beached boat in sight.

Just as I'm weaving in the last branch, I hear Hannah drop another armload of wood behind me. A minute later, she sighs, letting me know she's still standing there, waiting for me to say something. I keep my back turned and pretend to be working.

"Shelter looks good," she finally says.

I feign dissatisfaction with the last branch and pull it free and begin weaving it in again.

"You could say something," she says, "couldn't you?"

"I don't feel like it right now."

"Will you be mad forever?"

I turn around to face her. "You betrayed me, Hannah."

"Well, that's a little dramatic," she says.

"Really?" I ask, offended that she's putting this off on me. "You can't just go around doing whatever you want, you know. Maybe you could while you were spoiled here at the house, but you don't know anything about surviving out in the real world."

"And you do?" she asks.

"I know we have to trust one another."

"Like you and Jimmy do?"

"Is that what this is about? You're jealous of Jimmy?"

"Maybe," she says.

"Why?"

She steps up next to me and picks idly at the lean-to roof. "I don't know," she says, cutely.

13

"Why, Hannah?"

"Maybe because you wouldn't commit to spending forever with me unless Jimmy took the serum, too."

"Jimmy's my best friend."

"Shouldn't I be your best friend?"

The look of sadness on her face melts my anger, and I reach over and lift her chin. "Look at me. You need to listen. I'm not going to fight with you about Jimmy all the time. You got that? You need to ease up on him already. Okay? We've been through some tough stuff together, that's all."

She nods. "Can you forgive me?"

"Can you stop being a brat?"

"If you'll forgive me."

"Maybe you can talk to Jimmy?"

"About what?" she asks.

"Convince him to take the serum."

"Would you forgive me then?"

"Maybe."

She lifts an eyebrow and bites her lip.

"Yes, I'd forgive you then."

She smiles. Then she throws her arms around me and hugs her head to my chest. "Have I told you you're the best boy in the whole world, Aubrey Van Houten?"

"I'm not a boy," I say. "I'm almost sixteen."

"Well, you're the best man in the world then."

I laugh. "Compared to all the other men out here?"

"I'd have chosen you if there were a million men."

As evening falls we build a fire just outside the lean-to. Hannah managed to collect a surprising amount of wood, and even Jimmy is impressed with her. We sit inside and watch the sky go dark beyond the fire, eating a light dinner of more fish for us and more foraged plants and mushrooms for Hannah.

"I'd give anything for some algaecrisps right now," I say.

Hannah must be thinking the same thing, because I see her eyeing our fish as she gnaws on yet another root. I hold a hunk of pink trout meat out to her. She shakes her head.

"Come on," I say. "Just a taste."

"I don't like killing things."

"It's already dead whether you taste it or not."

To my surprise, she plucks the fish from my palm. Jimmy's eyes widen, his curiosity pricked. Hannah brings the fish to her nose and smells it. Then she bites off a tiny piece and quickly chews it with her eyes closed. I see her swallow, then she sticks out her tongue and shakes her head. "Ahk! No thanks."

Jimmy and I laugh. Hannah holds the rest of her uneaten fish out to Junior, and he rises from beside the fire, walks over, and scarfs it down, then licks her fingers. She pulls him onto her lap and pets him, his tired eyes closing with each stroke then opening again. Jimmy pulls around his netted sack and dumps out a pile of enormous pine cones that he collected. He begins plucking nuts from their spikey bodies and cracking them open between two stones. He eats a pine nut then hands one to me. Then he eats another pine nut and hands one to Hannah. The fire crackles, Junior's eyes open and close as Hannah pets him, and the quiet night is punctuated by the methodical cracking as Jimmy pounds open the pine nuts.

"Hey, wait a minute," I say, coming out of a near trance. "You're doing sneaky middles."

Jimmy looks confused. "Sneaky what?"

"Sneaky middles."

"I dunno what yer talkin' about," he says, cracking open another pine nut.

"Yes, you do. You eat one then you give me one. Then you eat another, and you give Hannah one. Then you eat one again. You're getting two nuts for every one nut we get."

Jimmy laughs and pops a nut in his mouth. "You wanna crack 'em then?"

I shake my head and smile. I catch Hannah's eye and nod, signaling that now's a good time for her talk. Then I palm her the case of syringes and scoot toward the door.

"Where ya goin'?" Jimmy asks, holding out a nut.

"I'm full," I say, waving it away. "I'm gonna go down and check on the boat."

Jimmy starts to rise. "I'll go with ya."

"No, you stay. I want to be alone for a bit."

Jimmy turns back to his pine cones and lets me leave.

The boat is just a dark silhouette now against the near black sky, and a gentle breeze drives small waves to lap against its side. I can hear Jimmy in the distance clacking his rocks together, splitting the pine nuts. I hope Hannah knows what to say. I sit on the edge of the small peninsula, where the grass used to be before the wave came, and look past the boat to the dark shadow of the dam far on the other side of the lake.

It's strange to think of those scientists entombed in the flooded Foundation beneath the dam. I try to picture it. The closed locks. Water to the ceiling. The sealed train tunnel gates. Then I think about those subterranean tracks leading south, where my people work away right now as I sit here, nearly five kilometers underground and still in absolute ignorance of what really lies above their heads. It's hard to imagine just how much

I didn't know. I wonder how much I still don't.

I reach into my pocket and pull out my father's pipe. I've got some of his tobacco left, but I don't feel like smoking it tonight. Instead, I just sit in the dark and feel the weight of the stone pipe in my hand, smelling the cool pine breeze and listening to Jimmy's clacking stones as I try to remember my father's face. It's harder to do than you might think. Mostly, I see his hands—strong and veiny, the fingers wrapped around his work reader, or maybe, on Sundays, wrapped around the bowl of his pipe. This pipe. My pipe.

I wonder where it is we do go when we leave this world, or if Hannah's right about there being nothing. Growing up, we were taught that we'd be together forever in Eden, so I guess I never gave any other afterlife much thought. I'd like to believe I'll be reunited with my dad some faraway day. My mom, too.

Even so, I hope Jimmy decides to take the serum, because although I'm curious about what waits for me on the other side of this life, I'm in absolutely no rush to find out.

CHAPTER 2
A Flood of Surprises

The lake is quiet when I wake.

The cold air smells of coming snow.

I sit up and swirl in empty space under a starless sky that gives no light. I can't seem to get my bearings until I spot the orange glow of the distant burned down fire on the bluff. I feel around in the dark and find my father's pipe and stuff it in my pocket before heading up to the shelter.

The fire is mostly embers, one small flame fighting to stay alive atop the heap of glowing coals. Inside, Jimmy is curled on his side, sleeping, with his arm around Junior, also asleep. I think Hannah must be sleeping too, until she opens her eyes and lifts her finger to her lips, signaling for me to be quiet as I duck inside and scoot next to her and sit down.

"How'd it go?" I whisper.

Hannah grins and holds up an empty syringe. Relief surges through me. The idea of living a long time without Jimmy was just too much to bear, but so was the thought of dying decades sooner than I had to. It's funny to think that when I was a kid down in Holocene II, thirty-five seemed impossibly old. Now ninety seems to be a cruelly short life. I guess it's silly to think anything could ever outgrow our rising expectations, even life expectancy.

Producing the remaining unused syringe, Hannah signals for me to roll up my sleeve. It occurs to me that it's her father's shirt I'm wearing, which seems fitting in some strange way. She clamps the syringe in her teeth and grabs Jimmy's canteen and pours water into a small circular impression dug in the dirt and lined with rawhide. Then she grabs a stick and rolls a hot rock forth from the coals, guiding it to the hole. Steam erupts as the rock rolls into the water. She tears a small piece of cloth from the hemline of her dress, dips the cloth into the boiling water, and pulls it out steaming into the air.

"Did Jimmy teach you that?" I ask, trying to be quiet.

"Shh . . .," she says, nodding.

She cleans the inside of my left arm with the hot cloth, scrubbing until my skin is red. Then she removes the thin sash from the waist of her dress and wraps it around my upper arm, looping it once before pulling it tight. I watch as the veins in my arm swell. Removing the syringe from her teeth, she uncaps it and holds it up, depressing the plunger until just a tiny drop of serum appears on the needle's tip. It looks like a drop of black oil in the low light of the coals. Then she turns to me and smiles, waiting for my approval.

I look from the syringe in her hand to the veins snaking down my arm. What is it that runs through them anyway? It seems strange to pump something inside of me, some foreign thing born in a lab long before I was born. My dad used to say nothing comes free without a price following along later. And usually a heavy one. I wonder what he'd say about the serum? I remember Mr. Zales drawing my blood sample the night before my test. I remember sitting at our kitchen table and talking with my dad about his pipe and about our ancestors, with whom he couldn't wait to be reunited in Eden. But Eden was just a lie. A fairytale told to keep us trapped underground, slaving away until we walked willingly up to our slaughter. We were the ignorant working at the hands of the wise. And what separated us below from those like Radcliffe here above, even more than the five kilometers of bedrock over our heads, was the knowledge that comes with age. They never let any of us get old enough to question things. They killed us when we turned 35. I don't know what my dad would say about the serum, but I do know that it's time for me to become a man.

I nod, and Hannah thrusts the needle into my vein. She holds it steady and depresses the plunger and the dark serum disappears into my arm. It's surprisingly painless.

Several hours later, I wake with Hannah in my arms. The fire is nothing but smoldering ash, and Jimmy is gone. Gray light filtering into the shelter announces the new day, and I ease myself away from Hannah, careful not to wake her, and scoot to the entrance and look down on the lake.

The boat is beached right where we left it, but there's no sign of Jimmy anywhere. I stand and stretch, stepping away from the shelter to piss. The morning air bites my cheeks, and my hot breath floats away from me in little clouds that hang in the stagnant air. An eagle screeches somewhere in the distance. I turn back and stir the coals and add some wood to the fire so Hannah won't be cold. Then I swig from the canteen and head down to the lake to inspect the boat.

It's a four-seat, enclosed cabin design, probably Radcliffe's backup boat for bad weather. The carbon-fiber skin looks like a solar-cell impregnated material we engineer down in Holocene II for highflying drones. Light and strong. I'm guessing the solar cells charge a liquid metal battery and that the battery runs an electric engine powering a jet drive. Other than a few dents, it looks to have weathered the wave with little damage.

I wade into the freezing water and am instantly awake. I manage to pop the cabin latches with no trouble, and the lid unseals and lifts easily on hydraulic hinges. I hoist myself up, slide into the cabin, and sink down into the pilot's chair. The instruments are simple—steering wheel, compass, speedometer, and a throttle lever. An LED battery indicator reads full. I press the start button, and jets hum to life. Then the boat violently rocks, and Jimmy is sitting next to me in the passenger seat.

"Let's see what she can do," he says, pulling the lid down and latching it.

"Where's Junior?"

"He's got a rabbit holed up, and he won't quit it. Stubborn little fella."

"Takes after you," I say, smiling.

I pull the throttle back and bang my head on the wheel as we jet backward off the beach. When I manage to neutral the throttle, we're floating fifty feet from shore. The engines make almost no sound. Jimmy nods, obviously impressed by the boat's power. Movement catches my eye, and I look through the windshield as Hannah appears on the hillside, her wild mane of red hair framing her sleepy face. She lifts a hand to us and then disappears again into the shelter.

I turn the wheel left and push the throttle forward, and the boat whips around, its nose lifting until all we can see through the windshield is gray sky. Then the water returns to our view as we plane level and take off like a rocket across the lake. The speed feels awesome. We cut through the glassy water like an arrow cuts through the air. And it sure feels much more like flying than traveling in a boat. When I glance over at Jimmy, he's grinning so big all I see are teeth.

Then I notice the dam across the lake, and I remember the giant monolith of stone crashing into the water and raising the wave that toppled Dr. Radcliffe's boat like a toy. My palms sweat on the wheel to think about it. I cut left, away from the dam, and cruise us toward the shoreline to survey the wave's damage. Everywhere we look the banks are stripped clean. And the closer to shore we get, trees and floating debris make our progress slow. It feels like some apocalyptic water tour.

When we finally get back to the peninsula, I slow the boat and run it onto the shore before killing the engines.

There's a moment of silence where I feel Jimmy staring at me. "Ya wanna go back down there, don't ya?" he asks.

"I do and I don't."

"I know what ya mean," he says.

"But I think we'll need to if I'm going to find a way to free my people."

"Well, ya can count me in."

"Thanks, Jimmy."

I look down and notice a handle beneath my seat. I pull it open, exposing a drawer filled with emergency supplies: food rations, thermal blankets, bottles of water. Jimmy opens the drawer beneath his seat and finds a first aid kit and a few flares, which he appears to be fascinated by. I grab the foil blankets and some food rations, and we head up toward the shelter.

Almost immediately we hear Hannah's scream and take off running. Jimmy is slowed some by his old thigh wound from the cove, and I actually outpace him up the hill. As I approach the shelter, I notice a trail of blood leading toward the door, and my heart jumps. I drop the supplies and clench my fists.

I see Hannah first, cowering in the back of the shelter with a look of horror on her face. Then I see Junior sitting in front of her with a dead rabbit hanging from his mouth. It takes several heart-pounding seconds for everything to sink in, then I laugh uncontrollably with relief. Jimmy races up beside me and looks in, and then he laughs, too.

"It isn't funny," Hannah says, looking as if she might cry.

"He's just showin' off his catch," Jimmy says, stepping in and rubbing Junior's ears and reassuring him he did good.

I turn back and collect my dropped supplies. Hannah's mood improves when I hand her the rations. She bites into a meal bar, spits the wrapper, and chews with her eyes closed, making little moaning sounds. Then she heads down to the lake with her breakfast—I'm guessing to freshen up. I collect more wood while Jimmy field-dresses the rabbit. Thirty minutes later, we're all sitting side by side at the edge of the bluff, looking over the lake with one of the foil blankets spread over our laps. I can feel the fire's warmth on my back and hear the hiss of sizzling rabbit juice as it drips into the flames behind us. None of us wants to say what we're thinking, but we're all looking across the lake at the dam.

"Think it's still flooded?" I ask, after a long silence.

"I dunno," Jimmy says, twisting around to turn the rabbit.

"You'd think the water would drain away pretty quickly," Hannah says. "At least I hope so."

"It sure would be nice to know, though," I say.

"You think there are bodies?" she asks.

"I'm sure," I reply. "Can't imagine where they'd go."

"If that's the case," Jimmy says, "we better be gettin' down there sooner than not. 'Fore they get too ripe."

"Gross," Hannah says, but then quickly adds, "although it sure would be nice to have supplies."

"And shelter," I say, reaching out and catching a single falling snowflake in my palm.

After a while, Hannah turns to me and asks, "What should we do about . . . well, you know?"

"Holocene II?"

"Yes," she says.

"We need to free them, of course."

"Have you thought it through?" she asks.

"Thought it through? What's to think through?"

"Well, how they'll react might be one example, " she says.

"I'm sure they'll be happy to be free."

She cocks an eyebrow at me. "Would you have been?"

Her question catches me off guard, and I stop to consider it. I don't know what I would have felt if we had suddenly been told that everything we thought was true was really lies and that the world had been up here all along. I mean, it was a huge shock for me, and I learned it the hard way—piece by piece, over an extended period of time.

I'm still thinking about Hannah's question when Jimmy says, "I vote for tomorrow mornin'."

"Tomorrow morning what?" I ask.

"Headin' over," he says. "I vote we go at first light."

Hannah tosses a twig off the bluff. "Works for me."

"Tomorrow morning it is then," I announce, glad to have finally decided on something. "Is that rabbit ready?"

"Jus' about."

Hannah scrunches up her face. "Hand me another bar."

By the time Hannah and I wake the next morning, Jimmy

is already up, tending the fire. He hands us each a makeshift bowl of hot tea, fashioned from the plastic upturned ends of the first aid kit that we found on the boat.

"Not bad," Hannah says, sampling her steaming tea.

I sip mine and taste the bite of pine. "Why pine needles?"

"Vitamin C," Jimmy says.

Outside the shelter, the lake sits like a steely gray abyss opened in a world of white. Everything surrounding the lake is covered with snow. The trees, the shoreline, the mountain peaks. The foundation of the old lake house has disappeared so beneath a thick blanket of white, I doubt even a trained archeologist would notice it had ever been inhabited at all. The boat rests on the shore, its roofline coated with snow. I notice Jimmy's tracks leading down and back and Junior's tracks crisscrossing his and heading off in every direction.

"Not a bad day to get out of here," I say.

"I used to love snow," Hannah sighs. She says it in almost a whisper, the bowl of tea forgotten in her hand. "My mom and I would sit in the living room and watch it come down out the window. 'Blowing like a banshee today,' she'd always say when it was a blizzard. Then she'd spend all afternoon fussing over her exotic plants. Covering them against a freeze."

"What about your dad?" I ask. "Did he like the snow?"

"He was always off working somewhere," she says. "And when he wasn't, he seemed to hardly notice what was going on around him. He'd rather read about the world than live in it."

Seeing the pain in her eyes, I lay my hand on her arm and say: "I'm sorry. I know how hard it is to lose your parents."

"I know you know," she says. "But you know what else? My dad really did turn into a monster. I couldn't believe he shot

Gloria like that. Oh! It makes me sick."

"Well, we've got a chance to make it right."

"I hope so," is all she says.

We stack the unburned wood in a far corner of the shelter, just in case we need to return, cover the fire with dirt, load up our few possessions, and head down together to the boat. The only sound as we leave is our cold breath and the crunch of our feet in the snow.

Jimmy scrambles onto the bow of the boat and clears the snow off the lid. Then he opens it and reaches down a hand for Hannah. I climb up next and sink into the pilot's seat. Jimmy puts his fingers in his mouth and whistles, loud and clear in the cold, quiet morning. Twenty seconds later, Junior bounds onto the bow of the boat, leaps into the rear seat next to Hannah, and shakes the entire cabin wet before lying his head on Hannah's lap. Jimmy and I laugh.

"Why are you so friendly when you're wet?" Hannah asks, wiping her face with one hand and scratching behind Junior's wet ear with the other.

Jimmy pulls down the lid and latches it. I back us gently from the shore and turn the boat so Hannah can get a last look out the window before we leave. She presses her hand against the glass, as if waving goodbye to her childhood home. I wait until she looks at me and nods, then I drop the throttle and steer us toward the dam.

Once again I'm surprised by the size of the lake and how long it actually takes us to cross it. It's a quiet trip, other than an occasional whimper from Junior, still hunkered down in the back with his head on Hannah's lap. As we approach the locks, I ease off the throttle, half hoping the mitre gates won't open.

But the giant steel doors part, and a black hole appears in the dam. I take a deep breath and notch the throttle forward.

"Wait!" Hannah says.

I jerk the throttle back, reversing away from the entrance. We sit there, rocking gently on our own wake, feeling small and insignificant floating beneath the towering dam.

"I just thought of something," Hannah says. "What if the Foundation is still flooded, and the locks take us down? Won't a wall of water bury us when the lower gates open?"

I stop to consider this. I remember Dr. Radcliffe telling us about the step locks on the downside of the Foundation cavern that lead out to the Pacific Ocean. I'm guessing that's how they drain away the water and lower the locks.

"I don't think so," I say, not sounding very reassuring even to myself. "I doubt the locks will bring us any lower than the water level of the Foundation bay."

"But are you sure?"

"No."

Hannah falls back into her seat. "Oh, sweet mother of Earth. Just go. If we die, we die."

I turn to Jimmy. "What do you say, Jimmy?"

"Whatever," he says. "I'm jus' along for the ride."

The shadowed locks wait in front of us, the white snow-covered world waits behind. I guide the boat through the doors and bring it to rest in the center of the locks. The doors grind shut behind us, sealing out the light, and all is quiet and black. Junior whimpers. Hannah shushes him, calming his nerves by humming a quiet song. I remember her father singing the same tune while Jimmy and I were stowaways in his boat heading down to burn Eden. A minute later, the LED lights pop on, and the boat begins to lower as the water level drops.

"So this is where we went?" Jimmy mumbles nervously from the shadows next to me.

"That's right," I say, "you never saw this part, did you? We were hidden in the bow of Radcliffe's boat."

"So it was you two who sabotaged Eden," Hannah says.

"We had to do something," I shoot back.

"I know it," she replies. "I was just saying."

We continue our slow drop in the shadowy locks until the lower gates appear dimly on the inside wall. Then we stop. The gates are only exposed at half the height I remember them. I feel myself tense, bracing for a wall of water. The gates slowly part, exposing the flooded tunnel, the water level much closer to the LED ceiling lights, but definitely passable in our small boat. The three of us collectively sigh.

I guide the boat into the tunnel, staying in the center to avoid hitting the ceiling where it slopes down at the edges. Small bits of floating debris litter the path and it feels like we've been shrunken down and are traveling through a subterranean sewer drain. When we reach the end of the tunnel, we idle into the pitch-black cavern bay. I guess the lights here went out with the flood. I stop the boat, and we float a few meters from the mouth of the tunnel in absolute blackness.

"Are there any lights on this thing?" Hannah asks.

I feel around blindly on the dash. "Shouldn't you know?" I ask, frustrated because I can't find anything.

Jimmy lifts open the lid, and the cool cavern air swooshes in. Junior whimpers again. Then I hear a crack and am blinded by a bright phosphorous flash as Jimmy strikes one of the flares lit. My eyes adjust, and the flare fades to a constant burn, casting a glow around our boat that is eerily similar to the red light that used to pulse up from Eden. Jimmy stands and holds the flare high while I idle the boat farther into the cavern. All around us is the floating wreckage of the Foundation. Overturned crates marked from various levels of Holocene II. Metal canisters half-submerged. A white lab coat. No. A dead scientist wearing a white lab coat. He's face down in the water, his bloated hands floating like two gray balloons at the ends of outstretched arms. I lean over and look back. Our wake lifts his left hand as if he were waving to us as we pass.

When we approach where the docks should be, they're either gone or underwater, and as we cruise onto what would have been the shore, the rooflines of the submerged buildings come into view. We pass the galvanized walls of the sintering plant and the munitions warehouse, then the scientists' living quarters with some of the scaffolding still in place. There are objects resting on top of the buildings, making it clear that the water was much higher, probably as high as the cavern ceiling, and that it is just now draining away.

I look back and see Hannah frozen in a wide-eyed trance and Junior sitting on the seat next to her, scanning the black water. The flare hisses in Jimmy's hand beside me as if it were the sound itself chasing away just a halo's worth of the darkness that swallows everything behind us as we pass.

We come at last to Eden, its domed roof singed by the fire to a bluish black, but largely still intact. I circle the structure, marveling at how large it is. It's hard to imagine the generations of Holocene II retirees that were slaughtered here: their brains enslaved, their bodies cast off like refuse. Somewhere in there still are my father and my mother, or at least the burnt remains of the chemicals that made up their brains—brains that met and loved one another enough to create me.

I ease the boat alongside Eden's sloping roofline. Jimmy jumps off and secures a line to a vertical vent protruding from the roof. It takes some coaxing to get Junior to leave the boat, but when we're all safely on the roof, Jimmy leads us up the dome with his flare. Eden's dome is the tallest structure in the Foundation cavern, and from its apex the flare casts a faint red glow onto the murky waters below, though the edges of the cavern are still hidden in shadow. We sit on the crest and take in the dim and dreary view.

"What are we going to do?" Hannah asks. Her words echo back to us above the sound of the hissing torch.

"I don't know," I say. "You think it's still draining?"

"Maybe," Hannah says. "I hope so."

"Do you hear that?" Jimmy asks.

"Hear what?"

"That banging," he says. "There. Listen."

I strain to listen, but all I hear is the hissing of the torch.

"I don't hear anything," I say.

"Shh," Hannah says. "I think I hear it."

"Where?"

Hannah points. "Out there."

As my eyes follow her finger, the sound comes into my head; it is a kind of metal clanging coming from beneath the water in intervals of three—clang, clang, clang.

"What do you think it is?" I ask.

"Definitely human," Hannah says.

"How do ya know that?" Jimmy asks.

"Duh," Hannah replies. "Only our brains can make sound

patterns like that."

"Ever heard a bird sing?" he asks, sarcastically.

"Stop it, you two. Let's just go out there and see."

When we return to the boat, the tie-line is strained, and the hull is partially beached on a newly exposed portion of roof, answering our question about whether or not the water is still draining. We untie and shove free and motor by flare-light to investigate the source of the sound.

"I can't hear it anymore," Hannah says, hanging her head overboard to listen.

I kill the jets and let us coast in silence.

"There," she says, pointing. "To the left."

I restart the jets and idle to where she pointed, reversing us to a standstill and killing the jets again. The sound is definitely louder and coming from somewhere near us, but there's nothing to see but black water.

Jimmy hands me the flare and strips off his shirt.

"What are you doing?" I ask him.

"I'm goin' down."

"What?" Hannah asks. "In the water? You have no idea what's down there . . ."

"That's why I'm goin'."

"But it's black as hell. You won't be able to see a thing."

"Thought ya didn't believe in hell," Jimmy says, smirking at Hannah as he steps out of his animal-skin kilt. "And besides, there ain't nothin' wrong with my ears or my hands, so I can listen and feel around. Seein' ain't all there is."

I hold the torch out to Jimmy. "Take this down."

"In the water?" he asks.

"It'll burn fine. They don't need oxygen."

"Ya sure?"

I nod, reaching over to grab a fresh flare from beneath the seat, just in case. Hannah holds the lit flare for Jimmy as he clamps his knife between his teeth and lowers himself into the water. He dunks his head to wet his hair, then comes back up and takes the flare from her. Junior joins Hannah at the edge of the boat and whines.

"Ahh," Jimmy says, through his clenched teeth. "How cute. You's worried about me."

"So what?" Hannah says, lifting her chin. "At least I'm adult enough to admit it."

"I was talkin' to Junior here," Jimmy says, trying to control a giggle. "But I'm glad you's worried too."

Hannah huffs, "Well, I knew that, and I was only . . ." She stops short when she notices Jimmy is gone.

As the flare descends underwater in Jimmy's hand, a cold and silent darkness swallows the boat. We watch the ball of red light move away from us, diving deeper beneath the surface, abbreviated by the elongated shadows of Jimmy's kicking legs. Then a larger shadow appears in the deep—something long and cylindrical. The boat tilts as the three of us lean over its side and watch. None of us dares to breathe, not even Junior, as if it might somehow help if we all hold our breath along with Jimmy. The light of Jimmy's flare moves around to the far side of the shadow, and the backlit silhouette of a submarine fades into view. Then the flare goes out, and all is black.

There is a moment of absolute silence, so still and quiet that I can hear the distant dripping of water somewhere in the faraway darkness. Then several things happen almost at once. The boat rocks, followed by a splash as something, or someone, falls into the water. I pull the cap and light the flare in my hand, the glare momentarily blinding me. And just as my vision returns, the submarine rockets from the water nose first, clearing the surface by several meters, and splashes down just five or so meters away. It sends a wall of spray into the boat, knocking me backwards onto the floor.

When I clamber to my feet, waving the flare in front of me like a weapon, the first thing I do is look for Hannah. She's picking herself up from the backseat, also stunned and soaking wet, but she looks unharmed. I rush to the edge and hold the flare up and look out, ready to dive in after Jimmy, but I see him treading water a few feet away with Junior paddling beside him. Behind them floats the surfaced submarine, its protruding sail emblazoned with the inverted valknut that makes up the Foundation crest. I reach out a hand and haul Jimmy up into the boat, and he turns back and heaves Junior aboard.

"What the hell happened?" I ask.

"It's some kind of a boat," Jimmy says.

"I can see that. You all right, Hannah?"

"I'm fine," she says. "Is Jimmy okay?"

"I'm all right," he says.

"Well, what happened?"

Jimmy fills us in excitedly: "This boat thing here was tied up to the docks down there and floatin' hard against the lines. I heard the tappin' from inside, thought there must be somebody in there. I was figurin' how to free her when my flare gave out. I already had a hand on the front line, so I jus' cut it."

"You sure freed it all right."

"Yeah, I wouldn't of done it neither if I'd seen that," he says, pointing to the valknut.

"The Foundation logo?" Hannah asks.

Jimmy shakes his head. "I dunno what you all call it, but that's the sign of the Park Service."

Hannah opens her mouth to respond, but I cut her off.

"You did the right thing, Jimmy. We don't know who's in there, no matter what the symbol's for."

The screech of grating metal turns all our heads to the submarine. The three of us stand together in the dark, watching, the flare held high in my hand, with Junior crouching at Jimmy's feet. A small door opens in the sail. Several seconds pass as we stare at the black opening. Then a man steps out into the flare's light. He's wearing white coveralls streaked with grease. And he's very old and very small. His long, white hair is frizzed out by humidity, giving him the appearance of someone being electrified. He's holding an enormous wrench.

I don't know why, but I shout: "Freeze right there, Mister! Don't you dare move."

He mumbles something unintelligible and then disappears inside the submarine again. We look at one another, confused and slightly panicked. I start the jets and bring us alongside the submarine. Jimmy jumps onto its deck and ties us off to a cleat still tied with the thick line that he cut. We scramble onto the submarine's deck and head for its door, stopping as we realize there's only room enough for one person to descend at a time.

"I'll go first," I say.

Jimmy pushes me aside. "No, I'll go."

"These people worked for my father," Hannah says. "If one of us has to go first, it should be me."

Just then Junior pushes past us and leans over the edge of the ladder, his bushy tail waving in the air for one moment before he disappears down into the black. Guess that answers that. I step onto the ladder next, but Hannah grabs my arm and takes the flare from my hand. "This can't go down there."

"Well, you stay out here and hold it then."

"No way. I'm going down." She hands the flare to Jimmy.

"Jimmy, give me your knife," I say. "If we're not back in ten minutes, come after us."

With Jimmy's knife in my teeth, I descend the short ladder into the dark submarine. I can hear Hannah climbing down after me. She places her hand on my shoulder and we creep along the narrow passageway. I begin to feel claustrophobic in the dark space, but soon a doorway comes into view, its hatch ajar and a triangle of yellow light slanting across the passageway ahead. When we arrive at the doorway, I stand back and grip the knife in my hand. Hannah gets a hold of the heavy door and looks to me for a signal. When I nod, she pulls open the door, and I step into the room, leading with Jimmy's knife.

"Shazbit and sheetle stick!"

The little old man sits in a control seat, mumbling strange obscenities as he fusses with nobs and levers. Junior is spread out on the floor at his feet, watching him intently.

"Hello." I don't mean to whisper it, but I do.

"You confounded fudderwacker!" The strange man slams the panel with his fist.

Hannah pushes past me and steps toward him. She says: "You'll respond this instant, rude sir."

Her commanding tone seems to get his attention, and he stretches out his arms and brings them together and interlaces his fingers behind his head, leaning back and turning to face us. He looks like some mad, frazzled scientist either surrendering or perhaps on vacation in repose.

I step up beside Hannah. "Who are you?"

He flashes us a strange and unsettling smile.

"That's an interesting question, young man. It could be answered in many ways. Who is anyone? Is anyone anyone? If a particle can be in two places at one time, couldn't a person? Or even a fox?"

"How about your name then?" I ask.

"Benjamin," he says. "Professor Benjamin Beckenbauer. But everyone just calls me 'Moody'." He slurs the word *Moody* while releasing his hands and holding them up, as if in some gesture of acceptance of a nickname which he hates. Then he spins around and returns his attention to the control panel in front of him, speaking over his shoulder to us. "Now, I'm not sure what you're getting into, you two here and that other I saw on the boat, or what you have to do with this fragnabbled flood, but I have no time for shenanigans, or they'll have me on the shock table again for sure. And if you see Dr. Radcliffe, please do tell him I'm working as quickly as I can."

"Dr. Radcliffe is dead," I say.

His hands freeze, and his head turns. He stares down for a moment, as if just now noticing Junior on the floor. Then he slowly swivels around to face us again. "I'm sorry," he says, "but would you mind repeating that?"

I cast Hannah an apologetic glance. "What I meant to say is that Dr. Radcliffe passed away."

He leaps from the chair, throws his hands in the air, and jogs a small circle around the room, surprisingly nimble as his spindly legs lift high off the floor in the manner of someone marching. "He's dead," he chants. "He's dead. The old boy is finally dead." He stops abruptly and turns to face us. "How do I know you're not lying? Wait. You're his daughter, aren't you? You look just like your mother. Yes, yes, you do. You wouldn't lie. Let me hear you say it. Tell me your father is dead."

"He's telling the truth," Hannah says. "He's dead. And I am his daughter, so perhaps you could appear a little less happy about it. Now tell us who you are and what you're doing."

He nods, seeming to calm down as he digests the news. "I'm sorry for my outburst," he says, straightening up and standing formally before us. "They call me Moody because my moods are a tad bit unpredictable. At least I think that's how it started. Anyway, it doesn't matter now. Moody it is. I'm a professor of theoretical physics, but for the last several hundred years they've had me in charge of maintenance for our fleet. It's quite beyond me as to why, really, except that no one else wanted the job. But I digress. May I assume, young lady, that you are in charge now? Professor Moody here, at your service. Although I'd like to officially tender my request for a new assignment, preferably one more fitting to my profession."

Junior gets up off the floor and trots past us. I turn and see Jimmy standing behind us in the doorway.

"You guys all right?" he asks.

"Well, well," the professor mumbles. "If it isn't Shadrach, Meshach, and Abednego."

"Who?" Hannah asks.

He waves her question off. "Just some old story."

After introducing ourselves, we circle up on the floor and discuss our situation, passing a water bottle and a welcome bag of algaecrisps produced from a cabinet by the professor. He shifts between manic rants, which he quickly apologizes for, and depressing claims that we'd all be much better off if we'd drowned along with the others. And although it's clear that he is slightly unstable, he proves very willing to submit, especially looking to Hannah for reassurance when answering questions.

We tell him all about the wave and about Dr. Radcliffe's apocalyptic doomsday plans, including flooding the Foundation, which happened, and flooding Holocene II, which didn't. He listens and nods and seems surprised by none of it. He says the water should drain back to level in time, and that we need only wait. And he seems little concerned about the lack of power, insisting that the flow of electricity from Holocene II where it's generated is constant, and that the batteries are capable of powering the Foundation for many years, even if there were an interruption. I ask why not use the dam for hydro power locally, which seems to impress the professor. He explains that it was used as such once, but that the turbines proved too costly in time and materials to maintain when the rail tubes between the Foundation and Holocene II proved to be a perfect transmission line for the power collected by us there from the Earth's magnetic fields. When we begin debating the advantages of Magnetohydrodynamics over geothermal power generation, Hannah and Jimmy begin to moan with boredom until we move on to discussing our more immediate plans. That's when I ask the professor how to stop the drones.

"Stop them?" he asks. "Why?"

"Because that's what we intend to do," I answer.

He scratches his chin, lost for a moment in thought. Then he turns to Hannah. "Do you agree with this? Are you officially abandoning our mission statement?"

"I certainly think it's time to review it," Hannah replies.

He furrows his brow and nods. "Well, then, I never was a big fan of old Radcliffe's radical ideas. I'm happy to leave the politicking to you three."

"But you did go along with Dr. Radcliffe's plans," I say. "You sure didn't protest if you maintained the fleet of drones."

He nods. "I did, I did. But you might have, too. He could be very persuasive, Robert could. Especially if you were here to see the destruction and horror mankind leveled on itself."

"Still, how do we know we can trust you?"

"Kid," he says, sighing. "I'm really, really old, and now I'm dying. I don't care two hoots what you do."

"Okay. Then tell us how we stop the drones?"

"That's no easy task," he says. "We'll need to wait for the power to come back on and reboot the system. Then we'll see what we can do."

"But you'll help us?"

"Keep me off the shock table, and I'll help you."

"Shock table?" I ask.

"Yes," he says, shaking his head and shivering at the very thought. "They claimed that it helped with my moods."

CHAPTER 3
Sorry, Jimmy, I'm with Hannah

The power does turn back on.

But I almost wish it hadn't.

For three days, we collect bodies. The dead scientists float bloated to the surface, or are exposed trapped in their rooms as water is pumped away. Jimmy and I use the boat to patrol the underground bay in the dim, gray glare of LED lights, towing the floaters back to shore where we drag them with ropes to what's left of Eden. The water from Radcliffe's flood had washed away most of what the fire we had set didn't destroy, but the steel-lined killing room is eerily intact.

It's hard for me. I remember looking into that monitor and seeing my father's head opened before his body was sloughed off into the trap door in the floor. Turns out that trap door leads to an industrial-grade meat grinder that renders bodies into a paste before flushing them down sewage pipes the length of the step locks into the Pacific. So we toss the dead scientists in and grind them up and send them as fish food out to sea. It's a much better burial than they deserve, if you ask me.

Fortunately, almost all of the materials used down here are either synthetic plastics or metals designed to resist corrosion, so there is very little damage from the flood. Hannah and the professor—we refuse to call him "Moody," like he asked—

spend most of their time restoring the critical mechanical systems around the Foundation: heating, lighting, waste-water pumps. But even though the computer systems are water-tight, designed with heat sinks instead of cooling fans, we decide to let them dry for several days, as a precaution, before rebooting to see if we can take control of the drones.

The professor walks us through the Foundation and uses his codes to unlock the few remaining rooms we haven't been able to check for bodies. He takes us into the sintering plant, where Hannah and I stood with her father and watched the missiles being built. Although pools of water remain on the floors, everything seems operational enough. Still, we all hold our breath as he opens the munitions room door. But there, too, everything seems to have been moved around by the water but hardly damaged at all.

"Why is that here?" I ask, pointing to the strange black box marked with red letters that read: ANTIMATTER.

The professor squats and peers into the box's blue-glowing window. "This little baby here," he says, running his hands over the box as if petting it, "contains almost a trillion dollars-worth of worldwide scientific work."

"What's a dollar?" Jimmy asks.

"A measure of currency, when the world used money."

"Oh. Like pearls or somethin'?"

"Like pearls," the professor says. "But the money aside, this represents an amazing accomplishment. Unfortunately, like everything we lousy humans did, it was only produced because of its potential use in weaponry."

"How much is in there?" I ask.

"A little over 200 grams," he says. "But don't worry. The design of this case, really a large battery itself, keeps it trapped in permanent suspension. Unless it's detonated, of course."

"Whataya mean by detonated?" Jimmy asks.

"Let's eat something," the professor says, changing the subject. "My stomach is growling loud enough to be rude."

We've scrounged up enough sealed rations to eat fairly well, heating our meals on the cook stove in the living quarters. But with the rooms still drying out, Hannah, the professor, and I sleep on separate bunks in the submarine, while Jimmy sleeps outside the submarine in the boat with Junior.

On the fourth day, with no bodies left to be found, Jimmy, Hannah, and I gather at the command center door and wait for the professor to let us in so we can reboot the computers.

"What's that say?" Jimmy asks, pointing to a metal plaque mounted next to door and engraved with the words:

<u>MISSION STATEMENT</u>
THE PARK SERVICE THUS ESTABLISHED SHALL PROTECT AND
CONSERVE THE NATURAL BEAUTY OF THE EARTH BY
EMPLOYING ALL AVAILABLE MEANS TO ERADICATE FOREVER
FROM THE PLANET THE VIRAL SPECIES KNOWN AS HUMANKIND.

To my relief, before I can read the plaque to Jimmy, the professor shows up and punches his code into the keypad and leads us inside the command center. It reminds me of the safe room at the lake house, only larger and more sophisticated. It has a concave wall lined with LCD screens in front of several cockpit-style chairs, complete with joysticks for controlling drones and fire switches to release weapons.

I sit in one of the chairs and notice that the seating surface is heated with buttons for vibration-massage settings, just in case you need to relax a little between kills, I guess. I imagine Dr. Radcliffe and his team of environmental terrorists spending countless hours down here "working." I wonder if they enjoyed the hunt. I wonder if they kept score of their kills. The thought of it makes me really dislike the professor, and I wouldn't be able to forgive him except he claims the command center was off limits to everyone except Radcliffe and a select few others, and I'm tempted to believe him because he doesn't seem very familiar with the room.

After mumbling many pseudo-profanities, the professor finally locates the mainframe racked up in a server closet and tells us to hope for the best while he reboots the "Big Iron."

The computers are noiseless. The screens flicker, then run a dizzying display of code before going dark and coming back on again with a patchwork of vibrant scenes from around the park: a snowy sunset high in the Himalayas; a gorgeous view of blue ocean waves breaking on a tropical coast; a prairie caught in the gold light of sunrise; a billowing dust storm in a desert; a peekaboo view of reflected moonlight in a tangled marshland as a drone glides on its mindless midnight mission. Lowlands and highlands, rivers and lakes—it's an orgy for my tired eyes, which have been four days in this gray and dreary underworld looking for bloated cadavers in the dark.

"Is all this happening somewhere right now?" Jimmy asks, stepping forward and reaching out to touch a screen.

"Yes," I say, reminding myself that he's never seen a video image before. "These are from cameras mounted on drones."

The screens change to new images every sixty seconds or so, and with the third changeover something terrible happens. All at once, the screens combine to create one image the size of the entire wall. The scene is of an ice sheet in the permanent twilight of early arctic winter. Several seal groups huddle beside blocks of ice next to their breathing holes. A handful of fur-clad hunters inches toward them, hidden behind a white, skin-covered blind that they push ahead of themselves on the ice. When they're close, the hunters spring out from behind the blind and rush to the seals and crush their skulls with clubs.

"Oh, no!" Hannah exclaims, beside me.

A few of the white pups rush for the breathing hole but are caught up and clubbed, then hung from hooks on the wood framing of the blind, and bled. Several moments of butchery follow, and an impressive radius of ice around the scene turns blood-red. Just as I'm about to ask how far away the camera is, crosshairs appear on the screen. A few seconds later, two of the seal hunters explode, their severed limbs skittering, along with hunks of blubber, across the bloody ice. Another hunter is left in the frigid water, clinging to the icy edge of the hole blasted by the bombs. He struggles and kicks to climb out, scrambling up and running across the barren ice. The camera follows him, the crosshairs zero in again. One moment he's running for his life, the next moment he's a pink mist, and only a blood-stained hole is left in the ice to mark his life.

The gory scene disappears as the screens change over to various peaceful views of the park. When I peel my eyes away and look around the room, I notice Jimmy clutching the back of a command chair, his face frozen in an ashen stare.

"What's wrong with him?" the professor asks.

"He's upset because he's seen this before in person," I say.

"Ah . . .," the professor sighs, "it never gets any easier to watch. Especially when they club the little whitecoats."

"He's not upset about the seals," I say.

Jimmy shakes his head and mumbles: "What in the hell's wrong with you people?"

"I'm sorry," the professor says, "I didn't mean to . . ."

"Let's just see if we can control the drones," Hannah says.

The professor hangs his head and approaches the panel of controls, mumbling as he types commands into the keyboard.

"I didn't mean to upset anyone. Stupid, stupid, stupid. Holy shrimp in the sea, there's nobody stupider than me."

Red letters pop on the screens:

COMMAND POST DEACTIVATED

SITREP MONITORING ONLY

"Oh, piffle!" He slams his hand down on the keyboard. "No good. No good at all."

"We're locked out?" Hannah asks.

"It appears so, young lady," he says. "Flood triggered the emergency system. Just as Radcliffe planned it to, I'm sure. The command and control lines are severed."

"What does that mean?" I ask.

"It means that the drones are now operating autonomously with their own internal software systems. They'll continue to execute their mission. All we can do is watch."

"How many can there be?" I ask.

"Many thousands of them," the professor answers. "We've substantially increased the fleet over the years to cover more ground as . . . well, as populations thinned."

"Don't candy-coat it," I say. "You mean as you killed more people." The professor nods, apparently untroubled by, or at least unwilling to refute, my statement. I continue, "They can't possibly run on their own forever, can they? How long?"

"No," the professor replies. "But they can operate in the theater for many years. The drones have solar skins and electric engines, and they're loaded with enough traditional munitions to perform many hundreds of kills each. They have backup lasers that are of reduced effect but can still incinerate a biped from quite a distance. The ships will last even longer."

"Can we use the drones here to target the other drones?"

"We might see what's left in the hangar," he says. "But when Eden caught fire they flew most of them as a precaution.

And even if there are any left, and even if they're salvageable, I doubt we could launch them with the system on lockdown, let alone program a new mission."

"What about the submarine then?" I ask.

"Research vessel," he says. "The weapons on board are strictly defensive. We didn't bother maintaining the fleet of ballistic submarines we found here, and they've long since been scuttled . . . them being of little use in targeting . . .," he pauses to look at Jimmy, ". . . ahem, well you know."

"But there must be some way to wrestle back control of the drones," I say. "Some way to reset the system, maybe?"

The professor covers his eyes with his fingers as if reading something written there. He inhales a long, deep breath, and when he removes his fingers his bushy eyebrows are raised above wide, staring eyes. He says, "We might try reloading the mastercode."

"What mastercode?" Hannah asks.

"The software that runs the system," the professor says. "But we'd need to get it first."

"Okay," I say. "Where is it?"

"In the basement."

"There's a basement here?" Hannah asks.

"Not here," he says.

"Then where?"

"Holocene II."

"That's perfect," I say. "We need to free them anyway."

The professor jolts back so fast he bangs his head against

the wall. "Free them?" he asks, rubbing the back of his head. "What in the name of science has gotten into you?"

"Nothing's gotten into me," I say. "It simply isn't right to keep them imprisoned down there."

"But they're happy," he says, a confused look on his face. "They have everything they need. They even have Eden to look forward to. Or at least they did. You can't take their ignorance away from them. What right have you? You can't burden them with the reality of their situation. It's not humane."

I shake my head. "They're not happy down there."

"How would you know?" he asks.

"Because I'm from there."

"Oh," he says, nodding, "you're the boy Radcliffe brought up. He told us you were lost in that derailment."

"I was, but I found my way here."

He clucks his tongue and chuckles. "Of all the wild places in the world to end up. Don't you sometimes think coincidence might just be us living out some cosmic destiny, over and over again, forwards and backwards, for eternity? It pains me to consider it, because this life really has been too long already. But you'll never know the pain of living a millennium, will you? Or did Radcliffe already infect you with his serum?"

I open my mouth to tell him we've all taken the serum, but Hannah jumps in: "Tell us more about the mastercode. Can we get it without letting anyone in Holocene II out?"

I grab Hannah's arm. "What are you saying?"

"I know, Aubrey," she says, pulling away. "We have to free

them. I agree. But have you thought it through? We need to stop the drones first. There's no room for everyone here. And there are no facilities for producing the things we need to survive, either. Think about it. Food, shelter, electricity. It's all down in Holocene II. You can't very well bring them up here to be slaughtered, can you?. The logical thing to do is deal with the drones first. Then we'll devise a plan for reintroducing the people to the surface. Don't you agree?"

I have to admit, she makes some sense. I hadn't thought about the logistics of bringing all those people up. I have an image of thousands of them stumbling around, confused and blinded by the sun, drones picking them off like eagles hunting fish caught in a puddle. She's right. We have no real system of government, no infrastructure, no formal economy.

The professor's voice snaps me back to the room: "Well, we have visited Holocene II undetected before. We control the train from here, for obvious reasons. And that's on a different system than the drones. The transfer station is vacated and locked down during rest hours. Elevator takes us to six, where another goes to the basements. Timing is critical, but it can be done. If that's what you really want?"

Hannah raises her hand. "I vote we do that."

I look at Jimmy. He shakes his head.

"What are you thinking, Jimmy?"

"It ain't our call to make."

"What do you mean?"

"I mean, we always done stuff by vote."

"But we're voting now," Hannah says.

"We is," Jimmy replies. "But they ain't." He points down.

"But they're not prepared to deal with this," she says.

"Why do we get to decide that for 'em?"

"Whatever," Hannah sighs, turning to me. "It's up to you then, Aubrey. You're the tie breaker."

I'm torn. I agree with Jimmy in theory. It isn't our decision to make on behalf of the people of Holocene II. But I also see Hannah's point. And no way do I want to be responsible for all those people starving to death up here. Or freezing. Or being slaughtered by drones, even. I reach into my pocket and grip my father's pipe. What would he do? I remember him telling me to always trust my heart.

"The brain is a powerful servant but a heartless master," he'd always say. But then I think of that day I saw him for the last time. The day he walked right into Eden to be slaughtered. I tried to tell him that we'd been lied to. I tried to reason with his mind. But his heart was set on meeting my mother, and it clouded his judgment. If he'd only listened to his mind instead of his heart, he might still be alive.

"Sorry, Jimmy, I'm with Hannah."

Jimmy looks at me and shakes his head slowly. "Figures," he says. Then he storms from the room and slams the door.

I start after him, but Hannah calls me back.

"Let him vent, Aubrey. That all can wait. We need to make some decisions here."

"All right. I can catch up with him later, I guess."

"Tell us about this mastercode," Hannah says.

"It's quite simple, really," the professor replies. "With the mastercode we should be able to restore the system and reclaim control of the drones."

"Then could we change their mission and stop the killing?" I ask. "Or even call them all home and retire them?"

"Well, there's not room enough for them all here at once," he says, "but I see no reason why we couldn't reprogram them to cease their fire and observe only. Then, as they cycle home for maintenance, you could certainly disarm them."

"Or maybe we keep them armed for defensive purposes?" Hannah suggests.

"Defense against what?" I ask.

"I don't know," she says. "But I agree that we need to stop this senseless slaughter immediately."

"And what about freeing my people?"

"Let's focus on one thing at a time," she says. "As soon as the drones are under our control again, we can put our heads together and come up with a plan for that."

"I'm only going along with this if we all agree: as soon as the drones are stopped, we tell the people of Holocene II the truth, and we set them free. Deal or no deal?"

"Fine," Hannah says. "Agreed."

"Professor?"

"Fine with me," he says.

"Okay then. When can we leave?"

The professor glances at his wrist then looks puzzled by

the fact that he isn't wearing a watch. He leans forward and reads the time on the bottom edge of a screen. Then he closes his eyes and talks to himself. "If we call the train now . . . five hours up makes nineteen hundred . . . rest hours begin at sixteen hundred . . . twenty-seven . . . subtract five hours down . . . twenty-two. We can leave in twenty-two hours."

"There was an easier way to do that," Hannah says.

"Yes, well . . . arithmetic never was my strong suit."

"But you're a physicist."

"Theoretical physicist, young lady. Theoretical."

I leave them to bicker about math while I go to look for Jimmy. I have a sinking feeling even before reaching the docks. The boat is gone, and Jimmy and Junior are gone with it.

I look across the empty, underground bay at the mouth of the tunnel leading to the locks. It's seems like an evil archway through which my departing hope has passed. My instinct is for pursuit, but I quickly realize the powerlessness of my situation. I'm trapped. Jimmy's gone up there, and I'm stuck down here. While the submarine can pass through the miles of step locks down to the Pacific, it is much too large to pass through the upper locks to the lake. I could build a boat, maybe, but there's no time. We leave on the train for Eden in 22 hours.

Several hours pass as I sit on the deserted dock and rerun everything Jimmy and I have been through. That delirious first encounter by the sea. Him teaching me to catch pigeons. The cove. Learning to swim. The horror of the drones slaughtering his family. The bodies and the blood. I remember tending his infected leg and praying to anything that might hear me to restore his health. I remember our long, depressing days of mourning as Jimmy recovered from his wounds in the cliff-side caves. I remember crossing the mountains together, and finding Junior on the trail. And as much as I don't want to, I remember betraying Jimmy when we first arrived at the lake house—lying, conniving, caught up in Hannah's spell and conspiring with Dr. Radcliffe. It's unforgiveable, really. But Jimmy did forgive me when he saved my life in that river. And he helped me blow up Eden; he helped me free my folks.

I feel Hannah's hand on my shoulder, and I'm suddenly aware of the cold. She sits down and puts her arm around me. I'd rather blame her than blame myself for Jimmy's leaving, and I'm prepared to yell at her the second that she speaks. But she doesn't say a word—she just sits beside me on the dock and stares across the bay at the empty tunnel, looking sad herself.

CHAPTER 4
Returning to Holocene II

"Did we really need all this?"

The professor hefts another pallet from the train onto the platform. "Most of it," he says. "But we also needed a reason to call up the train ahead of its scheduled monthly visit. You of all people should know how important routine is down there."

When the last of the supplies are finally offloaded, we eat a quick meal then retire to our bunks for some rest before the journey down to Holocene II. The professor has moved back into his room in the living quarters, so it's just Hannah and me left in the submarine. She makes an attempt to crawl in with me, but the bunks are just too narrow, and she jumps into the upper bunk and falls asleep within minutes.

I toss and turn beneath her.

Several times I get up and climb the ladder to the hatch and look out toward the tunnel, hoping to see Jimmy returning. But each time I'm alone with the eerie LED glow and the distant sound of dripping water. When I do get to sleep, it's restless, with dreams of Jimmy being killed by drones, or eaten by bears, so I'm grateful when the professor pokes his head into our bunkroom and announces that it's time to leave.

Hannah and I pull on our new zipsuits, brought up on the train from Holocene II. It feels funny to be wearing one again after all that time nearly naked in the cove, and later wearing Dr. Radcliffe's hand-me-down clothes. But while I'm clawing at the closed neck and uncomfortable, Hannah seems to be happy to have shed the threadbare dress she'd been wearing, admiring herself in her new zipsuit from every angle in the small mirror.

My pipe feels bulky in my zipsuit pocket, but I don't want to take it with me down to Holocene II anyway. If something happens, at least my father's pipe won't be buried down there forever with me. I remember Jimmy's look of shame that day in the cove as he apologized for stealing my pipe—shame over something so silly when I have done so much worse. I wish he were here now so I could tell him what he means to me. So I could give him the pipe to keep as a token of my thanks. He deserves it. He's a better man than I am.

I tuck the pipe and case of tobacco in a drawer beneath my bunk and head up with Hannah. I stop at the edge of the dock for one last look, before Hannah tugs me along by my sleeve.

Boarding the train is hard. I remember climbing in on the day I left Holocene II, and I remember Dorian with his clipboard locking me inside for the ride. I remember the terrible accident that came like a surprise bomb while I slept in my seat. And I remember crawling through the crippled car to get free.

The professor shuts the train car door, and I'm immediately claustrophobic. My heart pumps with panic, my head pounds with pain. What am I thinking? Back in a zipsuit and heading down to Holocene II? Remember the reasons, I tell myself. We're going to save lives. I sit in a metal seat and rest my head between my legs and breathe—I breathe good energy in, and I breathe bad energy out.

Hannah sits beside me for a while, but I'm in no mood to talk, and eventually she goes and sits next to the professor and they discuss the plan. I never knew five hours could last so long. I can feel the train moving deeper, as if the weight of the rock above were somehow increasing the air pressure as we descend. Fortunately, I drift in and out of a restless sleep, and just as I finally give up on wondering when we'll arrive, I feel myself press back into the seat as the train glides to a stop.

The door lock clicks free, and the professor stands and grabs the handle. "Straight to the elevators now," he warns, looking back at Hannah and me before opening the door.

We cross the dim-lit loading dock like thieves, walking on our tiptoes even though it's deserted. When we arrive at the elevators, they stand waiting and open, their polished steel interiors reflecting back our warbled shadows as we pass. The professor counts them off out loud, ushering us into the sixth. He reaches into his pocket and pulls out his hand, staring at his empty palm. He searches himself with increasing panic.

"Frickle nick. I just knew it. Stupid, stupid, stupid. Wait. Aha! There you are." He produces a keycard from some hidden pocket in the folds of his coveralls and waves the card in front of the panel. The doors slide shut, and the elevator begins its long descent.

"Why this elevator?" Hannah asks.

The professor waves his card. "Other than our once a year population exchange, only freight elevators operate between the levels. They're direct shafts, each connecting only one level to the transfer station."

"But why?" she asks.

"Well, to provide a modicum of control, I guess. It helps to prevent fraternization between levels."

"Smart," she says, nodding.

I shake my head. "Cruel is more like it."

The elevator drops for a long time. Maybe three minutes, if I were counting. When it finally stops, the doors don't open.

"Oh, no," I say. "Here we go again."

Hannah opens her mouth to ask me what I mean, but her question is cut off by the blast of disinfecting gas rushing into the elevator. She panics, just like I did my first time, and backs away from the vent. But there's nowhere to go. The professor's smile disappears in the white cloud, and I reach for Hannah and try to comfort her as I suck the gas in and try not to cough.

When the doors open, we pile out into the dim gray glow of the all-too-familiar LED lights and cough out the inhaled gas, fighting to catch our breath. Hannah looks upset, but she sucks it up without a word and walks with us onto a grated bridge. Below us, a channel of murky water meanders through the dim valley. I'm overwhelmed by the smell of human waste.

Hannah plugs her nose. "What is this place?"

"Sewage treatment level," I say, happy to know more than she does for once.

She points down. "You mean to tell me that that's crap?"

The professor laughs. "That's just gray water, young lady. The crap is coming up soon enough."

We wind our way over various walkways, past windowless buildings and islands of pipes and valves that seem to sprout from the ground. The rotten smell builds steadily as we go until the professor stops on a high bridge and points down to an enormous field of circular pools, bubbling and burping out hideous gases that are sucked up by giant vent hoods hovering above them like hungry, mechanical mouths.

"Gross," Hannah moans, her fingers still clasped on her nose. "This is disgusting."

"There's nothing disgusting about the beauty of bacteria, young lady," the professor says, playfully tapping her nose. "Did you know there are more bacteria cells in your own body than there are human cells? We have more in common with those fellas feasting on our shit down there than we do with anything else in the world up there."

"What do they do with the methane?" I ask.

"Good question," he says, smiling at me. "It's looped back and burned to heat the pools, thus speeding the decomposition process in a self-encouraging cycle."

"Very smart," I say, genuinely impressed. "You know all those years growing up on Level 3, I never even thought about what they did with our waste."

The professor nods. "Nobody ever does."

"Can we keep moving?" Hannah asks.

Once past the main treatment station, we cross another bridge and follow a footpath on the inside edge of the cavern. It is worn smooth as glass by a thousand years of boot marks left by workers trudging to their daily grind. As we round a bend, I get a glimpse down into the cavern valley where small apartment buildings cluster around an open square, their yellow windows appearing to wink as the residents' shadows cross in front of the backlit shades.

"Shouldn't the residences be on higher ground than the treatment plant?" I ask.

The professor shakes his head. "Methane rises."

After we pass the fork leading to the valley of apartments, the path turns hard left, and we enter a tunnel in the cavern wall. Unlike the well-worn workers' path, the tunnel seems neglected, mostly because of trash lying in corners and graffiti written on the walls. I notice one tag in particular that reads: JAMES + ERICA FOREVER, with a chalk line through "Erica" and the name BETH scrawled above it.

The professor stops at a steel door. A yellow warning label barely visible beneath the dirt and dust reads:

DANGER, BIOHAZARD.

He fumbles his pockets again for his keycard and waves it in front of a panel. The panel opens, exposing a keypad. He punches in a long code—nothing happens.

"Son of a sheep." He closes his eyes for a moment then tries again. This time the locks release, and the heavy door pops open with a woosh of pressurized air from inside. A short hallway leads to another door with another keypad. The professor unlocks it, and we enter a cavernous room lit with orange vapor lights, a welcome change from the gray glow of LED. The walls are lined with yellow barrels all marked with three interlocking black circles that I recognize from my lessons as the biohazard sign. It's a symbol that makes me instantly uncomfortable.

We cross the room quickly, our footsteps echoing in the quiet chamber, and enter yet another elevator, this one much smaller than the other. As the elevator descends, fear grips me again, and I lean against the wall and close my eyes. I try to calm myself by thinking about Jimmy. I imagine him kilometers above us, walking free beneath the bright winter sun. I imagine Junior gamboling along beside him, frolicking in the fresh snow. I imagine them making camp on the dry ground beneath a giant pine, huddling together in front of a warm fire. I think I'd give anything to be there with him right now.

As the elevator drops, the temperature rises, and sweat beads on my brow. Hannah grips my hand in hers, and I can tell by her clammy skin that she's nervous, too. The professor whistles, seemingly more comfortable the deeper we go.

After what feels like an eternity, the elevator stops, and the doors open to reveal a circular room humming with the sound of hidden fans.

"It's hot in here," Hannah says, fanning her face.

The professor nods. "Believe it or not, this is cool for this depth. If it weren't for the fans, we'd be cooked alive."

Several tunnels branch off from the room, all radiating in different directions and all with strange symbols etched into the walls above them. The professor stands staring at the tunnels, as if trying to remember the correct path.

"What language is that?" I ask.

The professor shakes his head. "I don't know."

"You don't know? Haven't you been here before?"

"Of course I have," he says, his tone edgy with offense. "But you might remember that Holocene II was a government research facility long before Radcliffe negotiated a private and public partnership for the Foundation to run it."

"What did they do down here before?" I ask.

"I don't know much," he answers, with a slight shiver in his voice. "And I what I do know I wish I could forget. I think it's this third tunnel. Follow me now. Let's hurry along."

We enter the tunnel, and I feel a noticeable and welcome breeze that smells of chemically conditioned air. The tunnel is dim, lined with closed doors on either side. Above each door are symbols in the same alien characters as were above the tunnels themselves. The professor stops at a door and puzzles over the symbol. He reaches for the handle, then hesitates. He changes his mind, pulls his hand back, and moves to the next door, mumbling to himself as we follow. Seemingly sure this time, he opens the door. A blue ceiling light illuminates glass, liquid-filled pods from which shadowed mutant humans stare with unblinking eyes, their grotesque faces pressed to the glass and watching the door with patience possible only to the dead.

"Verdammte!" the professor says, jerking the door closed.

He leads us back to the first door, clenching his teeth and opening it quickly, in the manner with which one might pull a bandage. Fortunately, the room is much less spooky. The LED lights come on automatically as the door is opened, revealing a mess of antique computers stored on racks. Cables spill from boxes; a file cabinet stands against a wall with its drawers ajar. The professor sighs with relief and leads us into the room. Hannah taps me on the shoulder and points to a bin filled with reading slates. They're of an earlier generation than the one I had growing up on Level 3, but they appear to be in working condition. I grab the one that looks the least abused.

We join the professor at the back of the room where he fuddles with a combination lock on an enormous free-standing safe. He spins the dial, stopping on random numbers, then immediately second guesses himself and curses as he spins it again. He continues like this for several minutes before Hannah reaches past him and tries the handle. The safe isn't locked, and the heavy door swings open. At first, my heart sinks because it appears to be empty. Then I see a small black box tucked into a corner of the bottom shelf. The professor slides the box out and holds it cradled in his hands. "Open it," he says.

I release the seal, and the glass lid jumps in my hand as the vacuum inside is filled with pressurized air. Then I reach in and remove a small solid-state hard drive, less than a third the size of the slate I'm holding in my other hand. It's hard to believe that such a small and mindless thing containing nothing but ones and zeros holds the mastercode for a software system that has systematically murdered millions of people on its relentless quest to eradicate all human DNA from Earth.

By the time I realize I'm standing there looking at the hard drive in a trance, I hear Hannah and the professor arguing.

"But I want to look around some," Hannah says.

"No," is his stern reply. "We've got to keep moving. I had to program the train's return departure from the Foundation before we left. If we miss it, young lady, we'll all be spending the rest of our lives down here."

That's all I need to hear. I'm at the door in a flash, holding it open and ushering Hannah and the professor into the tunnel. Hannah looks longingly at the countless closed doors we pass as we make our way back toward the elevator.

Up and out of the biohazard room again, I slip the hard drive in my pocket and clutch the lesson slate to my chest as we walk-jog our way across the sewage pools, retracing our steps. My panic doesn't subside until we're back in the freight elevator moving up, safely on our way to the transfer station and the waiting train. Hannah squeezes my hand and shoots me a sexy smile on the sly. Sometimes she can be very cute.

We stand hand in hand and take in the gas this time like pros. Then the elevator opens, and we step off and hurry in a single file line across the loading platform toward the train. The hydraulic hiss of another opening elevator door catches my ear, but before I can turn my head to look, something slams into me and knocks me to the ground.

I scramble to my feet and spin around.

"Red?"

"Aubrey?"

Standing before me with a look of panic on his face is Red, my old childhood nemesis from Level 3. He's shorter than I remember him, his boyish freckles faded and a new patch of red, wispy whiskers on his chin. But otherwise, his enormous head covered with thick, red hair remains unchanged. He looks me up and down.

"You look different," he says.

"What are you doing here?" I ask.

"I was fixing to ask you the same thing."

"I asked it first."

He looks down and kicks at the ground. "I was going to see my girl."

"On Level 3?"

"Yeah."

"But I thought you were moved down to 5."

He holds up a lanyard with a dangling keycard similar to the professor's. "I'm apprenticing in freight."

I laugh. "Still sneaking around during rest hours, eh? Good to see some things haven't changed."

The professor grabs my arm. "We need to keep moving."

Red looks at the professor, a confused expression falling over his face. "Hey, wait a minute. You're a senior, aren't you? A real, live senior. If you're only thirty-five, I'll eat my head."

"No small task," the professor grumbles, sizing up Red's

big head with an irritated glare. "Let's go, Aubrey."

"Are you all older up there?" Red asks. "And what are you doing down here?"

"Don't worry about it," I say, taking a step away. "And don't tell anyone you saw us here, either."

Turning away, I follow the professor toward the train.

We both stop when I hear Red scream.

I turn back and see Hannah leading Red along behind us, pulling him by his ear. They pass us by, Red flailing his arms and crying.

Hannah says, "No way is he staying behind."

Before I can protest, we're all on board the train and the door is closed and locked. Red slumps down in a seat and rubs his ear, already bright red and swelling. Hannah storms to the back of the car and sits with her arms crossed. The professor looks at me and shakes his heads, leaving me to sit down and explain things to Red. No easy task for sure.

By the time we approach the Foundation, nearly five hours later, I've somehow managed to confuse Red more than I've managed to enlighten him.

"So . . .," he scratches his head, "Eden wasn't really Eden, but now it's been destroyed by a flood anyway? And this guy's how old again?"

"Don't get hung up on the details," I say, not wanting to go over it for the thirteenth time. "Just know you're taking part in something big up here now. Okay? Something that you'll be remembered for forever."

"You mean freeing the people?"

"Yes, freeing the people."

"And what about these drones again?"

The train glides to a stop, and Hannah struts to the door and yanks it opens. We follow her onto the Foundation cavern platform.

Red looks around. "So where are we now?"

When Hannah shoots an annoyed look our way, the professor says, "I've got an idea. Why don't you let me show Red here around the Foundation, explain some things to the lad. Might be nice to dust off my old teaching skills, you know. That way you two can go get some rest."

"What about the mastercode?" I ask, holding up the hard disk. "Don't we need to load it?"

"I'll start a system backup," the professor says, taking it from my hand. "But that will take hours. I'll come and get you when things are ready to be rebooted." Then he nods to the lesson slate in my other hand. "Would you like me to give that a charge while I'm at it?"

"Please. Thanks. I miss reading a lot. And I am pretty beat. I think I will go get some rest."

"I'm not tired," Hannah says. "I'm going to go see what's salvageable in the lab."

Hannah takes off toward her lab, the professor leads Red away, and I head for the welcome relief of a submarine bunk.

I descend the ladder and make my way to the bunkroom, navigating by memory and not bothering to turn on any lights.

I crawl halfway into my narrow bunk and freeze. Someone's in my bed! I have one leg on the mattress, and one leg still on the ground, and all I can hear is my heart pounding in my chest. Then something warm and bristly rubs against my ankle. Still not daring to move, I squint until my eyes adjust to the low light, and I notice Junior lying on the floor by my feet.

Hope leaps into my heart.

I turn and look at Jimmy's shadow next to me, his sleeping face fading into view. He looks peaceful and calm, not a care in the world visible on his features. I'm reminded of those fearful days hidden away in that cave, nursing him back to health, hoping the homemade antibiotics would help. I remember the same innocence on his sleeping face then. And I remember the horrors of what happened in that cove flooding back into his eyes the moment he was awake. As much as I want to, I can't bring myself to wake him now. Instead, I do something that surprises me. I lean down and kiss his forehead.

Then I ease myself off the bunk, climb onto the empty one above, close my eyes, and fall fast asleep.

CHAPTER 5
Where Man Rises from the Sea

The professor's voice echoing down the hatch wakes me.

I lean over and look down on the bunk below, but Jimmy and Junior are gone.

"Aubrey!" the professor calls again.

"Coming!"

I jump from the bunk and rinse my face with cold water in the tiny submarine sink and run my wet fingers through my hair. A faceless outline of my head is dimly reflected in the small mirror. I wish I knew who I was supposed to be.

The professor lends me a hand out onto the deck of the submarine and presents me my lesson slate.

"Does it work?"

"Quite well," he says. "And it's loaded with our entire library now, even the books that were banned in Holocene II."

"That's great! I was sad to see Radcliffe's library washed away in that wave. There was so much I wanted to read."

The professor smiles approvingly. Then he says, "We do have a problem, however. Come with me."

"Where's Jimmy?"

"Oh, no," he says, "Jimmy's fine. He's in the supply room trying to find something for that fox of his to eat. We have a problem with the mastercode."

"What is it?"

"Come. I'll show you."

Following the professor toward the command center, I look around at the Foundation, wondering what the problem could be. It's remarkable how little evidence there is of the flood. You'd never know how many people drowned here if you didn't have to dredge them up and dispose of them like Jimmy and I did. I remember Dr. Radcliffe leading Hannah and me down here for the first time, taking us through the sintering plant on our way to the hanger to board that drone and tour the park. I remember seeing Eden and having doubts about its promises, but I pushed the doubts away. Never again. From now on, I trust my instincts.

We enter the command center and find Hannah and Red watching random lines of code scroll across the wall of black screens. Red's head bobbles up and down as he tries to follow individual lines of code, moving far too fast to read even if they weren't gibberish. Hannah has her balled fists on opposing hips and a frustrated look in her eyes. The professor waves at the passing characters as if presenting the problem.

I shrug. "What does it mean?"

"It means," the professor sighs, "the code is encrypted."

"Encrypted?"

"Impossibly so," he says.

"There's no way to unlock it?" I ask.

"Not unless you have the key."

"Well, where's the key?"

He tosses up his hands. "Probably at the bottom of the lake trapped inside Radcliffe's thick skull."

Hannah shoots the professor an angry look. "There must be some way to crack it," she says.

"We were using 14 rounds of 256-bit keys when this was

designed," the professor frowns. "I'm afraid there's no way to decrypt it with brute force."

Red shakes his head. "I should've studied more in school."

I step closer and watch the code roll down the screens— lines of random letters and symbols marching like armies across two-dimensional space. Could we possibly be doomed to die down here because of a missing key? A simple string of thought buried with Dr. Radcliffe and never to be exhumed?

"There is this," the professor says, stepping past me and tapping a command into the keyboard.

The code disappears in a flash, replaced by a static page of header text that reads:

THE HUMAN EXTINCTION PROJECT

ENCRYPTION KEY _____

"WHERE MAN RISES FROM THE SEA, IN THE RIGHT HAND OF DAVID YOU SHALL FIND YOUR KEY"

I read the strange clue aloud: "Where man rises from the sea, in the right hand of David you shall find your key."

"I'm not sure of its meaning," the professor says. "It appears to be some kind of clue to finding the encryption key."

Hannah casts a distrustful glance at the professor. "You must have some idea what it means," she says. "You were here when my father wrote it."

"I was indeed," he replies. "But there were many more of us back in those days, and I truly was very low on the pole for this kind of thing."

I turn to Hannah. "What are we going to do?"

She shakes her head. "I wish I knew."

The professor taps the keyboard again, killing the screen. "Let me dig around a little and see what I can turn up," he says. "Why don't you all try and take your minds off of things? Play some games or something."

"Games?" I ask.

"Well," he says, "whatever it is you young people are into."

"I like games," Red says.

Hannah rolls her eyes. "Of course you do."

"Come on, Red," I say, "I'll introduce you to Jimmy."

Hannah looks surprised. "Jimmy's back?"

"You didn't know?"

"No, I've been in the lab this whole time trying to make some sense of the mess there."

"Well, let's go welcome him back," I suggest.

"You go ahead," she says, waving Red and me toward the door. "I'm going to stay here for a bit and help the professor."

We find Jimmy near the docks. He's dragging a rabbit fur along the ground by a long string as Junior stalks after it. Every time Junior crouches to pounce, Jimmy jerks the string and pulls the rabbit from his reach. As we approach, Jimmy stops teasing the poor pup and lets him seize the rabbit in his mouth. Junior shakes the fur from side to side and algaecrisps spill out from inside. Excited, he laps them up and chews them with an audible crunching.

"Teachin' him to eat this awful food ya'll got down here ain't an easy thin'," Jimmy says.

I smile. "You get used to it."

"I sure as shit hope I never do," he says. "Who's this?"

Red sticks out his hand. "They call me Red."

"I can see why," Jimmy says, pumping his hand. "Where'd

ya come from?"

"Level 5."

"Huh?"

"He's from down below," I say, jumping in. "Holocene II. We grew up together."

"Oh," Jimmy looks him up and down. "You's the bully."

Red drops his head. "I said I was sorry."

"Well that's more'n most folks ever do," Jimmy replies, patting him on the back. "Welcome to our little club then."

"Thanks," Red says.

"Speakin' of apologies, Aubrey," Jimmy continues, "I owe you one my own self."

"No, you don't."

"Yes, I do," he says. "I acted like a spoilt kid. And you was right, I was wrong. It wouldn't be right bringin' them people up jus' to be slaughtered out there."

For all Red's apparent ignorance, he has the good sense to see what should be a private moment, and he says, "If you don't mind, I'd like to go play with the dog."

Jimmy nods, handing him the string. "He's a fox. His name's Junior."

Red lumbers away, dragging the rabbit fur, and Junior tears off after him, yipping and swatting at it as they go.

"Junior's getting big," I say, wanting to lighten the mood. "Remember when you wanted to eat him?"

Jimmy smiles. "He might be my fox now, but he missed you, too. Kept lookin' back and whimperin' the whole time we was gone up there."

"Are you saying you missed me?" I ask.

Jimmy dips his chin, then looks back up into my eyes. He

says, "I got as far as our river. You know, where you's almost drown. Anyway, we made camp at dusk, and no sooner had I lit a fire when that whole river got dark with a passin' shadow. I looked up and could've damn near spit and hit the underside of a drone. I swear it was brushin' the treetops. Evil lookin', I tell ya. And I ain't too proud to say I's scared. I's scared as I ever been. And the first thin' I thought, before I even thought about dyin', was I thought how much I wished you was there."

Now my eyes well up. "I had the same feeling here," I say, my voice cracking a little. "I'm glad you're back."

"You forgive me?" he asks.

"I couldn't ever not forgive you," I say.

Jimmy laughs. "I think you jus' said you'd forgive me, but I ain't quite sure about it the way it come out."

We both laugh, then an uncomfortable silence follows—nothing more to say. We stand there looking after Red, as he kneels on the ground, trying to wrestle the rabbit fur from Junior's mouth.

After a minute or so, Jimmy says, "We'd better get on and catch up 'fore ol' Junior there decides he likes the taste of Red better'n those awful algaecrisps."

The next two days pass in a blur of boredom.

The professor spends most of his time locked away in the command center, messing with the computers. Whenever he does come out to use the restroom or get some food, we can hear a string of muffled profanities echoing across the cavern as he moves. Red proves very useful busying himself with loading the supplies into the storeroom, even though he does eat almost as much as he manages to organize. Jimmy and Hannah seem to get on fine, both treating the other with a polite distance at meal times, but I feel as though something has come between Hannah and myself. Deciding the submarine was too cramped, she moved into a sleeping room next to the professor's, which is still just too creepy for me, since we found dead people in there, and she spends most of her awake time working alone in the lab.

Today, I find the lab door locked as usual, and I knock for three minutes.

"What's up?" she says, finally opening the door, but not inviting me in.

"Nothing. I just wanted to talk."

"I'm kind of busy right now. Can we talk later?"

"Actually, I thought maybe we could get away for a bit."

"Get away? Where?"

"Come on," I say, my tone bordering on pleading. "Just say yes. It won't take long."

She takes a deep breath then lets it out in a sigh. "Okay, but I need a few minutes to wrap up here."

"Cool. Just meet me at the dock."

Her few minutes turns into more than half an hour, and I have everything ready and am waiting long before she arrives at the dock. She sees the boat and stops.

"Where are we going?"

"Just out for a little picnic."

"A picnic? Up top?"

"Yes, up top. I need a little break from all this gray down here. And I'm sure you could use one, too."

Hannah hesitates, looking across the bay at the tunnel leading to the locks. "Fine," she says. "But only if you promise we won't be gone long."

We don't say much until we're out above, cruising on the lake. Most of the snow has melted away, replaced with a winter frost that catches the setting sun and sparkles like pink and gold ornaments on the trees that line the shores. The lake is calm, almost like an inverted second sky over which we fly, breaking the clouds into ripples and sending them rolling in our wake. Both our moods begin to lift, and Hannah remarks about how beautiful everything is.

I purposely take us away from the lake house site, toward the eastern shore where I run the boat up on a bank far enough for us to step out onto dry ground. It's cold, but invigorating. I lay out one of the foil emergency blankets and gesture for Hannah to sit down. Then I wrap another blanket around her shoulders and ask her to wait while I run for wood.

"I'll help," she says.

"No. Stay here. I'll be fast."

The wave's line of destruction is littered with limbs left behind, and although covered in a light frost, they seem to be mostly dry. When I get them arranged in front of our blanket, I realize that I forgot to ask Jimmy for his strike-a-light. But then I remember the flares, and I grab one from the boat and use it to light the fire.

I offer Hannah a meal bar, but she laughs and waves it away. She seems much more interested in the bottle of algae ethanol I smuggled from the storeroom. I get the top off and hand the bottle to Hannah.

"What's this?" she asks. "No glass?"

I recall our first dinner together, outside the lake house, beneath the mosquito net, and I remember the bottle of port and the fine crystal glasses. I feel suddenly unsophisticated.

Hannah must see the shame on my face, because she laughs and passes me back the bottle and says, "I'm only kidding. It's fine. But you first."

I tilt the bottle to my lips and take a long pull. It burns my throat and makes me feel instantly sick. Too embarrassed to show it, I control my expression until most of the pain passes. Hannah takes a swig next, and her head jerks to the side and she spews the ethanol out onto the sand. She thrusts the bottle at me. "Ugh! That's terrible."

Relieved, I recap it and stow it away in my bag.

Hannah opens her blanket and invites me to scoot next to her. We sit together and watch the last of the pink light fading behind the mountains where the sun has set.

"This was a good idea," she says.

"Kind of cold, though."

"Yeah, but still a good idea."

A few minutes of silence pass. A coyote calls somewhere. I take a deep breath and smell the cold, pine air.

"Hannah?"

"Yeah."

"You know how when we first met, we kind of fell for one another really fast?"

"Yes, I remember," she says. "It wasn't very long ago, although it feels like it was."

"Well, that's just it. Do you think . . . well, never mind."

"Do I think what, Aubrey?"

"Was it too fast? Us, I mean. I'm just saying, I guess . . . well, I mean it seems like you don't really like me like you did."

Hannah sighs and leans into me. "I still like you the same, Aubrey. I always will."

"Well, what's going on then?" I ask.

"I don't know," she says, her voice faraway. "It's just been a lot. We've been through a lot. And, you know, you were the first boy I'd ever seen. The first person I'd ever seen, other than my parents, of course. And, well, it was kind of all set up for us. I mean by my dad . . ." Her voice fades away with her gaze, obviously thinking about her dad now.

"Do you miss him?"

"Maybe the idea of him," she says. "But mostly I just miss my mom a lot."

There doesn't seem to be much else to say, so we sit and watch the light drain from the sky. A duck lands on the lake not far away, its feet skipping across the surface several times before it touches down and slides to a halt.

"Do you want to break it off?" I ask, after a while. "Break us off, I mean. Do you want to just be friends?"

"Friends?" she asks. "But I thought we were friends. How about we just start over and take it slow?"

I feel Hannah's warm breath on my cold neck. I turn and our lips meet. She tastes of salt and just a faint bite of leftover ethanol. I lie her down on the blanket and kiss her. It feels nice, but my mind is thinking about other things. I'm thinking about our predicament with the drones. I'm thinking about freeing Holocene II, and about where we'll live once we do. And I'm thinking about Jimmy. About the debt I owe him for saving my life. About how terrible it was for me to abandon him when I met Hannah. About how sad I was when he was gone.

Hannah stops and pulls away. "Are you cold?"

"Yeah, I'm pretty cold." I look up and see the sun is fully set, our fire bright against the dark blue lake. "We better get on back," I say, standing and brushing dirt off my butt. Hannah helps me fold the blankets and gather our things.

The sky is fully dark by the time I steer the boat into the locks again. I turn and look back as the doors close out the clear, cold night, and I catch a glimpse of our fading fire on the faraway shore, burning like a lonely candle on a sea of black. And then it's gone.

The minute we enter the cavern, we see Jimmy waiting for us on the dock, waving his arms frantically.

"What is it!" I shout, pulling up to the dock.

"The professor," he says. "Something's wrong."

When we enter the command center, Red is leaning over the professor, slapping him in the face. "Wake up! Wake up!"

I push Red aside. "What are you doing?"

"He won't wake up."

The professor appears lifeless enough. Drool hangs from his mouth, clinging to his white, bristly stubble. His unblinking eyes stare off somewhere far beyond the walls of the room. Hannah removes a handkerchief from the professor's pocket and touches the corner of it to his eye. He blinks instinctively.

"He's catatonic," she says. "We need to get him to the infirmary for an ECT."

"An ECT?" I ask.

"Just help me carry him. It's not far. Next to the lab."

Red grabs the professor's legs, Jimmy and I each take an arm, and with Hannah supporting his head from behind, we carry the catatonic old man to the door. We somehow manage to angle him through outside, where a comedy of errors ensues over which way is left and which way is right when half of us are facing backward, until we finally agree and the whole procession heads toward the infirmary with Junior running in circles ahead of us, as if it were the most exciting game. The professor is heavier than he looks.

Hannah has us rest the professor on a metal chair that reminds me of the dentist's chair I used to lie in for cleanings down in Holocene II. But when she straps his arms and legs into metal cuffs, I'm suddenly reminded of Eden's killing chair that I saw my father butchered in.

"What are you planning to do to him?"

"Electroconvulsive therapy," she says, opening a cabinet attached to the chair and connecting two electrodes to the professor's head.

"You're going to shock him? He made us promise not to."

Hannah pushes me away, ignoring my protest. "I don't care what we promised," she says. "We're saving his life here."

"He made it sound like it was torture."

"My father would never torture anyone," she says, stuffing a rubber bite-guard into the professor's mouth.

I look to Jimmy, but he shrugs.

"How's it work?" Red asks.

"It induces a seizure," Hannah says, turning the machine on and adjusting the dials.

I shake my head. "And a seizure's a good thing?"

"In this case, it is," she replies.

"Well, how do you know so much about it?"

"Because my mother had to have them from time to time, too. Stand back, please."

Hannah throws the switch, and the professor jumps on the table, his back arched, his limbs shaking in their cuffs. Then it's done. Just like that, I guess. The professor looks up at us and moans, his eyes blinking with an unsettling rapidity.

"Are you okay?" I ask him.

"Who are you?"

"I'm Aubrey."

"Funny name for a boy," he says.

Hannah grins. "Sometimes a little short term memory loss happens. He'll remember you soon enough."

"Catherine? Is that you, Catherine?"

Hannah removes the electrodes from his temples. "Hello, Professor Beckenbauer. I'm Catherine's daughter."

"Well, no need to be all formal about it," he says. "Just call me Moody."

"I can see why," Hannah laughs. Then she turns to us. "Maybe you two could help me walk the professor to his room for some rest. And, Red, how about you run and get some water and meet us there? I'm guessing the professor is thirsty."

With the professor tucked in and sleeping, we all gather in the command center again. It's littered with laminated maps and waterlogged journals laid out open to dry, pages torn free and arranged in odd patterns on the floor. The strange scene, coupled with the professor's apparent psychological problems, has me believing that maybe he's madder than we originally thought. It's time to start thinking for ourselves.

"You can't even read most of this old junk, it's so faded," Hannah says, holding a moldy journal up to Jimmy. "Can you read any of that, Jimmy?"

Jimmy looks embarrassed. "No," is all he says.

I thought Hannah knew Jimmy couldn't read. I hope she's not just being mean. The mastercode header page is up on the screens, the words spreading across the monitors and covering the entire wall. Just reading the title makes me sick:

THE HUMAN EXTINCTION PROJECT

"So," Red says, scratching his head and looking at the screens, "what does ex-tink-tee-on mean?"

"You're reading it wrong," I say. "You have to sound it out: ik-stink-shun."

"Ex-stink-shun," he drawls. "Like something used to stink and now it doesn't."

I can't help but laugh. "Something like that."

Hannah reads the encryption key clue out loud: "'Where man rises from the sea, in the right hand of David you shall find your key.' What do you think it means?"

"'Where man rises from the sea'? Does it have something to do with evolution, maybe?" I suggest. "And who's David? And why would the key be in his hand?"

"Maybe it's a volcano or somethin'," Jimmy says.

Hannah scrunches up her face. "A volcano?"

Jimmy shrugs. "Heck, I dunno. But my pa said there was places where volcanoes rose right up from the sea. He said that's how lots of places got made in the beginnin'."

"That's silly," Hannah says.

"No, it's not," I jump in, not just to defend Jimmy, but because I also think he might be onto something. "He actually makes a good point."

Hannah scoffs, "Why would an encryption key be hidden in a volcano?"

"You tell me," I say, irritated with her constant jibing of Jimmy. "It was your crazy dad who left the stupid clue."

"Jus' forget about the volcano," Jimmy says.

"Does an encryption key open some kind of coffin thing?"

Red asks, either more ignorant than I thought, or purposefully trying to diffuse the situation with humor. Hard to tell. "No," I say, deciding he must not know what it is. "We need the encryption key to unlock the software so we can take control of the drones and stop them from killing humans."

"Then we can free the people below?" he asks.

"Yes, then we can free the people."

He smiles. "Good. I miss my girl."

Bang! The door flies open and slams into the wall. We all spin around in unison and look. The professor stands in the doorway with a crazed look in his eyes, his wild hair appearing more electric than ever. "The Isle of Man!" he shouts, so loud we all flinch. Then he storms into the room and points at the screens. "The Isle of Man," he says, again. "That's the clue. 'Where man rises from the sea.' It's the Isle of Man."

"Are you sure?" I ask, still suspicious of his mental state.

"Das ist so offensichtlich, sonnenklar," he says, so excited he doesn't appear to realize he's speaking some other language. "I can't believe it took me so long to figure it out. Radcliffe used to go there all the time. And always alone, too. Not long after we launched this latest software, he ceased his visits. But it remains a black zone. As we speak, no drones can fly near it, and the ships stay a mile from its shores. Our satellite software even blurs it out when they pass overhead. Don't you see? 'Where man rises from the sea.' It's the Isle of Man."

His enthusiasm is catching, and I feel my pulse quicken.

"Well, what about the second part?" I ask. "'In the right hand of David you shall find your key.'—?"

The professor's shoulders slump. "I'm afraid I still have no idea on that," he mumbles.

Worried that he's lapsing into a mood again, I pat him on the back and smile. "It doesn't matter," I say. "You've done it! You've solved the most important part, and we owe you big time. You might have just saved us all."

He grins a little. "You think so?"

"I sure do. We all do. Don't we guys?"

The professor looks from face to face as everyone nods. "No more shock table?" he asks.

Hannah jumps in: "That was for—"

"No more shock table," I say, cutting her off.

The professor staggers to a chair and sits down and sighs. "But I'm afraid my little epiphany is of little use unless you can get to the Isle itself and solve the second half of the riddle."

"Then that's just what we'll do," I say.

"But how would we get there?" Hannah asks, sorting through a stack of laminated maps. "Isn't it halfway around the world somewhere?"

"It's at least 8,000 kilometers," the professor says. "And that's if you could fly. The drones left in the hangar are pretty banged up from being tossed about in the flood, and even if they weren't, there's no way to fly them with the system locked down. I'm afraid we're stuck here."

"Cain't we take the submarine?" Jimmy asks.

The room falls quiet. The professor rocks his head from side to side. "It's possible, though you'd be navigating manually without the ability to tap into the guidance system."

"Would we go around north?" I ask.

"Good gracious, no," the professor responds. "Beneath all that awful ice."

"So what then? All the way around South America?"

"You've learned your geography well, young man."

"Wait," Hannah interjects. "My dad said something about the old Panama Canal being used by our ships."

"And you've learned yours even better, my young lady," says the professor. "It's about 8,000 kilometers through the canal to the southwest tip of . . . well, what used to be Florida. And another six or seven thousand to the Irish Sea."

"Irish Sea?" Red perks up. "My dad says my ancestors were fighting Irish."

"Well, then . . .," I add up the two trips. "That's about 15,000 kilometers total. How long would it take to get there?"

The professor closes an eye. "Fifteen thousand kilometers makes about eight thousand nautical miles. Figure an average speed of maybe fifteen knots gives us 533 hours, by twenty-four hours . . . you're looking at twenty-two or twenty-three days each way, give or take."

"I thought you said you were no good at arithmetic?"

He smiles. "I have my moments."

"When can we leave?" I ask.

The professor sighs. "Well, it'll take some time to teach you how to pilot the sub. I'm guessing several weeks. And then you'll need to learn chart navigation—"

"No," I shake my head. "When can *we* leave."

"You mean me? You want me to go with you? No, no, no. I'm afraid that's not possible. Not possible at all."

"It's our only chance," I say. "You have to do it."

"I couldn't."

"You could too."

"Come on," Hannah says, "don't be chicken."

"I won't go," he says.

"You'll go if I say you will," Hannah replies, planting her hands on her hips.

The professor shakes his head.

"Listen," I say, trying to sound as threatening as possible, "I'm not opposed to strapping you down to that table again and shocking you into next week, if that's what it takes."

He tosses up his hands. "All right, I'll think about it."

"I'll take that as a yes."

CHAPTER 6
It's Okay to be Afraid

The professor hands me another list.

"Gee, Professor. For someone who didn't want to go, you sure seem excited about this trip."

"On the contrary, young man. I loathe going outside, but today just seems to vibrate with energy, wouldn't you say?"

He rushes off, making his rounds to check our progress.

We send the train down to Holocene II twice for supplies. The communications liaison for Level 5 sends a message up through the system informing us of a missing citizen, but we decide it's best not to mention Red. Instead, we send a message back explaining that a minor flood has damaged Eden, and that retirements will be on hold for several months while repairs are being made. At least it's half true. Fortunately for us, because the scientists needed to hide their age and keep up the illusion of Eden, communication between the Foundation and the other levels is limited to emails on the closed computer system.

After the supplies are offloaded and inventoried, we start the slow work of storing them away on the submarine. With only four bunks, it would be a squeeze for five people anyway, without all the supplies. We load meal bars and algaecrisps in every empty drawer. We stack canned goods on the floor in the passageways and lay metal strips recovered from the scaffolding over the cans so we can walk on top of them. Vacuum bags of freeze-dried vegetables make perfect fillers for empty nooks.

When we finally finish, there's hardly room to move, and I get the feeling it's going to be a long several months at sea.

The professor explains that the submarine manufactures its own fresh water, and the electric engines that turn the screw run on liquid metal batteries that recharge via solar cells molded into the sub's outer skin.

"Wouldn't you need to be on the surface for that?" I ask.

"Only close to it," he says. "They're very sensitive."

I ask the professor about breathable oxygen and he shows me the systems that use electrolysis to separate the oxygen and hydrogen molecules from seawater. It's all very interesting, and I could spend months learning about how everything works, but by the third day of preparation, the professor announces that we're ready to leave the following morning. Or at least when we wake from our next sleep, since it's impossible to tell night from day down here.

A hush falls over the group the eve before our departure. Hannah hides away in her lab as usual, the professor goes to his room, and Jimmy disappears with Junior somewhere in the maze of buildings. Red falls into a panic about some perceived shortage of supplies and spends the evening counting cans in the submarine, constantly losing track and having to begin all over again. I lie in my bunk listening to him count, trying to imagine what it will be like to spend two months in here.

There's a tap on the door.

"Come in." The door opens and Red steps in. "Geez, Red. Give it up already. How many times do you need to count what's in here?"

Red sighs and sits on the edge of the bunk across from me. "Can I talk to you?"

"Sure, Red. What's up?"

"I don't know. It's just that something's on my mind."

"Better share it then and lighten the load."

"Well," he says, scratching his head, "it's just that I'm thinking maybe it might be best if I went back down to Level 5. I mean, don't get me wrong—this seems like a great adventure and all, and I really want to go more than anything. I do. But I'm just thinking about the others, really. Because I've been counting, you know, and there aren't enough supplies. There just aren't, no matter how I do the figures." When he finishes talking, he stares at me with a hopeful expression.

I lean up in my bunk and look him in the eye. "It's okay to be afraid, Red."

"Afraid?" He asks, placing his hand on his chest. "Me? I'm not afraid. Not at all."

"I am."

"You are?"

"Sure."

"What are you afraid of?"

"I'm afraid of being trapped in this tin can at the bottom of the sea. I'm afraid of dying. Hell, I'm afraid of what we might find if we do make it to the island."

"Wow," he says, his eyebrows lifted with surprise, "I never thought you were afraid of anything."

"I'm afraid of lots of things. I'm even afraid of confined spaces. That's why I'm in here now, before we've even left, trying to get used to it."

Red drops his head. "You remember when we used to bury you in the sand at the electric beach?"

"Yes, I remember."

"Well, how come you never seemed afraid then?"

"Because I wouldn't let myself show it."

"But if you wouldn't show it then, how come you're okay telling me you're scared now?"

It's a good question, and I take moment to consider my answer. "I don't know," I finally reply. "I guess I've just been through so much that it seems silly to be afraid of being afraid."

Red nods, thinking over what I've said.

After a long pause, he says, "I think I'll go spend my last night in a regular bed." Then he stands to leave, hesitating in the doorway. "Aubrey?"

"Yeah?"

"I am afraid. But I feel better now. Thanks."

Smiling to myself, I close my eyes and lay my head back on my bunk. I feel better, too.

I'm woken sometime later by another tap on the door. Assuming it's Red again, I sit up and prepare for another talk, but Jimmy steps in. He sits across from me and sighs. My first thought is that he must be having second thoughts also. And that scares me, because he's always so much braver than I am.

"What's up, Jimmy?"

"Somethin's worryin' me," he says.

"We're going to be fine," I reply. "I'm nervous, too, but we've been through worse with less. We've got plenty of food on here, and the professor seems to know what he's doing."

"It ain't about me," Jimmy says. "It's Junior."

"What about him?"

"It ain't right to take him."

"What do you mean?"

"He's already showin' signs he ain't happy jus' bein' down

here. I cain't imagine makin' him spend near two months on this here submarine."

"What else can we do?" I ask.

Jimmy looks down and picks at the mattress seam. "It's killin' me to even think it, but we need to let him go."

"Let him go? You mean leave him behind?"

"I jus' think he'd have a better chance up at the lake."

Right away, I know Jimmy's right. With five of us trapped on here having to take shifts for the bunks, and hardly enough room in the submarine control room for all of us at once, it would be cruel to make Junior come along.

"We better hurry then," I say, pulling on my shirt. "Won't be long before the others are up and ready to go."

Jimmy holds Junior while I pilot the boat. Usually, the trip up the locks seems to take forever. Today it goes too fast. When the upper doors open, we cruise out into early blue dawn on the mist-covered lake. Strange, billowy clouds hover not far above us, brighter than the dark sky they're hanging in, as if illuminated by some light of their own.

I look over and see Jimmy's bowed head buried in Junior's fur. Junior sits there unaware and almost smiling as he looks out the window. I steer us toward the site of the lake house, figuring familiar territory might provide the best chance of survival for a fox on its own. I go slow, reducing my speed as we approach the peninsula. Still, the shore seems to rush upon us as if some current were carrying us there against our will.

I kill the jets and run the boat onto the gravel. Jimmy sighs and looks at me. A single tear runs down his cheek. He doesn't bother to wipe it away. I know he won't be able to do it, so I release the latch and lift the lid on its hinges. Junior wiggles free from Jimmy's arms and bounds across the bow and leaps onto the shore, taking off like a terror down the beach.

It's just another adventure to him.

The sky is a lighter blue now, the clouds a darker shade of gray, as if they somehow soaked up the darkness like so many sponges in the sky. We watch as Junior races away, stopping occasionally to sniff at things he passes before glancing back toward the boat and then racing on again. He's obviously happy to be free from the darkness of the cavern bay.

Jimmy's voice cracks with emotion: "We'd better get on back now, while we still can."

"You sure?"

Jimmy nods, pulling the top down and latching it. I start the jets and back from the shore, turning us toward the dam.

"You remember when we found him, when he was jus' a pup followin' us along that river?" Jimmy asks.

I smile just thinking about it.

"You remember what ya told me?"

"Yeah, I told you to not look back."

"Then you's looked back yerself."

I laugh. "I sure did."

"Will ya tell me again?"

"Tell you to not look back?"

"Yeah. I need you to tell me."

I shake my head. "I won't tell you that, Jimmy."

Tears well up in Jimmy's eyes again, and he covers his face with his hands. "Oh, God," he moans, sobbing. "I'm sorry. I'm so damn sorry. I'm cryin' like a baby."

"It's okay to cry," I say, touching Jimmy's shoulder. "He means a lot to you."

"He was all I had when you left me on my own," he sobs.

What he says hits my chest like a hammer.

"I know I was a jerk," I say, not strong enough to take the blow, "but it was you who left, Jimmy."

"You coulda come after me," he stutters.

Now I'm crying, too.

"I'm sorry, Jimmy. I really am. I'm sick over it still. I was all caught up with Hannah and my own stupid hormones. You have to understand, I'd never even met a girl before who liked me. I betrayed you, and I'm sorry."

"I know it," he says. "We each done stupid stuff."

I wipe away my tears and focus on the water ahead. I think about when Jimmy took off with Junior from the lake house and made camp in the woods. I remember how Gloria came to cut my hair and how I asked about Jimmy, and she told me that Jimmy had been asking about me, too. And I remember him pulling me from that river and saving my life, and how he said it was Junior who followed me. I crank the wheel and whip a one-eighty and drop the throttle and speed back toward shore.

Jimmy looks up from his hands. "What are ya doin'?"

"I'm looking back again."

Jimmy's face breaks into a huge smile.

We're still pretty far from shore when we run up on Junior swimming after us. He's obviously exhausted from paddling, and I doubt he'd have had enough energy to even make it back to dry land. Jimmy pops the top and leans out and scoops him dripping from the water and pulls him into the boat. Junior lies limp in his arms and licks his face. I peel off my shirt and hand it over, and Jimmy uses it to dry Junior's coat while I pull the top down and continue on toward the dam.

When we arrive back at the underground docks, no one appears to have noticed that we even left except the professor who pops his head out from the submarine and says, "I was about to start offering odds on whether or not you two had run off for good."

"Where is everybody?" I ask.

"Red's still snoring loud enough to wake all of Holocene II, and Hannah's in the shower. Why don't you boys pull that boat up on the lift there, since it won't be needed while we're gone."

After we've stored the boat, Jimmy takes Junior on board the submarine and hunts up a spot for his bed. I hang my wet shirt to dry and, as much as I hate to do it, change back into my zipsuit. Red arrives shortly with a renewed enthusiasm, even laughing at himself when I ask if he wants to count the supplies one last time. The professor tinkers with the controls, emerging several minutes later to announce that we're set for departure. We all gather on the submarine deck and wait for Hannah.

"I'll go get her," I suggest.

"She'll be along," the professor says. "Give her a little time to prepare. It's a long journey for a young woman crammed in here with four men and a fox."

And soon enough, she does come.

She walks toward the dock with her head bowed and her long, red hair, still damp from her shower, hanging over the shoulders of her gray Holocene II zipsuit. She stops on the dock below the sub and looks up at us. "I'm staying."

"What?" I ask.

"I'm staying here."

"Why?"

"Because someone needs to be here," she says. "And I've thought about it all night. It just doesn't make any sense for all of us to go, wouldn't you agree?"

"What do you mean?" I ask, jumping down to the dock and facing her. "We're all in this together."

"What if something happens to us out there?" she asks.

"Then it will happen to all of us."

"Yes," she says. "But have you thought it through? What will become of Holocene II? With no one left here to call the train up and set them free, won't they be trapped down there forever? That's not a very good plan."

"But Hannah—"

"She's right," the professor says. "And not just that, but someone should be here to respond to any queries from them also. I'm sure our delaying their upcoming retirements has put them on edge already. Routine is very important down there, as you well know, Aubrey."

"Well, what if something happens to you here?" I ask.

Hannah shrugs. "There's nothing to worry about here. You're the ones taking all the risks. The only thing I'll need to contend with is boredom."

"But what will you do for two months?"

"I've got plenty to keep me busy in my lab," she says. "And there's lots to be done yet around here after the flood."

"No." I shake my head. "I won't let you stay."

"I'm not asking you," she says. "I'm telling you."

I look to Jimmy, but his face is expressionless, as if to say this is my decision. The professor frowns, but nods, agreeing with Hannah. I storm to the edge of the dock and look at the dark tunnel leading down the step locks toward the Pacific.

How many miles, how many months? Anything could happen.

The professor clears his throat. "Ahem. We need to get moving now, I already set the locks to lower."

I turn back to Hannah. "Fine, but I'm not letting you stay here alone. No way. Someone either stays on with you, or none of us goes at all."

Hannah drills me with an angry stare, but I stand my ground. "You need the professor to pilot the sub," she says. "And there's no way Jimmy would let you go without him. I know that much. So I guess that leaves Red."

I look at Red, having entirely forgotten for a minute that he was even there. He raises his hand meekly, almost as if he were asking permission to speak.

"Yes," I say, "what is it, Red?"

"I just want to say, for the record, that I'll stay if you need me to, but after last night I'm ready to go."

I smile, remembering our talk. "I know you are."

Several quiet moments pass with only the sound of our breathing audible in the almost absolute silence. A fan turns on in a building somewhere.

I step to Hannah and wrap my arms around her. She leans her head on my shoulder and I smell her wet hair, the scent of shampoo. My guts are knotted up and aching with heartbreak already, but I don't cry. We stand together hugging for a long time, neither of us moving to pull away. I know when we do it will be time to say goodbye, and I have no idea what to say.

I think about the first time I saw her from the bluff. It was sunny then and she was wearing that white skirt and knocking tennis balls across the net. I remember Jimmy hoisting me up to look over the fence and her standing there with her hands on her hips. She told me Aubrey was a funny name for a boy. Man, it seems like ages ago already. Almost like another life.

"Give us ninety days," I hear the professor say. "If we're not back by then, bring up some help from Holocene II and make a plan. I'd suggest any of the managers from the loading bay. They're practical people."

Hannah nods, her head still resting on my shoulder.

"Other than that, try to have as little contact as possible with them. They don't expect to hear much from us up here."

Suddenly, I feel Red standing beside me on the dock. I pull away from Hannah and turn and look him in the eye. He nods, seeming to understand what I want to say but can't. With just his eyes he promises to look after her.

Then I turn and climb aboard the submarine and descend into the hatch without looking back.

Part Two

CHAPTER 7
Whales, Sharks, and Great Apes

The door eases open.

"I don't want to talk."

Junior slinks in and lays his head on my bunk, even though I know Jimmy cracked the door to let him in.

I'm upset with everyone right now. I'm upset with the professor for pressuring us to leave. I'm upset with Jimmy for not helping me convince Hannah to come along. I'm really upset with Hannah for staying behind at the last minute. But mostly I'm upset with myself for being relieved that she didn't come. There's just been so much arguing between us lately.

Oh, well. At least she'll be safe.

Juniors licks my hand.

"You're a good boy, Junior," I say, scratching his ears. "What do you think? Will we be able to find this key and get back safely and put all this behind us?"

He whines, turning his head for a deeper scratch.

"What's that? You've had enough adventure? Me too, little fella, me too. Let' go see what Jimmy's up to."

Panic grips me when I discover the submarine is empty. Then I notice the open hatch and climb out onto the deck and find Jimmy and the professor sitting with their backs against the sail, watching the dim cavern walls slide past. The only light comes from the water itself, which seems to be glowing green, and it throws moving reflections onto the rock walls, painting a watery silhouette of the passing submarine there.

I drop down beside Jimmy.

"You okay?" he asks.

"Yeah, I'm okay."

We sit silent for a time, listening to the bow wave splash softly against the cavern walls. It's very hypnotic. We seem to be moving at a steady clip, but if the submarine is throwing a wake, it's too far back for me to hear it.

"Hey, wait just a minute." My voice echoes off the walls. "How come we're not going through any locks?"

The professor chuckles. "Good question, young man. We are passing through locks, we're just not stopping."

"I don't understand."

"That's the beauty of these step locks. The journey's length of nearly three hundred kilometers combined with its 1,400 meter drop, allows for very long locks. So, you see, the water lowers while we're moving and we roll into the next lock without pause. It's all timed perfectly for a sixteen hour trip at ten knots."

"Seems funny to call them step locks then, if there aren't even any steps," I reply.

"I see your point there," the professor says. "Perhaps we should call them escalator locks."

"What's an escalator?" Jimmy asks.

"Oh, just an old moving staircase that they used to put in

shopping malls."

"What's a shopping mall?"

"Ha!" he says, looking over at Jimmy and me. "Mostly just a place where kids like you could hang out and get into trouble. Something from long before your time."

We spend the next fourteen hours or so getting used to life on board the submarine. The shower is small and cramped, but I feel much better after letting the hot water run over my body. My shirt smells like wet fox from Jimmy's using it to dry Junior, but I pull it on along with Dr. Radcliffe's old pants and happily stuff my zipsuit away in a drawer next to my pipe.

I teach Jimmy to use the electric cooktop in the galley. At first, he won't go near it, fearing the red, glowing swirls beneath the glass. But I explain that it works just like a cook fire, and soon he's stirring up a pot of potato soup that he insists on picking himself from among the cans, even though he can't read the label. The galley even has a rack of spices, synthetically produced down in Holocene II, and Jimmy gets so excited by their exotic smells that he mixes everything in, making the soup nearly inedible when he's finished. Still, the professor and I choke it down and tell him it's good. Only Junior won't lie, leaving his bowl untouched on the floor.

I'm reclining in my bunk with my lesson slate, reading an ancient collection of stories that chronicle the lives of fictitious people on Mars, when the professor pokes his head into the bunkroom and says: "We're almost out!"—meaning, I assume, free of the tunnel and into the Pacific Ocean.

Jimmy and I climb onto the deck. The channel is no longer illuminated, and the dark stretch of water ahead leads to an arched opening that shimmers with a silvery brilliance. As we near the end of the long tunnel, small waves meet us, lapping at the side of the submarine. We glide beneath the cavernous arch and spill out into the wide expanse of the moonlit Pacific.

The moon hangs low above the horizon to the southwest, sending a silver highway across the water's surface to meet us. Jimmy takes a deep breath beside me then lets it out. In the silver light I can see his eyes are closed, his hair rustling in the salty breeze. He's smiling.

The professor guides the submarine several kilometers out to sea before leaving the silver highway and turning us south to follow the coast toward the southern tip of the continent and the Panama Canal. The distant shoreline rolls past, shrouded in deep shadows, gradually growing clearer as the eastern sky fades from black to deep blue. I'm somewhat relieved when the professor calls for us to come back down, because I wouldn't be surprised if our course takes us past the cove where Jimmy's family was slaughtered. We don't need to be reminded.

The professor seals the main hatch behind us and pushes us toward the control room where he waves us into chairs and sits himself in front of the controls. Then he throws a switch and floods the ballasts, and the submarine drops beneath the waves and all becomes quiet.

"How deep can this sub go?" I ask.

"Submarine," he corrects, cocking a busy eyebrow at me.

"We say submarine or boat, but never sub, and never ship."

"Okay," I say, rolling my eyes at Jimmy. "How deep can this *submarine* go?"

"Maybe three hundred meters or so," he replies. "Used to dive deeper before we installed the acrylic windows."

Jimmy's face lights up. "It has windows?"

The professor grins and reaches for a switch.

Near the front of the submarine, on either side of Jimmy and me, interior wall panels slide open, revealing the blue ocean beyond. A strange sight out the windows makes my heart skip.

The morning sun slants into the blue water with gorgeous rays that cut like luminescent blades through a sort of floating forest. Giant, black cylinders, that look themselves like vertical submarines, hover with their upturned noses just beneath the surface. The professor cranks the wheel and dodges left to miss hitting one, and I get a glimpse of how truly enormous they are. He quickly floods the ballasts with more water and drops us beneath the behemoth floating obstacles.

"That was close," the professor says. "I'll need to check the sensors and see why the alarm didn't sound."

Jimmy and I stand glued to the windows, looking up at the floating forest, now just dim shadows above us.

"What are they?" Jimmy asks.

"Physeter macrocephalus."

"Physter what?" I ask, assuming the professor is speaking German again, or whatever language he uses when he's excited.

"Sperm whales," he says.

"Are they dead?" Jimmy asks.

"No, no. They're just sleeping."

Jimmy shakes his head with awe. "I seen a lot of whales," he says, "but I ain't never seen one sleepin' before."

After the excitement of the whales, we spend the next six days in relative boredom, trapped on board the submarine. The professor teaches us each to operate the controls, and we work into an easy system, taking turns relieving him so he can sleep, although it seems he only takes the shortest of naps.

We stay at a shallow depth most of the time, but still, the silence is almost absolute. Junior spends many hours lying in the corner, looking depressed with his head on his paws. During the afternoons, we plead with the professor to take us up to the surface and he usually agrees, but only after much grumbling about the wasted energy consumed by the friction of the bow wave and wake, which I'm happy to point out costs nothing since the batteries are recharged by the sun.

"Nothing costs nothing," the professor says.

Every day when we pop the hatch, the eastern landscape visible in the distance is more arid, and the air feels warmer. It's torture to sit on the deck and watch the blue water sliding by without being able to get in, but the sun feels good on my face, and the salty breeze is a welcome relief from the unnatural purity of the submarine's filtered air. Even though it's winter, Jimmy goes bareback, and his skin takes on its former deep tan. Mine picks up a little color, too. We spend many hours on deck, watching the white churn of water disappear into a glassy calm behind the submarine. Junior joins us most days, pacing the borders of the small deck, stopping only on occasion to look into the water or to hold his nose in the air and read some important news sent on olfactory channels only he can receive.

Jimmy nudges me. "You see that?"

"See what?"

"There!" he says. "Starboard side ahead."

I chuckle because until yesterday's boating lesson from the professor, neither of us even knew what starboard meant. I stop laughing when I turn and see what he's pointing at.

Not ten meters from us and coming up fast is a giant octopus bigger than any I've ever imagined existed, its floating carcass being ravaged by a pack of thrashing white sharks. The octopus's orange flesh bobs in the low swell, and countless fins and open mouths of razor teeth encircle it, jostling for position. As we cruise past, I catch sight of an open mouth, big enough for a man to dive into and disappear, and when it clamps down and tears into the dead octopus, the shark's visible eye rolls back into its head with gluttonous ecstasy before rolling back and focusing its milky stare on us as we pass.

I shiver at the sight. "I'm never asking the professor to stop and let us swim again."

"I dun' think we need to worry about swimmin' any time soon," Jimmy says, pointing to the horizon ahead.

A dark wall of clouds races toward us, pushing enormous swells ahead of it. The first set crashes into the submarine just as Jimmy seizes Junior by the neck, nearly sending all three of us overboard. Soaking wet and panicked, with images of the sharks still swimming in my head, we scramble to the hatch and descend into the safety of the submarine, double checking the seal before stumbling down the listing passageway and joining the professor in the control room. He floods the ballasts and drops us beneath the waves into the calm and quiet world that forever resides just below the surface.

Two days later, we arrive in the evening at the entrance of the great canal. The professor brings us to the surface, and we all gather on deck and gaze at the canal in the lingering light of a phenomenal sunset. The canal looks like an enormous river inlet, except the water is flowing into it instead of out.

"Why's it flowing the wrong way?"

The professor doesn't respond for a long time, and I begin to think he didn't hear my question. Just when I've forgotten that I even asked it, he says, "Water never flows the wrong way. There used to be a series of locks that lifted ships up to a manmade lake, allowing them to cross Panama before being lowered into the Caribbean on their way to the Atlantic. The system was useless by the time we discovered it after the war, the dam having been bombed and the lake long since drained out to sea. So we did something the old French once wanted to do, back when man still thought he could shape and control the land. We cut a sea-level canal from one ocean to the other."

I'm startled by an audible spray of mist and notice a pod of passing porpoises, their humps rolling above the pink sunset water before diving quietly beneath the surface again.

The professor continues: "The Pacific side is slightly higher, mostly due to water density, so what you're seeing here is the world's only river that flows constantly from one ocean directly into another. It was an unhappy necessity for us to cut it. We have charges buried somewhere in the channel walls to cave it in once we no longer need it. And the sooner we blow it the better, if you ask me."

"Why's that?" I ask.

The professor ignores my question. "We can wait out here for daylight, or cross in the dark. I don't much care either way. It's up to you two." Then he disappears into the hatch.

"What do you think?" I ask Jimmy, now that we're alone on deck. "Wait 'til morning or go now."

"I dun' see no reason to wait," Jimmy says.

"Me either. Hey, does the professor seem nervous about something to you?"

"Maybe," Jimmy says. "But he's prob'ly jus' in one of his moods. This was the first time I even seen him up here."

"Yeah, me too," I say. "I don't think he likes the sun."

The canal is too shallow in places to traverse its entire length fully submerged, and Jimmy and I stay topside and watch as the dark jungle creeps by on either side of us. The submarine is being pulled by the strong currents and, without the bow wave or wake, an eerie silence descends over our crossing. As the red horizon behind us bleeds fully into black, the jungle recedes into the night ahead, and only a wide swath of winding starlit sky is visible above the high edges of the flowing canal.

"Sure is peaceful," Jimmy says, breaking a long silence.

I reach into my pocket and take out my father's pipe, using the last of the tobacco he gave me to load the bowl.

I nudge Jimmy. "You got your strike-a-light?"

There's no wind at all, and it only takes two good sparks to coax the pipe lit. We pass it back and forth, tasting the sweet tobacco on our tongues. Jimmy takes to it right away.

The night is so calm, and the air so still, that it would be hard to tell that we are even moving if the smoke didn't leave our mouths and rush aft, passing in clouds of shadow through the light of the open hatch before making its way out into the night. Or maybe the smoke stays still and it's us who moves. Depends on where you're standing, I guess.

When the last of the tobacco is gone to ash, I tap the pipe clean against my palm and pass it to Jimmy.

"I want you to have it."

"No way," Jimmy says, trying to give it back.

I hold up my hands, refusing it. "I mean it, Jimmy. I want you to have it."

"But it was yer dad's."

"Yes, it was. And he would still be imprisoned in Eden, in that awful brain tank, if it weren't for you helping me set him free. And you know what else? That pipe would be clogged up in the gullet of some vulture that picked apart my corpse if you hadn't saved me when I stumbled into your life."

"You more'n paid it back," Jimmy says. "You's saved me

now at least twice."

"Still, I want you to have it."

"How 'bout I hold onto it for ya?" Jimmy says, slipping the pipe somewhere safe inside his clothing.

I'm about to tell him again that it's his to keep when something hard slams into the deck right beside me. Before I can even react, another missile whips past my right ear and bangs against the deck behind us. Suddenly, it's raining rocks. Rocks and clods of dirt. They hammer down on the deck in a thunderous riot from both directions on the banks above.

Jimmy and I scramble toward the open hatch with our arms over our heads. A stone rockets past us and ricochets down into the passageway. We manage to get inside and seal the hatch just in time to shield an even heavier hailstorm.

With the barrage still echoing into the submarine, we lurch into the control room and find the professor there feverishly consulting his instruments. He finesses the lever that controls the ballasts and submerges the submarine just enough so that the pounding turns to the soft thud of sinking rocks slowed by several feet of water. Junior rushes to Jimmy's side and stands guard over the passageway with his fur bristled up.

"What the hell was that?" I ask, still catching my breath.

"Hominidae," the professor slurs, fear etched on his face.

I hold out my hand and show him the stone that I scooped from the passageway floor. "You mean to say that people threw these at us?"

"Close," he says. "But no. The other great apes."

"Apes ain't no people," Jimmy jumps in.

"That's exactly what many of my colleagues argued," the professor replies. "But others of us worried that the apes might evolve to fill the vacuum left by humans. We considered adding them to the extinction project. It was a close vote."

"You voted?" I ask. "I thought you said you weren't very involved in the decisions?"

"Well, I wasn't," the professor answers, turning back to his instruments as the pelting from above fades away. "But apes still scare the sleep out of me."

I look at the rock in my hand and wonder at the thoughts that must have been bouncing around in all those sub-human heads. Why on Earth would they set up to ambush the canal? Or was it simply for sport that they attacked us? Either way, I'm just happy that it's behind us now.

We cruise into the Caribbean Sea just before daybreak. For the next two days we navigate relatively mild seas, heading north until we enter the Gulf of Mexico and turn east, following a deep-water channel toward the Atlantic. On the morning of the third day, we pass the southernmost island key where Dr. Radcliffe brought Hannah and me for our overnight tour of the park. I scan the shoreline for the bungalow, and I'm almost certain I catch the morning sun reflecting off the windows. But when I try to point it out to Jimmy, he seems unconvinced.

"If you's say so," he says. "But I jus' dun' see it."

"How can you not see it?" I ask. "The sun's glinting off

the glass. Look. Right there!"

"Maybe ya jus' miss her."

"You think I'm making up seeing the bungalow because I miss Hannah? Well, that's just silly."

"It's normal, ya know," he says, after a brief silence.

"What's normal?"

"Missin' someone."

"I guess. Maybe I do miss her a little. And I'm worried too, you know. You think they're all right?"

"Her and Red?"

"Yeah."

"I ain't sure about Red 'cause she's prob'ly runnin' him around like a slave, but I'll bet my skin she's jus' fine."

"Really?"

"Yeah. Dun' worry so much."

"Okay. I'll try not to."

"Oh!" he calls. "There it is."

"What?"

"The bungalow. I see it now."

CHAPTER 8
Discovering 'Merica

"Did he answer?"

"No," Jimmy says. "He's still locked in the bunkroom."

"Come on, it's been two days already. I'm tired of sitting at these controls. It's boring."

"Why you tellin' me? I'm sittin' right here with ya."

"Sorry. I'd just like to go up top and get some air."

"Bring us up," he says. "I'll watch the controls."

"No. It's okay. We'll stay together until he snaps out of his stupid mood. I wish we had a shock table on board."

Jimmy steps up beside me and nods to the throttle lever. "Let's see how fast she can go."

The look of mischief in his eye makes me smile.

"Okay," I say.

We've been submerged and moving at a steady fifteen knots for over two days, and it feels good to press the throttle down and feel the screw wind up and push us faster through the water. The gauge climbs to twenty-five knots, then to thirty, but other than the brief acceleration, it's just as boring as going fifteen. I back the throttle off. As we slow to around ten knots, a pod of dolphins overtakes the submarine, one of them swimming alongside the window and looking straight in at us.

When the dolphins veer right, Jimmy says: "Follow them."

I turn the wheel and adjust our course, hitting the throttle and speeding after them. We quickly overtake the pod, so I drop our speed again and allow them to catch up. Several of the dolphins take turns swimming to the windows, looking in and tapping the glass with their noses, as if playing a curious game. Then they break left and swim away again. Again I chase after them. Jimmy points up through the windows. "Up there!" he shouts. "They're runnin' on the surface."

I flip the switch to blow water from the ballasts and use the planes to steer us toward the surface. But I miscalculate the angle, and we launch from the water like a giant dolphin, the windows going sky-blue before the nose of the sub slaps down hard onto the surface. We stabilize at our normal surface-level depth and continue on. I shoot a glance at the door, expecting to see the professor storm in at any second.

Jimmy regains his footing, laughing uncontrollably, and rushes to the windows, which are now just beneath the water's surface. I set the throttle at ten knots and leave the controls and join him. We watch as the dolphins stampede all around us, riding the bow wake, leaping into the air, appearing to double in size from our vantage point beneath the water's surface, their silhouettes trembling there on the liquid lens above like melted version of themselves, only to shrink again to their normal size before piercing through the waves and racing on ahead of us. I count ten, twenty—no, there must be at least fifty dolphins rushing ahead of us in some kind of aquatic jubilee.

Then a terrific screech is followed by a terrible boom, and

Jimmy and I hurl forward at a frightening speed, and my head bounces against the acrylic window with an explosive cracking sound that makes me sick to think it came from my own skull. I fall, seemingly in slow-motion, forever toward the floor.

"You little idiots!"

The professor stands over me with his hands on his hips. I can feel every heartbeat in my aching brain. Jimmy lies next to me, and Junior cowers in the corner licking his paw.

I reach out and shake Jimmy. "You okay?"

He moans. "I'm all right."

As we pick ourselves off the floor, the professor storms to the controls and shuts down the engines. The submarine isn't moving. It is, however, tilted slightly on its side with the port window fully beneath the water and the starboard window half above it, showing blue sky. I stagger to the window and lift to my tiptoes and look out above the water line. A small set of waves rolls past the submarine, obstructing my view, but as they get farther away, they shrink into the horizon, revealing an island. Just a glimpse of green. Then a new set of swells blocks the view again.

I turn and see Jimmy checking Junior's paw. The professor inspects his charts, a look of furious consternation on his brow.

My head is still throbbing with an audible pulse of pain and I can hardly hear my own voice when I ask the professor, "What happened?"

"What happened?" he slurs, mimicking me. "Nothing happened. Rather, what ensued as a result of your idiocy, and I mean idiocy in the classical definition of one who hasn't enough apparent intelligence for simple self-survival, is that you and your simpleton sidekick here ran us up on a reef." Here he pauses to turn his anger toward the chart book, which he tosses against the wall. "Which makes even less sense when there isn't even supposed to be a reef here."

While the professor rants, I wave Jimmy to the window and point out the island.

"What?" he asks.

"Wait for the wave to pass."

"There," he says. "I see it."

"What are you two gawking at?" the professor asks, storming to the window himself. "Just great," he says, when he glimpses the island. "Just fricken great."

We pop the hatch and climb onto the tilted deck. The professor pokes his head out and immediately withdraws back into the submarine, shielding his eyes with his forearm. It hits me that not once has he been above deck when the sun is up.

"Are you feeling alright?" I ask.

"I'm fine," he replies. "Just tell me what you see."

"Well, it looks like there's a wide lagoon of sorts. It's pretty calm, protected by the reef. And there's an island. Pink sand. Some kind of green grass on the hills. Palm trees."

"How far are we on the reef?"

"I can't tell from here. Wait. Jimmy just dove in to check it out. I'm gonna go check it out, too."

The professor calls from behind me as I head toward the

edge of the deck: "Be careful; that stuff will cut you to shreds."

I dive off the back, and swim around to join Jimmy on the protected side, facing the island shore. The water is cool but refreshing after so much time stranded inside the submarine. Jimmy points toward the nose where it appears to be resting on the reef, and we both take a deep breath and dive under.

The clear water provides nearly limitless visibility at this shallow depth, and we follow the submarine's hull all the way around, seeing that nearly the front quarter is stranded on the reef. The titanium hull of the submarine has ripped through the white and pink coral, exposing a deep gash of darker layers beneath. A glint catches my eye, and I swim closer and brush aside the crushed coral, uncovering what looks like a piece of brass. Brass? In coral? I surface for air and bob in the water, waiting for Jimmy, since he can hold his breath much longer than I can. Finally, he comes up looking like a seal with his dark hair slicked back against his head.

"It's stuck pretty good," Jimmy says.

"Hey, does something seem funny about this stretch of reef to you?" I ask.

"Whataya mean?"

"Well, for one thing the part we're stranded on is much higher than the rest of the reef. And it appears to be a kind of patch of its own in the middle of nowhere. I mean, look—the natural reef starts over there."

"I dunno," Jimmy shrugs. "Let's dive again and look."

"Okay, but let's swim out on the deep side and see if it

looks different from out there. Plus, we'll be able to see how bad the sub is hung up."

"Submarine," Jimmy corrects me, laughing as he mimics the professor's voice. "Never sub and never ship."

We swim around to the seaward side and paddle about twenty meters from the stranded submarine. Then we gulp lungs full of air and descend beneath the waves and look back toward the reef. Sure enough, only about the front fourth of the submarine is resting on the reef, but it's the reef itself that has my attention. It's a hulking rectangle of coral, seemingly out of place as it towers above the line of much lower reef near the seafloor. Then it hits me. The familiar shape. One end wide, the other end angled nearly to a point. The side a sheer wall of coral-filled windows, waving with strange sea flowers and odd tentacled creatures. The narrower base. The nearly perfect cylinder rising from the reef like a giant coral smoke stack. It's a ship! Or at least it used to be a ship before the sea turned it into the very reef it wrecked upon. I know what kind too. I've seen images of these cruise ships before, in educationals, down in Holocene II.

"Unbelievable," the professor says, shaking his head as we stand dripping before him. "All the pristine ocean in the world to travel upon, and you manage to strand us on top of another stranded ship. Get back in the water. Both of you."

"What? Get back in the water?—"

"Why?" Jimmy asks.

"To lighten the load while I try to back us off."

We climb out the hatch and jump back in and tread water, watching from a safe distance as the professor full-throttles the screw in reverse, managing to churn up a noticeable amount of wash, but not budging the stranded submarine an inch.

Next, we try to kedge. At least that's what the professor calls it. He releases the anchor from where it tucks into the aft ballast, and Jimmy and I take turns diving down and walking it along the bottom, away from the reef. When we've walked it out as far and deep as we possibly can, the professor wrenches it back, trying to get it to grab. We nearly exhaust ourselves to the point of drowning, dragging the anchor out again and again, but it just won't take hold in the soft bottom. I suggest we try hooking it to the coral ahead and maybe pull ourselves sideways off the shipwreck-reef, but the professor says it's too likely to compromise the hull. So we all gather again in the control room while the professor consults his tide charts.

"Hey," I say, looking out the window again at the island. "I've got an idea."

"This should be good," the professor mumbles.

"What if we swim to the island there and chop down one of those palm trees and float it back? Maybe we could use it as a kind of lever to lift our nose off the reef while you reverse the engines, and we might just slide off."

The professor looks up from his charts. "You know, that's not a half bad idea. But you've got one major problem."

"What's that?" I ask.

"Well, since you asked," he says, straightening his stance

and clearing his throat as if he's about to begin teaching a class. "Archimedes said 'Give me a place to stand, and I shall move Earth with it.' You might have noticed that we're here on the thing that is stuck. The load force, if you will. You can't get any mechanical advantage without having a place to stand."

"Sure we can," I answer, "if we wedge the tree beneath the front of the submarine, using the coral itself as a fulcrum."

"How would you apply any force?" he asks.

"Easy," I say. "We'll just climb out to the end of the tree. Our own weight will be multiplied as a force on the other end."

The professor scratches his head. He turns over one of his charts and writes on its other side.

"Let's see," he mumbles. "You two together—maybe 150 kilograms—figure two meters from fulcrum to load—eight meters to the effort—divide by point-two-five—makes a load force of over six hundred kilograms." He looks up from his equations. "By Jupiter, that may just be enough to do it. Very impressive, young man. But I'm afraid you have one larger problem yet to solve."

"Oh, yeah?" I say, feeling confident. "What's that?"

"How will you cut down the tree?"

"What do you have on board for tools?"

The professor leads us to the engine room and shows us the collection of tools, mostly wrenches and electrical supplies, but nothing in the way of an axe or a saw. Jimmy snatches up a coil of titanium wire and a small cutter. "We'll jus' use this."

"To fell a tree?" the professor asks.

"Sure," Jimmy says.

"It's your plan," the professor shrugs.

We eat a quick meal and drink our fill of water and climb the ladder to the submarine deck, carrying nothing but a coil of wire and a pair of cutters. The professor stands in the shadows below watching us go. "Try and be back before high tide."

"When's that?" I ask.

"An hour after sunset," he calls up.

"We better be back before that," I reply.

Jimmy leans into the doorway. "Hey, leave the hatch open so Junior can get some fresh air, will you?"

I hear the professor mumbling profanities as he walks the passageway back to the control room.

"It doesn't look too far," I say.

"Nah," Jimmy answers. "We've swum farther."

Junior sits on the deck whimpering as we slide off into the water and push away from the submarine.

Of course, it's a longer swim across the lagoon than we figured and by the time we drag ourselves panting onto the warm, pink sand and look back, the stranded submarine is just a black dash that could easily be a piece of floating driftwood if it weren't suspiciously sticking out motionless from the water.

"We better get on," Jimmy says.

We climb the sandy bank to the grassy edge of the island and walk up a gentle hill toward the palm trees that cover the upper plateau. Jimmy stops along the way and uses his knife to hack down a cedar sapling, carrying it with him and stripping off the little branches as we go.

"We're gonna need something a little bigger than that to pry the submarine free," I say, picking fun with him a little. Jimmy just smiles and keeps on whittling his piece of wood.

Soon we come upon strange lumps on the ground, almost like abandoned turtle shells, if turtles had hair. I kick one over and see it's some kind of shell. By the time we reach the grove of palms, we realize that they aren't just palms after all—they're coconut palms. Clusters of coconuts cling to the treetops, and coconut shells litter the ground, making it impossible to walk without stepping on them.

We select a tree that is tall and straight, thick enough to be sturdy, but not so thick that we won't be able to carry it back by ourselves, or at least roll it down the hill to the water's edge. Jimmy takes out the spool of wire and measures out a length a little more than twice as long as the piece of cedar he's been cutting on and snips it free. He folds the wire in half and wraps one length of wire around the other in a continuous spiral, finishing it off with a loop on each end. Then he bends the cedar sapling and slips the wire loops into angled notches he's cut into its ends, and when he finishes, he holds up a perfect wire bow-saw.

"Brilliant!" I say, genuinely impressed. "Think it'll work?"

"Never know 'til ya try," he says, setting the wire against the palm's trunk and sawing back and forth.

It's slow going, sawing through the tough outer bark. Jimmy saws until he's exhausted, pausing to wipe the sweat from his brow before handing the saw to me. I work for half an hour or so and make about half an inch of progress. Then the wire breaks. Jimmy cuts another length of wire, and we start over again. We work for several hours—taking turns, breaking the saw, remaking the saw—then something catches my eye and stops me cold with the saw frozen in my hand.

"Is it stuck again?" Jimmy asks.

"Did you see that?"

"See what?"

"Over there. Behind those trees."

Jimmy follows my gaze toward a thicker grove of coconut trees farther into the island. Several minutes pass, but nothing shows itself. "What'd you see?"

"Thought I saw something over there watching us, but it must've been my imagination."

"I'll bet you's dehydrated," Jimmy says.

"I am pretty thirsty."

Jimmy walks over to a shorter, thicker tree and looks up at the coconuts hanging there. Before I can ask him what it is he's thinking, he wraps his long arms around the tree and shimmies to the top and starts tossing down coconuts. I catch them and gather them into a pile. Jimmy slides down the tree and uses his knife to carve holes in the tops of two coconuts, and we stand and drink their sweet water.

"This is the best water I've ever tasted."

"Same here," Jimmy says. "Hey, I thought I saw somethin' from up there, too." He nods toward the other grove of trees.

"What was it?"

"Somethin' movin' around in them palms."

"Well, let's get this tree sawed down and get out of here."

"Good idea," Jimmy says, pointing to the horizon where the sun has dropped low, its light already more orange than it was just ten minutes ago.

We return to the saw with renewed vigor, a silent sense of urgency communicated between us. The second the sun dips into the Atlantic, a cold breeze blows in from the ocean and stirs the palms. I remember the professor telling us high tide was a half hour past sunset. I saw faster. My gaze keeps drifting back to the other grove of trees, and soon there's no mistaking dark shadows darting low to the ground between the trunks. Jimmy stands watching, too, his knife ready in his hand.

As the light fades, the shadows moving in the trees grow bolder. They come closer, making quick runs to nearer trees, betraying themselves with squeals and grunts. Soon, they seem to be all around us. My hands are raw and blistered but I keep working through the pain, falling into a kind of frenzy.

The sky grows dark, the palms sway in the wind. The loud rustling of the treetops mixes with a raucous chorus of strange squeals coming from the shadows, and it suddenly seems like we're in the center of some haunted hallucination.

Then the saw jams and the wire snaps.

I'm about to grab Jimmy and suggest we make a run for it, empty-handed, when there's a loud crack from the tree as the wind bends it into the cut. It splinters, then snaps, tipping over and falling to the ground with a thud.

"Let's grab it and go!" I shout, above the wind.

Jimmy jogs to the far end and lifts the tree as I kick the cut end free of its base and wrap my hands around the trunk. We stagger off toward the water with our prize.

It's heavy work. We take baby steps, making slow progress toward the edge of the hill where I hope we can roll it the rest of the way down to the shore. The shadows follow us, their grunts coming from all sides now and no longer even bothering to stay hidden in the trees. Jimmy is at least six meters behind me on the tree and I can't hear him over the wind, but I feel him pushing faster, so I pick up my pace. Stronger wind, louder grunts, closer shadows—pushing faster, faster, faster. Then I'm stopped in my tracks by the full weight of the tree as Jimmy's end drops to the ground.

I drop my end and rush back to see what's wrong, but Jimmy is nowhere to be found. The shadows rush at me then and I stagger backwards, seeing them now for feral pigs. They surround me, herding me toward nearby trees. I stop and plant my feet, ready to fight if I have to.

"Jimmy!" I call out. "Where are you!"

A particularly vicious pig rushes me, and I see the glint of its tusks in the low twilight. I dodge its slash, but fall to my knees. I'm surrounded on all sides now. "Jimmy!"

The grunts and squeals are deafening. I hold my hands up to protect my face. I see strange flashes through my fingers. Cloven pig hooves. Glinting tusks. Bloated human feet. Before

I can make sense of anything, something is pulled over my head and everything goes dark. I'm being strangled. I can't breathe. I panic—struggling, kicking, screaming. My arms are pinned. My legs being tied. Now strange lights. Where? Lights inside my head. Pulsing. Fading. Blackness.

When I come to, I'm lying on cold stone with a smelly sack over my head. Something lies struggling next to me. I hear a muffled cry and realize that it might be Jimmy. I nudge him with my elbow. "Jimmy?"

"Aubrey? Is that you?"

"Yeah. Are you okay?"

"I dunno," he says. "Where the hell are we? And what was those things?"

"Looked like pigs."

"I ain't never seen no pig tie someone up," he says.

"Yeah, me either. Shh . . . someone's coming."

Padding feet approach, accompanied by obscene grunting and labored breathing. Something nudges me, sniffing loudly.

"Is this the only two?" a deep and phlegmy voice booms.

"Seems so, Chief," is the squeaky reply.

"You think they's spies?" a third voice asks.

"What was they doin'?"

"They chopped down a tree."

"Well, that isn't any big crime."

"But they's guilty of something for sure," the squeaky one says. "You know they is."

"Why say you that?"

"They ran from us, Chief."

"Well, that tells us only that they're not very brave."

"Lack of bravery aside, sir, they's definitely foreigners."

"Heave ho, then," the deep one belts out, "pull off those hoods, and let's have a look at them."

I feel hands loosening the rope around my neck, then the sack is ripped free, and I'm blinded by the light of a lantern. As my eyes adjust, three ugly faces fade into view. They're people, but their features resemble those of pigs. Beady eyes peering out from above upturned noses. Thin lips quivering on mouths that stick out just enough to resemble snouts. The fattest of the three leans in and sniffs my hair, his sweaty nose trembling.

"Smells like the sea, this one does."

"Mightn't I surmise, Chief, that they's came to us across the ocean?" the squeaky one asks.

"Surmise as you want," the leader says. "Why should I give a coconut's care what goes on in that little head of yours?"

"But from where?" the third chimes in. "There isn't any other land out there."

"Can they talk?"

"This one was cussing, Chief."

The leader pokes me. "What's your name?"

"Aubrey," I answer.

"How about your friend here?"

"That's Jimmy."

"Are you spies?"

"No, sir, we're not spies."

He turns to his fellows. "They're polite."

"But how do we know they're not dangerous, Chief?"

He turns back to us. "Are you dangerous?"

"No sir. We were just minding our own business."

"You mean chopping down my tree?"

"Well, yes. We did do that. But we didn't . . ."

"Untie them," he says. "This is no way to treat guests."

"But, Chief? We don't even know where they's from."

"I said, untie them!" the big one shouts, losing his temper. "Show some small hospitality, I tell you. You'd not have us be thought of as rude, would you? What would the elders say?"

"As you wish, Chief. As you wish."

"We can interrogate them after the show." Then he grunts and waddles off, moving almost as much like a pig as a man.

"You heard the Chief," the squeaky one says to the other, his pride obviously hurt. "Help me untie the filthy things."

They lean over us, grunting as they struggle with the knots. When we're both free and standing on our feet again, the men, if I can even call them that, snatch up their lanterns and herd us from the cave into some sort of passageway.

The one in front constantly glances back to see that we're following, and the one behind keeps grunting to remind us that he's there. They're much shorter than we are, perhaps because of their hunched backs, and they're both wearing clothing made from gray, bristly pigskins so that it would be easy to mistake them for pigs themselves if they hadn't just been speaking.

I lean forward and whisper in Jimmy's ear: "Maybe we

should try to take them while we can?"

"Less talking, more walking," the one behind us grunts.

The passageway shrinks little by little until we're forced onto our hands and knees. Claustrophobia sets my heart racing, but the passageway opens suddenly onto a giant crystal cavern like no other cavern I've ever seen. And I grew up in one. The cavern is lit by coconut-shell candles everywhere—propped on shelves in the rock, lining pathways on the floor, some even floating in dark pools of water. Their light sparkles on crystal-flecked walls, illuminating stalactites dripping from the ceiling. But much stranger than the cave itself are its inhabitants.

Pig people. Everywhere. They shuffle around, preparing for some kind of event. Lighting candles. Setting up a buffet. Manning cook fires. Herding squealing children into groups. And there are pigs everywhere among them, too. Pigs rooting around at their feet, pigs snorting and snatching up scraps.

"This is weird," Jimmy says.

"I know it."

I feel a hand push me from behind. "Move along."

We wind our way down into the cavern until we arrive at a place where people sit in rows on the floor looking at a raised slab of stone lit with lanterns. It appears to be a stage. The wall behind the stage is crudely painted as a scenic backdrop, with a misshapen sun hanging in a purple sky. It looks like some scene I might have finger-painted as a child. The strange set is framed with palm fronds, creating the illusion of trees.

A hush falls over the small crowd as they become aware of

us. They whisper and stare. The two pig men sit us on the floor in the front row next to the fat one they refer to as Chief.

"Hi-dy," he says, shaking our hands. "I'm William. Sorry about the rough treatment back there. Uh-huh. I am. The boys get excited sometimes. No hard feelings, I hope."

"No hard feelings," I say, "but we really would like—"

"Hush!" he holds up his hand. "They're starting."

The babbling crowd falls silent as a solemn procession approaches the stage, led by a small boy pounding a pigskin drum that's hanging from his neck. Behind him is an old man struggling to keep up, his legs swollen and his feet gnarled with gout. Following the old man are several plump girls, wearing only grass skirts and coconut-shell bras, fanning themselves theatrically with dried palm fronds.

Jimmy nudges me. "Do ya see a way out?"

"I don't dare turn around," I whisper back.

"Shh . . .," William hisses, holding his finger to his lips.

The procession reaches the stage, and the old man stands before the crowd while the girls line up behind him. The old man ceremoniously holds up his hands, and the drummer stops. Then the old man scans the crowd, draws in a long breath, and speaks:

"Many centuries ago, uh, our forefathers gathered together on a night just like this, uh, possibly in these very caves. And, uh, they begun an ancient tradition that continues to this, uh, very day. We honor them now by refusing to forget their, uh, sacrifice. Their wisdom was greater than ours. Their discipline mightier. Their, uh, spirits filled with holy grace. And so here now I give you their story lest we someday forget."

I risk a look around. Everyone's head is slumped forward on their fat necks, their pig mouths hanging open as they loudly breathe, their eyes locked on the stage. I wish we weren't in the front row so we could slip away. The old man continues:

"Once we were a great country. Our ancestors worked the dry and ugly land until they had, uh, produced a vast paradise as close to heaven as, uh, any place can be without being heaven. You could climb a hill under purple skies and look down on endless fields of corn. Streams flowed with buttermilk. Honey dripped from trees, their branches hanging low and offering, uh, sweet meat. But men quarreled even so. And some refused to honor God's decrees. They were, uh, lazy. They laid down in the mud and rose only to eat and to fornicate."

Several people gasp with apparent shock when he says the word *fornicate*. I notice a few mothers with their hands clamped over their children's ears. He continues:

"And soon the land was, uh, reduced to nothing more than a sty. And God was angry. And so He sent the rains." Here the old man pauses, and the drummer boy hands him a coconut-shell rattle filled with sand. He holds the rattle high in his gout-mangled hand and shakes it, producing a sound effect of falling rain. Behind him, the showgirls look to the cavern ceiling with mimed horror and hold their palm fronds up, as if to shield themselves from the imaginary downpour. He goes on:

"And the waters rose. Uh. And the lands were covered up.

Uh. And the greatest country in history was destroyed by God's flood. And still the lazy among us laid in their filth, moving only to higher ground when forced by the rising waters. And like so many fish in a draining pond, uh, they were all crowded together in the last remaining bit of dry land, forced to live together with the pigs they had become. And so they turned on one another. Uh. They did. They ate the flesh of their own and so angered God further. And God in his rage sent down the plague. I said plague, I did. Great mechanical birds swept from the purple skies and cut the greedy sloths to shreds. Massive sea monsters rose from the deep and laid them to waste upon the tiny patch of remaining, uh, sand. For little else was left above the waters that covered the Earth."

The girls fall to the stage behind him and writhe on the ground, as if being ravaged by imaginary adversaries from above. The old man waves his fat, knobby finger in the air and speaks now in a hushed voice:

"But the story does not end there. No, no, no. God, uh, took mercy on the few worthy men who remained. Gradually, he slowed the rains. He called the machines away. And peace fell again on the tiny patch of land. That's when our forefathers gathered here, possibly in these very caves, and renewed their commitment to the decrees of God. Gone are the days of corn and streams of buttermilk. But they will come again. Gone are the days of honey trees filled with sweet meat. But they will come again. Uh. I tell you. They will come again!"

The crowd chants it back: "They will come again!"

"They will come again!" the old man says.

"They will come again!" responds the crowd.

Someone nudges me, breaking my trance, and the strange surroundings fade back into view. William slurps milk from a coconut shell and passes it to me. I hold the shell in my hand and look at his milky slobber coating its rim. I want to pass it on without drinking, but William is watching me with his beady eyes. I raise the shell to my lips and sip the milk, trying not to vomit as I pass it on to Jimmy.

The old man holds his arms up. "They will come again!"

"They will come again!" comes the response.

"We must only be patient, and never forget our history," he says, his stutter disappearing as his voice rises like someone giving a sermon. "And the good times will indeed come again. The dreaded waters will lower. Our promised land will be uncovered. The ships and dragons will disappear for good, and we will once again be free to leave these caves and rebuild the great nation of 'Merica!"

"Rebuild 'Merica!" the crowd chants.

"I said: rebuild 'Merica!"

"Rebuild 'Merica! 'Merica! 'Merica!"

The drummer boy beats his drum as the old man shambles off stage, appearing to move with considerable pain. The girls fall in line behind, shaking their grass skirts and waving their fronds, and the odd procession heads back the way it came.

I turn to William beside me. "Did I understand that right? Do you think this island you live on is America?"

"Think?" he grunts. "Where else would it be? Come now, it's time to eat."

He leads us through the noisy crowd to the other end of the cavern, where a long buffet is set up on the floor. Coconut shells filled with food line the center, and each seat is marked by a personal trough carved into the stone. Jimmy and I sit where we're told. William slumps down next to us.

"That's my wife, Annie," he says, pointing to an enormous woman lying across the way. She has a baby in her arms, and the baby is clamped onto her nipple, feeding. Because of the way she's slouched, her other breast hangs nearly to the floor and a piglet stands on its hind legs suckling, too. I watch as it loses its balance and falls, only to get up and stretch to the dangling nipple again. Even if it weren't for the piglet, I'd probably be creeped out, because babies are formula-fed down in Holocene II. Jimmy, on the other hand, doesn't even seem to notice.

The food bowls are passed around, and everyone reaches in and scoops out portions and slops them together in the troughs in front of them. They eat with their fingers, slurping so loudly that the entire cavern echoes with the sound. Trying not to be rude, I pick out tiny pieces of the least repulsive foods and set them in my trough. Everything seems to be made from two ingredients only: coconut and pork. Bowls of boiled pig feet pass by, followed by bowls of blood pudding. Then a strange gelatinous substance riddled with tiny piglet snouts. Something that looks like liver, something else that looks like tongue. Most of these I let pass without touching.

Then come cooked meats that actually smell pretty good. Chops and bacon, sausages and ham. The meat is followed by bowls of shaved coconut, and others filled with coconut oil or coconut cream. They pass community drinks down the long, floor-laid buffet. I avoid the milky drinks, and wipe the ones filled with coconut water with my sleeve before raising them to my lips. Jimmy seems to be enjoying himself. He sits beside me and eats without reservation, even making conversation with one of the portly dancing girls on his other side.

"Whatcha celebratin'?" Jimmy asks, leaning across me and addressing William.

"Come again?" William grunts, his mouth filled with food.

"The feast," Jimmy says. "What are ya celebratin'?"

William looks confused. He slurps up a piece of pale flesh dangling from his lips and leans closer to Jimmy, crowding me. "Nothing special," he says, his stinky breath wafting over me. "We do this every night 'cept Sundays."

When William turns away, I lean into Jimmy and speak in a low voice: "We've got to get out of here."

"Why?" Jimmy asks. "Let's jus' go with the flow."

"But don't you see what this is?"

"What what is?"

"These people. That whole skit back there."

"Seemed like some kinda show to me," Jimmy says.

"Remember that ship we saw? The one in the reef?"

"Yeah. I remember."

"Well these must be the descendants of the cruise ship passengers. It's all pretty clear, isn't it? Some of them must have survived the Park Service drones by imitating pigs. Now they've evolved to look like them."

"Yeah," Jimmy says. "So what if?"

"Well, they've got it all wrong. There wasn't any flood. And this sure isn't America."

"Well, how do we know it ain't?" Jimmy asks.

"How do we know? Don't be stupid. This isn't all the land that's left. You know that much. And we just came ourselves from North America."

"Maybe," Jimmy says. "But didn't you grow up bein' told none of this was up here period? And that sure ain't true. How do we know how anythin' really happened, 'cept by what we's told?" He pauses to drink from a bowl passed by the girl on his other side. "And besides," he continues, wiping his mouth with the back of his hand and passing the bowl to me, "no one likes a know-it-all."

William whistles to quiet the crowd.

Hands freeze, suspended halfway between troughs and mouths. Bowls clatter as they're set down. A baby cries, but is quickly hushed by its mother.

"It's time to give thanks," William says, nodding to the old man, now seated at the other end of the floor-table.

The old man reaches over and seizes up a baby by the legs and lifts it flailing above the table and holds a knife to its neck. Before I can even open my mouth, a woman screams—

"No!" She leaps from her seat and pulls the baby away from the knife. "You old blind bastard!" she shouts, cradling the baby in her arms. "That's my baby, not a piglet."

The old man mumbles an apology and turns and reaches into the wallow beside the table and, with some labor and much squealing, manages to snatch a piglet and lift it up to the blade. He leans in close and inspects the piglet with one milky eye, as if performing a public display of due diligence. Then he slashes its throat and catches the gushing blood in a bowl.

I feel my stomach retch, but I hold down my vomit. Even Jimmy looks a little pale. When the flow of blood slows to a trickle, the old man hurls the dead piglet into the wallow where it is immediately set upon by other hungry pigs. Then he sips from the bowl, wipes the blood from his chin with a gouty knuckle, and passes the bowl of blood. I begin to panic as it makes its way toward Jimmy and me.

I elbow Jimmy. "I'm not drinking that."

"We better jus' do it," Jimmy says. "Seems like it's custom or somethin'."

When the bowl of blood reaches Jimmy, he holds it in both hands, pausing to scan the crowd. All eyes are on him. He glances at me and shrugs, then lifts the bowl to his mouth and drinks. He passes the bowl to me with a look of silent apology. I immediately pass it on to William.

William hands it back. "You must drink," he grunts.

I shake my head. "I'm not drinking this."

An even deeper hush falls over the group. I feel everyone's

eyes on me as I hold the offering out, my hands trembling, the thick red blood sloshing around in the bowl. William won't take it, so I set it down in front of him. He slides it back toward me.

"You drink," he says. "Otherwise God will punish us."

I push it back. "I'm not drinking that poor pig's blood." The defiance in my voice surprises me. "And besides, there is no God. At least no God that would flood any place. So you don't need to worry about being punished for anything."

William takes a long, stilted inhale through his quivering nostrils, then stretches open his mouth and lets it out in what might be a silent roar, or maybe just a yawn. He turns his beady eyes on me. "You tire me with these childish antics," he says. "Just drink so we can move on to the entertainment."

"I won't drink that blood."

"Eh then!" someone calls. "Let's drink his blood."

"Pigs' feet and human snouts!" the squeaky one shouts. "Let's cut the spies and bleed them out."

William reaches into his trough, grabs a fistful of slop, and hurls it down at Squeaky, silencing the racket. "Enough!" he bellows, his lips pulled back and his incisors showing. "You act like children. Show some consideration to our guests."

"But what if they's spies?" squeaks the sheepish reply.

William turns back to me. "Are you spies?"

"We already told you we're not," I say.

"They're not spies!"

"If they was, they wouldn't say it."

William shakes his head. "Tell me where you're from?"

I'm relieved to finally be asked one civilized question.

"We came on a boat, well, a submarine, really. From the west coast of North America. And there was no flood. There are all kinds of other lands out there. This just happens to be an island you're on."

William looks confused. "The stories tell of no other lands. And none are visible from the hill. But if there are other lands, there is certainly no other 'Merica."

"With all due respect, sir, this is not America."

"Lies!" someone screams.

"Blasphemy!" another shouts.

"I told you they was spies, Chief," the squeaky one says.

The old man snatches up his knife and crawls down the floor-table toward Jimmy and me. I'm frozen with disbelief. Is he really going to cut us? William pushes us back and meets the old man with balled fists. Then Squeaky leaps onto William's back. William's wife casts her baby aside and seizes Squeaky's dangling leg and sinks her teeth into his calf. Someone pounces on Jimmy. I'm hit on the head. Arms grab me from behind.

It's all gnashing teeth and swinging fists and kicking feet. Then, suddenly, the entire mad brawl comes to an immediate halt, and all heads turn to stare behind Jimmy and me.

Their faces are frozen with horror.

Their beady eyes bulge.

My captor releases me.

As my senses return to my swirling head, I slowly crane my neck to see what it is they're looking at. Junior crouches on the path behind us, his hackles up, and his canines exposed. He's growling, bless his little heart. And his effect on the pig people is astonishing. They back away, coming together and crouching against the wall in a mass of pale flesh and pigskin.

Jimmy picks himself up. We walk backwards toward Junior and the path. We're almost to Junior's side when one of the pig people lets out a hair-raising scream. The crowd parts, and I see Squeaky has caught his clothes on fire with a candle. He dances in circles, the fire getting worse as he does, and the others chase after him swatting at the flames.

We turn and run.

Junior races ahead of us, and we follow him up the path and into the tiny passageway, crawling on our hands and knees until it widens, then clambering to our feet and rushing through the pitch-black cave, following the sound of Junior's yapping. Soon, we're on an incline that steepens with every step until we're climbing with our feet and our hands. I feel a cool breeze on my face. Then Jimmy reaches me a hand, and I scramble to my feet, above ground and free.

As we rush in the direction of the beach, we nearly trip over our felled coconut tree. Without a word, Jimmy grabs an end, I grab the other, and we run with it toward the hill. Maybe it's just the adrenaline pumping through my system, but this time the tree seems to weigh nothing at all. We carry it down the hill until we stride onto the warm sand and plunge with it into the cold water. We each wrap an arm around the tree and swim it in the direction of the submarine. Junior treads water beside us, taking turns going ahead to check on Jimmy and coming back to check on me. Then Junior climbs onto the floating tree and hitches a ride. He deserves it.

We seem to be swimming forever, the tree moving slow in the dark water. I work my way up the trunk toward Jimmy so he can hear me. "Are we headed in the right direction?"

"I think so," he replies, sounding as breathless as I am.

"But are we making any progress?"

"I dunno," he says.

We swim for another twenty or thirty minutes, and I'm about to suggest we dump the tree and try to make it alone when I hear the professor shout from the deck of the stranded submarine. "Boys! Is that you?"

We call back and adjust our course and five minutes later, we're climbing aboard.

Junior shakes himself dry next to us. Jimmy and I fall to our knees and hug his neck and kiss his wet face. He wags his tail with pride.

"What on Earth happened to you?" the professor asks.

"We'll fill you in later," I say. "Let's hoist this submarine off the reef and hurry up and get out of here."

"The tide's dropping," he says, "but we can give it a go."

It takes all three of us and a rope from below to drag the coconut tree around to the front of the submarine. Once there, we hold the tree steady with the rope while Jimmy jumps in and helps lower the cut end down onto the reef, beneath the angled nose of the submarine. Thankfully, there's plenty of tree above water to keep it weighted down. Once it's wedged there good, Jimmy climbs back on deck, and we remove the rope.

"I think we're ready," I say, inspecting the tree where it's wedged in front of the submarine, slanting away over the water.

The professor returns to the control room and floods the rear ballasts and maxes out the engines. Then he shouts from inside the control room.

"Did he say 'now'?" Jimmy asks.

"I think he said 'now.'"

Jimmy goes first, scrambling up the leaning tree. When he reaches its end, he straddles the tree and calls back to me. The light from the open hatch doesn't reach much of the tree, and it's slippery climbing in the dark. I feel the tree bending beneath my weight. When I join Jimmy, we both cling to the top of the tree, bouncing to try and exaggerate our weight. It reminds me of an old childhood seesaw game in our underground park, except it's Jimmy and me on the upside end and a submarine on the downside end. We bounce and we bounce. I hear the screw churning water against the back of the submarine. Junior stands on deck and yips encouragement up to us. Then Jimmy slides a little farther out on the tree, where it's too narrow to sit, and rolls off and hangs there. I slide out and join him. We hang together, swinging our legs above the black water below. It feels and looks strange. As if the tree were growing from the black lagoon itself. Or perhaps as if in some alternate reality where the pig people's flood really happened after all, this was the last holdout tree and Jimmy and I are clinging to it, refusing to surrender to the rising waters below.

There's a loud crunching sound, and the tree drops a foot. It takes everything I have to hold on. Then Jimmy lets out some kind of tribal yell and flails his legs. I join him, screaming into the night and swinging from the treetop. Another crunch, another drop, and then the submarine slides free from the reef and the tree falls over into the water with us still clinging to it.

I'm momentarily tangled beneath the fronds of the floating tree, but I feel Jimmy's hands in the dark water, pulling me free.

"You okay?" he asks, once we're treading water.

"I'm gonna have another bump on my head," I say, "but otherwise, I'm all right."

We swim back to the freed submarine and climb onto its deck. Junior greets us with a round of licks to our wet ankles. As the professor carefully backs us into deeper water, I scan the dark island hillside for any sign of pursuit from the pig people. I think I see a light moving between the trees. But before I can point it out to Jimmy, it's gone, and I can't be sure.

Jimmy throws his wet arm around me. "You jus' had to tell 'em they was wrong, didn't you?"

"You mad at me?"

"No," he says, smiling.

"Good. I don't like it when you're mad at me."

"But that sure was crazy close."

CHAPTER 9
Meteors and Antimatter

"Wake up!" The professor shakes me in my bunk.

"Ah, come on," I say, rolling over. "It took me three hours to fall asleep. And why is it so hot in here?"

"Because your little misadventure on the reef damaged the cooling system," he replies. "I'm working on it. Now get up already. You sleep like a dead man."

"Is it my turn at the helm, or whatever you call it?"

"No," he says. "You need to join us on the deck."

"Why?"

"Just come up," he says, abruptly leaving the room.

My head still aches from the other day's punishment. First, I slammed it into the submarine window when we wrecked on the reef. Then one of those pig people clobbered me. And, as if that weren't enough, the coconut tree fell on top of me when we freed the submarine. Thinking maybe I'm dehydrated too, I hop off my bunk and drink from the bathroom faucet before pulling my shirt on and heading for the deck.

Jimmy and the professor are already there, the submarine left pilotless, moving at fifteen knots on a set course. The night sky is punctured by a million twinkling stars, some so bright they're actually reflected in the black water.

"This is why you woke me?"

"Look," Jimmy says, spinning me around to face the back of the submarine.

A green phosphorescent trail glows in the water behind us, brightest directly behind the screw, fading as it narrows into the distant night. It appears we're painting the ocean with light as we cut a shimmering path through the black water.

"What is it?"

"Phytoplankton," the professor says. "Tiny creatures that are responsible for much of the oxygen you're breathing. These ones happen to be bioluminescent."

"We called 'em sea ghosts," Jimmy says. "I used to swim through 'em and watch myself glow."

"Oh, how sweet to be clothed in the nakedness of youth," the professor opines. "But as beautiful as these plankton are, they're not why I called you up here."

"Why did you?"

"Look up and you'll see," he says.

I stare up at the starlit sky and search the constellations. It never gets old, the novelty of looking at the stars. I remember growing up down in Holocene II and gazing up at the glowing benitoite in our cavern ceiling and squinting to pretend that they were stars. I never believed I'd really see one, let alone a night sky ablaze with them.

A streak of light catches my eye.

Then another.

Appearing to originate from a single point, shooting stars blaze their fiery arcs across the night. It's an amazing scene, to be standing on the dark deck of the submarine moving through the black water with a tail of green following us and meteors streaking overhead. It wouldn't be hard to imagine us riding on a comet through the deep mysteries of space.

"My mother said those were souls returnin' to Earth," Jimmy says. "But she didn't know nothin' about science and stuff, like you two do."

"Who knows," the professor says. "Your mother may have been right after all."

"But aren't they meteors?" I ask. "Particles of cosmic dust entering the atmosphere and burning up?"

"They're certainly that, also," he says.

"But how can they be both?" I ask.

"How could they be only one?"

"I don't understand," I say. "Are you telling us you believe in human souls?"

"No," he says, "I'm telling you I believe in physics."

"Did you ever believe people had souls?" I ask.

"That's a long story," he says.

"We've got time," Jimmy replies.

There's a drawn out silence where I'm sure the professor has decided to keep his long story to himself. But at last, he clears his throat and speaks: "I was raised by my German grandmother in Michigan."

"Where's that?" Jimmy asks.

"Nowhere now," the professor says. "Do you want to hear the story or not?"

"Yes," I say. "Please continue."

"Yeah, sorry," Jimmy adds.

"My grandmother was a devout Catholic and brought me religiously to Mass. She was a woman of very few words, but her actions spoke loudly of her love. I don't know if I believed in God, or human souls, completely, but I sure believed in my grandmother." He lets out a long, sad sigh. "The fire started in the neighbor's bedroom. Probably a cigarette, they said. By the time an alarm was raised, it had traveled across the shared attic into the other townhomes. I don't remember anything about my escape except standing in the snow and looking back at the entire block burning. I was nine."

He pauses as a particularly bright meteor crosses the sky, his head turning to follow it. Then he continues:

"I'll never forget the neighbors blabbing on and on about how they'd been spared by God. 'Thank God this, and thank God that.' Even so, I prayed for the first time ever that night. I prayed that God had also saved my grandmother. I searched through the crowd, becoming frantic with each stranger's face that looked down as I tugged on familiar nightgowns. My bare feet went numb in the snow. My young teeth chattered out of my head. A man caught me up and took me to his home. We warmed ourselves beside the stove. He told me it was a miracle that I'd survived."

"What about your grandmother?" I ask.

"It was three days before they officially broke the news. She'd likely died of smoke inhalation, but there was little left of her to bury. In that moment, I gave up on believing in God."

"I felt jus' the same way when the Park Service killed my family," Jimmy says.

There's a long silence where I wish I could make out the professor's face to see if he shows any pain of responsibility for his and Jimmy's shared horrors, but it's too dark.

"I'm sorry about your family," he says, finally breaking the silence. "It somehow seems different, having met you. Amazing how detached things seem when they're on a little screen."

"Thanks," Jimmy says.

"What happened to you?" I ask.

"To me?"

"Yeah, after your grandmother was gone?"

"I went to live with a foster family."

"Did you like them?"

"They were fine as far as foster parents go. They had a lot of state kids, so none of us got much attention. But we were looked after all right. I dove into my schooling then. I think the sciences appealed to me because I wanted to disprove God, at least to myself. It seemed better that there be no God than a God that I could only hate. But then I discovered physics and a new world of possibilities opened in my brain.

"I was young. Easily excited, perhaps. My mind began to see mysteries in science. Questions began to keep me up late at night. What if there was no single judging force that controlled worldly events? No God like we'd been taught? But what if it wasn't all pointless chance, either? Perhaps the universes were ruled by a cosmic set of likelihoods? Clouds of probability? What if there were multiple realities, only one of which we perceive? Then perhaps my grandmother was saved from that fire after all. Or perhaps the fire never even happened."

"What do you mean, never happened?" I ask.

"If a particle can exist in two places at once, couldn't a person be both dead and alive?"

"Dead and alive?" I ask, thinking about my mother and father and hoping it could be true. "How could that be?"

"Well, it might have been juvenile thinking, and many of my contemporaries certainly laughed me out of their collegiate discussions. Still, I wondered. If we were able to truly transcend what we perceive, might it be argued that anything possible is not only possible, but in fact, is? If my grandmother believed in a heaven where her soul would carry on for eternity, is it too much to think that her belief made it so? What if everything that could possibly happen is happening and always has been and always will be? What if those meteors are particles ablating in the upper atmosphere? But what if they're also the reentering souls seen by Jimmy's mother?"

"So you do believe in souls," I say.

"I don't know what I believed then," he replies. "But I've learned enough now to not believe in anything."

"I hope I never learn that much," Jimmy says.

"Me either," I say. "But I do like your idea about multiple realities. About nothing really ending, but going on forever and ever. If that's what you meant."

"It has a darker flip side," he says. "Might not suffering be also eternal? Might not evil play out again and again?"

"Is that why you agreed to go along with Dr. Radcliffe and the Park Service?"

"I'm not sorry," he says. "If that's what you're asking me."

"Well," Jimmy pipes in, "ya should be."

"You didn't see the horror of humankind," he says. "I did. When we came up from Holocene II and began touring the devastation, I went back to my hometown, but my hometown wasn't even there. Then I went to the cities. I'll tell you here and now I saw the apocalypse on display. You have no idea the destruction leveled by thousands of thermonuclear bombs. Bomb isn't even the right word, they're such hell. And there were many more of them than anyone thought, too. How ignorant we were to feel safe all those years before. And if you were a survivor, you'd have wished to have been inside the blast radius instead. Awful mutations. Cancer. And the crimes we unearthed! You'd be surprised what people will eat when no crops will grow under a blacked-out sun."

"It sounds to me like you don't agree with our stopping the drones," I say. "So why are you helping us?"

"I don't know what's right anymore," he sighs. "But I have no interest in leading anything, so I'm happy to let you try and figure it out. And who knows, maybe we were wrong. It doesn't look as though it's worked after all these years. Plus, as I'm sure you know, my brain is suffering now after nearly a millennium of thought, if you can call it that. I used to believe I'd get wiser with all this time, but it doesn't seem so. Besides," he says, pausing to lift his shadowed arm up toward the night sky, "I'm ready to join my grandmother up there. Or wherever she is or isn't, alive or dead, always being or never having been."

The meteors fade with the close of his story until we're all standing in the sparkling dark, listening to the screw churn up the glowing waves behind us. After a short while, and without another word, the professor leaves us and heads inside. Jimmy and I linger for a few quiet minutes, watching the stars.

I toss and turn in my bunk, trying to fall back to sleep. My mind is running with images that I'd rather not see. Nuclear blasts catching cities by surprise. The professor's grandmother burning in her townhouse. Eden on fire and my mother and father's brains melting away in the boiling pool. The slaughter of Jimmy's family in the cove, the pile of their burning corpses. Dr. Radcliffe shooting Gloria. Mrs. Radcliffe setting off the wave. The images roll across my mind and melt into each other like some kind of kaleidoscope of horror. I lean over the edge and look down on Jimmy. "Are you hot?"

"Yeah," he says. "Not as bad as earlier though."

"It's hotter than hot up here."

"Go bunk in the torpedo room."

"Torpedo room?"

"That's what the professor called it when he chased me outta there. Last door in the forward passage. It's nice n' cool. But take yer pad, the floor's got them traction thingies on it."

The torpedo room is dark and cool, but the only place to

lay my mat is between the stored torpedoes themselves, which means I'm cuddled up to a damn warhead.

I press my cheek against the cold metal casing and imagine the destructive power hidden inside, just inches from my face. Would I even feel it? No way. It's strange to think what things we build with our big brains. That someone once picked up a rock and realized it could do much more damage than their fists alone. Then they sharpened it. Then they attached it to a stick. And here we are all these centuries later, and I'm sleeping next to a live torpedo.

There are times when I can almost understand where the Foundation was coming from when they dedicated the world as a park and formed the Park Service to protect it. But violence can't be the right solution to violence. Or can it? I don't know. Sometimes I wish other people would just tell me how to think. Tell me what to believe. I can see why it was so easy for the professor to go along with Dr. Radcliffe.

I open my eyes and see a blue light pulsing against the ceiling in the far corner of the dark torpedo room. At first, I think it must be my mind playing tricks on me. Some lingering view of glowing plankton, or a strain on my eyes from staring at too many shooting stars. But then the light begins to annoy me, and I'm already feeling short on sleep.

When I get up and turn on the LED room light, of course the blue light seems to disappear, making me hunt around for its source. I step over torpedoes, kick around the miscellaneous supplies stored between them, finally coming to a tarp covering something in the far corner. I pull the tarp free, exposing the black box labeled ANTIMATTER. Its translucent window glows with a rhythmic pulse of blue light.

I storm into the control room, shouting: "What is that damn thing doing on here!"

The professor's head jerks up from his chest, where he'd been sleeping at the wheel.

"Huh? What?" He checks the controls frantically.

"I said what is it doing here!"

"What are you talking about?" he asks, once he's satisfied by the gauges that we haven't run up on another reef. "And more importantly, why are you yelling?"

"In there!" I shout, pointing. "In the torpedo room. The antimatter. Why is it here? With us? On the submarine?"

"It's nothing," he says, waving it off as no big deal. "Just a simple precaution is all."

"A precaution?"

"Yes. We thought it would be wise to have a deterrent on board, in case something goes wrong."

"Who's we?"

"Myself and Hannah, of course."

"Oh, is that so? You and Hannah? You mean Hannah who didn't even want to come with us? Hannah who's back safe at the Foundation, but she sends the antimatter along instead?"

"It's perfectly safe," he says, trying to be reassuring.

"I don't care. I should have been told. And since when did you take orders from Hannah anyway?"

"Since Dr. Radcliffe was her father."

"Well," I huff. "We'll see about that when we get back."

"If we get back," the professor corrects.

"What do you mean 'if?'"

"I mean we have absolutely no idea what we'll find on the Isle of Man. And that's precisely why Hannah thought it wise to have some insurance on board. A bargaining chip of sorts. And frankly, even though I wouldn't have challenged her either way, I agree with her reasoning."

"Is that right? Her reasoning? Well, aren't you two just thick as thieves? I'm beginning to distrust you, Professor. And when exactly did you find the time to haul that thing on board beneath our noses anyway?"

"We looked for you, but you we're gone."

"Gone where?"

"Your little boat trip with Jimmy. The morning we left."

"Well, even so, you could have told us."

"It didn't seem important at the time."

"Important?" I ask. "I'm not the physicist here, but I'd say enough antimatter to annihilate us and the entire Isle of Man is important. Wait! Is that the deterrent? If we find people there, you intend to threaten to destroy the island?"

"There is no plan," he says. "It's just another tool. Let's not forget the mission. We need to get that encryption key, if it's even on the island. And then we need to get back safely with it so you can take control of the drones. Otherwise, it's business as usual up here, and your people are stranded down in Holocene II. Isn't that why you came? To free them?"

"Yes, but—"

"But nothing," he says. "Every tool we can bring that may help is worth having. Wouldn't you agree? I should say you would. Let's just hope we don't need it."

"Is everything okay?" Jimmy stands in the doorway with his eyes half shut and his hair tousled. Junior skulks at his feet.

"It's fine," I say. "Sorry if my yelling woke you."

Jimmy turns without another word and shuffles off back the way he came. Junior follows him.

I spin back to the professor and speak in a lower voice. "We're going to have a talk about not keeping things from one another when we return. You can bet on that."

"Whatever you say," he shrugs. "But that sounds like a talk you'll need to have with Hannah."

CHAPTER 10
The Isle of Man

Cold winds and high swells meet us in the Irish Sea.

This is a shame because I just catch a glimpse of the steep cliffs on Ireland's distant southern coastline when the professor calls us down to close the hatch so we can dive.

It's strange seeing everything for the first time. I have a strong sense of déjà vu because I've been building these images in my mind ever since I could read. And sometimes they're just as I'd imagined. Other times, they're not. The most shocking difference is that I always imagined the world in the past, as it was written about in the old books—a world filled with people. But not so up here now. Other than our misadventure with the 'Mericans, as they called themselves, we haven't laid eyes on a single ship or any coastal signs of civilization for the twenty-three days we've been at sea. It's a far cry from the busy but humdrum routine of my childhood life in Holocene II.

I'm in the head—that's what the professor calls the shitter, although I don't know why—when Jimmy comes knocking on the door. "Hurry up," he says.

"You feel sick, too?"

"No," he shouts through the door. "We're here."

"Where?"

"The Isle of Man."

Junior lies in the corner of the control room, chewing on something (probably the professor's slipper), and Jimmy looks over the professor's shoulder at the controls. I step up to the professor's other shoulder and look over, too.

A pop-up LCD screen displays a rugged coastline covered in snow. And the snow is still falling, being driven in flurries by the wind, providing only peekaboo views through the digital periscope. Waves crash against rocks. Steep banks rise from the water. Hills roll inland like so many snow-covered swells.

"Doesn't look very friendly," I say.

"No," the professor replies. "The weather is unfortunate. It's usually much milder here, I think."

"How big is it?" Jimmy asks.

The professor sighs. "Quite large, I'm afraid. I suggest we patrol the coastline at periscope depth. See what we can see."

"Sounds like a plan to me," I say.

Other than brief restroom breaks and snack runs, we stay glued to the periscope's screen. But my hopes sink with each passing kilometer. More jagged shoreline, more unwelcoming cliffs, and more falling snow. Eventually, Jimmy drifts away and passes the time by running down the passageways dragging his rabbit fur for Junior to chase. Every time they come skidding into the control room, the professor jumps with surprise then mumbles profanities, as if he were caught completely off guard, even though it just happened moments before. In time, Jimmy and Junior head off to hunt up food, and the professor nods off in his chair and snores. I stay alert and watch the screen.

It's mesmerizing to stare at the coastline as it crawls by, its rugged beauty enhanced by the anticipation of what might roll next onto the scene. In a strange way, I feel like I'm back down in Holocene II, watching some ancient educational in our Level 3 theater. I have to keep reminding myself that what's on the screen is happening right now, and that I'm only five meters beneath it underwater, not five kilometers underground.

I think about the people in Holocene II, going through their daily motions and still believing that this is a wasteland up here. I can't wait to get this encryption key and stop the drones and invite them up to see for themselves how gorgeous it really is. My thoughts drift to my father—to his dreams of someday seeing a butterfly. I wish more than anything he were still alive. He and my mother. Then I think about Hannah and Red back at the Foundation. I'm pretty pissed with Hannah right now, not just for staying last minute, but for letting the professor bring the antimatter along without talking it over with Jimmy and me first. But that doesn't stop me from worrying.

"Is that a light out there?" I ask, turning to the professor, only to remember that he's sleeping. His response is a snore.

Nightfall came to the winter world above while I was daydreaming, but I swear that I catch a glimpse of light on the dark screen. I reach over and shake the professor awake. He yawns, rubs his red-rimmed eyes, and blinks at me.

"What is it?" he asks.

"A light. On the screen."

"I can't see it."

"Wait for the snow to clear for a second. There!"

The professor springs to life, adjusting the controls and bringing the submarine to a halt. He zooms the camera as far in as it will go. The light grows on the screen from a tiny speck to a square glow, as if from a high window. But the driving snow and darkness make it impossible to discern the light's source. And moments later, it disappears. The professor drops anchor and marks our position just in case we drift overnight. Then he stands and stretches, yawning.

"Good eye, kid," he says. "Nothing to do now but wait for morning. Let's get some rest."

If the others really sleep, I'm not sure how. I toss and turn all night, wondering what we'll find in the morning. I'm curious. I'm nervous. Several times I lean my head over the bunk and look down on Jimmy, but his shadow is as still as can be, his arm flopped over the bunk and resting on Junior's back. I hear the professor snoring across the way, and once he gets up and stumbles to the head. But otherwise, it's just dead silence and an occasional light rocking as the submarine is pulled against the anchor chain by the currents. At least the cooling system seems to be working again.

I'm the first one in the control room, anxiously awaiting sunrise. Jimmy shows up next, carrying cups of hot algae tea. By the time the professor joins us, the dark screen has lightened to gray. And that's all it does—gray and more gray. The entire island is swamped in with a thick fog. We rotate the fiber-optic periscope every which way, but can hardly even see the water more than a few meters from the lens. I suggest we move the submarine in closer, but the professor says it's best to stay put, after mumbling something about the impatience of youth. And maybe I am impatient. But it seems to me that every extra hour we spend looking for this encryption key is an extra hour that the drones spend hunting humans.

"Let me take over," Jimmy says, several hours into my vigil at the screen. "Go take a shower or somethin'."

"You saying I stink?"

"No," he laughs. "Jus' that you need to relax a little."

Despite my protest, it sounds like a good idea. So I head for the shower and let the hot water wash away my worry. I hadn't realized how anxious I am until Jimmy noticed it for me. I wonder what else he notices about me that I can't see? It's a strange feeling, standing in a small, cramped shower, beneath a stream of steaming water, knowing that just a few feet away is the frigid water of the Irish Sea and above that the snowy Isle of Man shrouded in fog and mystery.

When I arrive back in the control room refreshed, Jimmy and the professor are pressed up close to the screen.

"What is it?" I ask, pushing myself in between them.

"Hard to say," the professor says. "It's just now clearing."

Sure enough, the fog is thinning. I can make out the waves hitting the shore. But it's not a rocky shore. Rather, it's a stone seawall of some kind that runs straight out of the water. Waves crash against the wall, then roll back out and slam into other oncoming waves, creating a turbulent sloshing of white-capped water. The fog clears a bit more, and a set of stone steps comes into view, cut through the seawall and leading into the water. Then a sloping terrace covered in snow. Then another set of steps. Another terrace. Then the wind sweeps in and pulls away the foggy veil, and a sprawling castle appears from the gray.

"Is that a castle?"

"It appears so," the professor says.

"What's a castle?" Jimmy asks.

"Basically, a big fortified residence," the professor answers, "mostly popular during the Middle Ages."

I'm sure Jimmy has never heard of the Middle Ages, but he accepts the professor's explanation with a polite nod anyway and then asks, "What's a castle doing here?"

The professor shakes his head. "Your guess is as good as mine. Although I'd be willing to wager this was an ancient site that's been reclaimed and restored."

"Restored?" Jimmy asks. "Like fixed up? By who?"

The professor tosses up his hands. "I don't know. Perhaps King Arthur is immortal after all."

"Who's King Arthur?"

The professor appears frustrated with Jimmy. "Just an old myth from these parts of the world. I was making a poor joke. It's not important. All right. Enough questions already."

"I never heard of King Arthur either, Jimmy," I say. "But regardless of whose castle it is, what are we going to do?"

"I say we go on up there," Jimmy suggests.

"You mean sneak up and spy?" I ask.

"No. Go on up and say hi-dy."

"Just knock and introduce ourselves? That's crazy."

"Maybe," he says. "But if we'd of caught people sneakin' on us, I know for sure we'd treat 'em like enemies. When folks approached us needin' help, we usually lent 'em a hand."

"He actually makes a good point," the professor says. "As hard as that is to believe. Nothing removes suspicion as well as an honest plea for help."

"So you're saying we should just walk up to the castle and tell whoever lives there why we're here and then ask for the encryption key? That's goofy!"

The professor shakes his head. "I'm not saying that. I'm suggesting that you could approach them as a stranger in need. Keep your mission secret. Tell them you've shipwrecked and washed ashore. Or tell them you come from another part of the island and are lost. Ask for help. Then, once you're inside, you can snoop around and discover what you can."

"You want us to lie?" Jimmy asks.

"No," the professor says, "just bend the truth a little."

"The truth dun' bend, it breaks. That's what my pa said."

The professor looks up as if addressing the ceiling. "Great, he's a philosopher, too."

"I think he has a point, Jimmy," I say, jumping in before they start arguing. "It's smart to keep our business private."

"Fine," Jimmy says, "I'll jus' keep my mouth shut. How's that sound? You's better at talkin' anyhow."

The professor checks his charts. "Sunset is in four hours,"

he says. "It should be dark enough to go in five."

"You want us to swim to shore after dark? In this cold?"

"We have to be sure they don't see the submarine," he says. "Plus, it will help your story, won't it?"

"Well, how will we get back?"

"Let's triangulate some landmarks with the periscope now, while it's light. After nightfall, we'll surface long enough for you two to get on deck, then I'll submerge again and re-anchor. I'll wait here for you."

"For how long?" I ask.

"For as long as it takes."

"What if we never come back?"

"That's a good question. Okay, I'll wait for a week."

"And what then?"

"Ah—ah—ah," he stammers. "I don't know what then."

"How about you wait two weeks then head back without us and take care of Hannah and Red?"

"All right then," he says. "I'll wait two weeks."

"Hopefully, we'll be back in a day or so, though. Right?"

"Wait a minute," Jimmy says. "How we gonna get back in the submarine when we swim out?"

"Another good question. What's wrong with me? Stupid, I tell you. Just stupid." The professor paces the control room for a minute, pulling at his hair. "I've got it. Stones. Three stones."

"Stones?" Jimmy asks. "What for?"

"There's bound to be no shortage of stones on the island. Or right off shore for that matter."

"Yeah. So?"

"You just swim out here with three stones and drop them on the roof of the sub, and I'll surface and pick you up."

"Submarine," I say.

"Yes," he replies.

"No," I correct him. "You said sub."

"I did not."

"You did so."

"Well, it doesn't matter. Three stones and I'll surface."

"What if yer sleepin'?" Jimmy asks.

"I'll try not to."

"Try not to sleep?" I question. "For fourteen days?"

"I'll sleep light. I'll stay at five meters. You can easily dive that depth and pound on the walls if you have to."

"Okay," I say, more nervous than relieved. "We've got a plan then. We'll leave an hour after sunset. But let's make sure we get some good landmarks before that fog comes back."

After identifying landmarks and then committing them to memory, I pace the submarine, playing potential scenarios out in my head. Who might answer the door? What might they ask us? How will we answer? As the hours creep past, fear creeps in. Jimmy disappears into the bunkroom, and I know he's there saying goodbye to Junior. The professor keeps coming out from the supply room and checking on me, looking me over in a strange way before leaving again. I finally figure out why when he comes out carrying homemade pants and shirt stitched together from fabric scraps.

"What's this?" I ask.

"You look entirely too civilized in those clothes."

"What about Jimmy?"

"Have you seen what he wears? Ha! He'll fit right in, no doubt. He could eat his outfit in a pinch."

"Good point," I say, chuckling.

When I enter the bunkroom, I find Jimmy lying on his bunk, petting Junior. He turns and props his head on his elbow, watching me change. "Where'd ya get those ugly clothes?"

"The professor patched them together. Said I looked too civilized, if you can believe that."

"What's he gonna do about yer attitude?"

"You think my attitude's too civilized?"

Jimmy laughs. "Not the exact word I'd use, but I ain't too good with words anyhow. Hey. Are you worried? I mean, do ya think we'll make it back safe and all?"

"I don't know," I answer, not wanting to lie. "But I'm not coming back without that encryption key."

"I'm not even sure what an encryption key is."

"It's just a set of numbers, I guess. A password, basically."

"And you expect to find that in the castle?"

"All we have is that clue to go on."

"'In the hand of David' or whatever?"

"Yep. 'Where man rises from the sea, so in the right hand of David you shall find your key.'"

"He dun' like algaecrisps, but he'll eat the bars."

"I got it," the professor says, getting annoyed with Jimmy's never ending list of instructions about caring for Junior.

"And he gets restless, so ya gotta run 'em with the rabbit."

"Roger that,"

"Huh?"

"It means I understand. Run him with the rabbit. We need to hurry, in case someone sees the boat."

Jimmy opens the hatch and disappears out into the dark. I follow on. A cold wind whips across the water, driving sea spray into my face, and the surfaced submarine heaves up and down on the swells, unsteady beneath our feet.

"I cain't see nothin'!" Jimmy shouts.

"We just swim straight ahead, and we should make it to those steps no problem. Don't you think?"

The professor remains just inside the open hatch, shielded from the weather. "Remember the clue," he calls out, his voice quickly carried away on the wind. "'In the right hand of David you shall find your key.' Take your time. I'll be waiting for you right here until you find it."

I see his face in the glow coming from the open hatch and could almost swear his eyes are wet with worry beneath his bushy brows. Or maybe it's just the wind. He forces a smile and then pulls the hatch shut.

We stand on the dark deck and listen to the waves rolling past. It's much colder and much wilder here than our swim to fell that coconut tree. Neither of us moves to dive in.

"Ah, crud! How'd you get out here?"

I turn to Jimmy. "What?"

"I'll bet he put him out on purpose."

Jimmy bends and lifts Junior from the deck and carries him toward the hatch. But he never makes it. Waves rush onto the deck as the submarine dives, and in mere seconds we're all three floating in the freezing water.

No going back now, I guess.

With no time to waste, we paddle toward shore. My feet go numb almost instantly. The frigid water constricts my chest, making it hard to breath. My instincts want me to race for dry ground, but I steel myself against panic and maintain a steady pace. It's nearly pitch black. I can hear Junior paddling between us, breathing hard and blowing water out his nose.

Then something rough brushes against my leg. At first, I'm relieved, thinking it must be a rock, signaling that we're close to shore. But my feet are nowhere near touching, and I can just make out the shadow of the seawall looming above, still many meters away. Again, something hits me. Harder this time. Like something passing by and woodenly knocking against my thigh.

I look over at Jimmy. I can barely see him in the dark, but I can see the fear in his eyes. Without a word between us, we each reach out a hand and grip Junior's fur and kick furiously, paddling with our free arms and dragging Junior along between us as he struggles to keep his head above water.

A primal fear erases every other thought in my brain, and I think only of reaching dry land. A furious thrashing follows us in the dark as we kick like mad for the seawall and the steps. If I'm hit again I can't feel it in my frenzy, but I'm consumed with the feeling of being pursued. Then my hand strikes something, and I recoil with fear. But Jimmy paddles by me, and a moment later he's reaching his hand down and pulling me onto the step.

We scamper, slipping and sliding, several steps up from the water and slump down on the cold concrete and look back—nothing but blackness and the sound of waves rolling in. I'm trembling with so much adrenalin, I don't even feel cold. But poor Junior sits between us, soaked and shivering, so tired he's not even bothering to shake dry.

"We better get on 'fore we freeze," Jimmy says.

Junior is too weak to walk by himself, and he looks like a dead seal draped limply over Jimmy's arms as we follow the steps up and across the various snow-covered terraces toward the dark castle. Neither of us mentions what happened in the water just now, and I begin to wonder if it wasn't a lone piece of driftwood tossed by the waves. Or maybe my imagination.

The path ends at a massive door. Even in the dark of night it looks ancient and rough compared to the refined materials we manufactured down in Holocene II. My teeth have begun to chatter, and my fear of the castle is quickly overcome by my fear of freezing to death. I lift the iron knocker and pause. I look over at Jimmy, soaking wet with his hair hanging in his face and Junior in his arms. Even in the dark I can see his smile that seems to say: "Too late to turn back now."

I pound three good whacks on the door.

We stand on the stoop for a long time, listening to the wind whip at our backs and the distant waves crashing against the seawall. My legs ache. My teeth chatter. My arms shake. I'm reaching for the knocker again when the door swings open and a triangle of light washes over us.

A small man stands before us, dressed in an odd vest-suit made from some type of wool. His eyebrows and hair are black as night, but his neatly trimmed beard is gray. He looks us over without a word. Then he leans out and looks up at the dark sky, as if perhaps to explain our condition by looking for rain.

At last, he says, "May I be of service?"

"Um—well—yes," I stammer, completely forgetting what I had planned to say. "At least I hope so. We're a little bit wet, and we wondered if you might be able to help us out."

"Of course," he says, as if the request needed no thought at all. "By all means. Come in, come in." He steps aside to let us enter the foyer then shuts the heavy door behind us. "Let's get you sorted. You'll need dry clothes straight away. Straight away. And something hot to drink as well, I would presume."

"That would be great," I say.

"Yes. Follow me."

We follow him across the grand foyer and down a long

hall to a cozy room with a roaring fire. The room is sparsely furnished but comfortable, the floors covered in carpets, the walls hung with colorful tapestries. Giant, shaggy hounds lie everywhere, sprawled in front of the fire or draped over chairs. The man shoos one of the hounds off the sofa, and it moans and bellows in protest, stopping to stretch before sliding to the floor and shooting us an annoyed look as it trots off and flops down in front of the fire on a rug. Junior whimpers, and Jimmy protectively pulls him tighter in his arms.

"Don't worry," the man says, closing one eye and peering closely at Junior. "They haven't been trained to hunt anything but deer for generations. Is she a fox?"

Jimmy nods. "He."

"Well, he's different from the ones we have around here, that's for certain. I would imagine he'd enjoy some warm milk very much? Perhaps some fresh venison?"

"I'm sure he'd like that a lot," Jimmy says.

"Yes, then. Straight away. You two just make yourselves at home now. Anything you need. I'll be back momentarily with dry clothing and a service of tea."

He retreats from the room with a bow, leaving us alone with the fire and the dogs.

We sit on the couch and let the fire's warmth waft over us. It feels nice. Jimmy holds Junior in his lap and pets him, and I notice that his coat is already beginning to dry. The hounds are mostly sleeping, but occasionally one will open its dark eyes, as if checking to be sure we haven't moved. True to his word, the man is back in almost no time with a tea tray balanced in one hand and his other arm draped in clothing.

"First things first," he says, setting the tray on a small table next to the couch. "Let's get you two into something dry before the cold gets into your bones. Here we are, then. These might be a bit large but should do nicely, I think."

He hands us each a pair of pants and a shirt. He doesn't offer us anywhere private to change, but he turns away and busies himself with the tea. I strip, grateful to be rid of the professor's soaked and ugly patchwork clothes. Then I slip on the new pants. They're loose and short, coming just past my knees, almost like a pair of long shorts, but I tie them off at the waist with the attached sash, then slip on the puffy shirt. I feel like a pirate in some old storybook from my lesson slate. Jimmy looks equally ridiculous.

When I turn around, Junior is already on the floor, lapping milk from a bowl, and the man signals for us to sit and hands us each a cup of steaming tea. It tastes of mint and sweet cream. The man bows and leaves us with our cups. The warm room smells slightly of wet dog. The clothes are soft, and the fire feels nice on my bare legs.

"What's that?" Jimmy asks.

"What?"

"On your leg?"

I lean forward and see a nasty scrape on my calf. The skin is rubbed off as if by sandpaper, and the exposed flesh is angry and red. A trickle of blood runs down to my ankle. "I don't know. I guess something did hit me in the water."

"I felt it, too," Jimmy says. "But I got nothin' on my legs."

The man comes back with a platter of food and slides the small table closer and sets the platter in front of us. It's covered with cheeses, crackers, meats, and pickled vegetables. I'm not sure whether swimming for our life worked up my appetite, or whether it's just because of weeks with nothing but algaecrisps and canned food on board the submarine, but my mouth fills with saliva at the sight of fresh food, and I rudely dig in without even saying thank you.

The man stands several paces away with his arms behind his back, gazing idly at the fire, as if waiting to fill any request we might make.

"I'm Aubrey, and this is Jimmy," I slur, my mouth full of crackers and cheese. "The fox is named Junior."

"Yes. How thoughtless of me not to introduce myself. My name is Riley. At your service, young sirs."

"May I ask you a question, Riley?"

"Of course," he says.

"It might sound strange."

"Ask anything, sir."

"How old are you."

"Oh. Well. Let's see then." He looks down and bobs his head from side to side as if tallying invisible figures lying on the floor. "I believe this spring will make fifty-three, sir."

After such a seemingly odd question, I expect Riley to ask us some questions of his own, but he doesn't. He just stands at the ready and asks us if we'd like any more food and then takes the empty tray away. He comes back some time later with two small glasses of warm milk laced with something sweet.

"This should help you get to sleep," he says.

"You don't mind if we stay?"

"Quite on the contrary, sir," he says. "His Lordship loves entertaining houseguests. I'm afraid I must apologize, though, for his absence, and for the depressed nature of the house in general. We're waiting on death to pay a visit."

"Waiting on death?"

"I'm afraid so. His Lordship is mourning at the bedside as we speak. Sometimes the trip mont da Anaon can be long."

"Well, it's very kind of you to take us in," I say.

"Pleasure, sir. And whenever you two are ready, I'm happy to show you to your rooms. I've already kindled the stoves and warmed the beds for you."

"We're ready now," I say, finishing the last of my milk.

"Straight away we go, then."

"What about Junior?" Jimmy asks.

"Your fox? Oh, he should be quite comfortable down here with the deerhounds. The fire stays lit constantly, and they're let out for a quick run at sunrise, before their breakfast. And what time would you two like to breakfast?"

I look at Jimmy, then answer. "Whenever is fine."

"I'll come by for you at nine. All set then? I'll see you up."

Jimmy pauses to look back at Junior, but Junior is already spread out on the rug in front of the fire, sleeping.

"He'll be fine," I say.

Riley leads us up a wide and winding staircase to the floor above and down a long hall lit with oil lamps hanging from the walls. He stops at a door and opens it. The room is small but warm. A small window, a sideboard with a pan for washing. A lantern hangs next to a chair beside the bed.

Jimmy and I step inside.

Riley clears his throat. "Excuse me, but I took the liberty of assuming you would be needing separate rooms."

"Of course," I say, stepping back into the hall. "I'll see you at breakfast, Jimmy."

"See ya then," he says, looking a little worried as he presses the door closed.

Riley leads me past several other doors, stopping to point out an open sitting area with a lantern and desk. "I'm afraid it's just me tonight, so I'll be right here if you need anything at all." He continues on to the last door at the end of the hall. "Here we are, then. Any special requests for breakfast, sir?"

"Anything should be fine."

"All righty, then. Full breakfast it is. See you at nine, sir."

Then he pulls the door shut, and I'm alone in the room. I cross to the window and pull the shutters open. The moonless sky shows no shape beyond the window's ledge. I don't even know which direction I'm looking. Since there's nothing at all to see outside, I turn and inspect the room.

There's a ceramic stove in one corner, a mirror and wash pan on a desk in the other. A small elevated door in the outside wall makes itself out immediately to be a toilet when I open it and get wind of its odor. It's a kind of closet you step into and squat over a crude hole in the floor. Unfortunately, I know I'll likely need to take advantage of it later.

After three weeks in the submarine bunk, the bed feels like floating on a cloud. It must be feathers. I lie on my back and watch the lantern flame cast shadows on the stone ceiling. I almost wish we didn't have to worry about the drones, or about freeing my people from Holocene II. I hate myself for feeling it, but it would be so nice to just be here with Jimmy and have none of the other anxieties weighting me down. There are moments when I forget why we came on this adventure. Times when I'm caught up in the excitement of it all and actually having some fun. Then the sudden unexpected image of drones slaughtering people rips away the feeling of well-being like a forgotten diagnosis of impending death.

I have no idea who these people are or how we'll find an encryption key on this island, if it's even here. And why was this Riley guy so nice to us? He didn't ask anything. Not one question. As if he'd been here all night, waiting for us to arrive. And who's this Lord he's referring to? And who's dying? I guess all we can do is take everything as it comes and do the best we can. I sure hope Hannah and Red are all right.

I get up and turn the lamp down until shadow envelops the room. Then I do something that surprises me. I get on my knees beside the bed and I talk to my dad. Not out loud, but in my head. I tell him that I miss him. I tell him that I'm scared. I tell him that I feel guilty for not trying harder to save him. It feels silly at first, but then tears come into my eyes, my throat constricts, and I hear his voice as sure as if he were sitting in front of me. I hear him tell me that he's proud. I hear him tell me everything will be okay. And I hear him tell me to breathe good energy in and breathe bad energy out.

I'm woken much later by a scratching sound somewhere in the room. I lie perfectly still and listen. It sounds like a kind of muffled rustling near the wall, across from the bed. I jump for the lamp and turn the flame up, but only shadows are chased from the dark room. I'm laughing at myself and my overactive imagination when I hear it again. It's coming from inside the wall. I follow the sound with my ear and notice the outline of a narrow door in the wall, a hidden panel with a recessed handle. I take a deep breath and pull the panel open.

Riley gasps but doesn't scream. He's flattened against the wall of a narrow passage with a lantern in his hand and a basket hanging from straps over his shoulders.

"I pray I haven't woken you, sir."

"What are you doing in here?"

"My apologies, sir. The stoves must be fed throughout the night. The passageways allow the wood to be loaded without disturbing you." He lifts the lid on his basket, showing me a stack of split wood. "At least that's the idea. I'm afraid Angus is much lighter on his feet than I am, sir. But he'll be back at his duties tomorrow."

"Sorry," I say. "You just spooked me a little. Goodnight

again." I pull the panel closed.

After the excitement, I can't get back to sleep. I have no idea what time it is. I look out the window, but it seems even darker than before, if that's even possible. After testing out the bathroom, which is quite a chilling experience with the dark hole beneath me and a cold wind rushing up, I wash my hands using the water jug and bowl on the table.

I wonder if Jimmy's awake, too. I'm tempted to go and check, but I'd have to pass Riley at his desk. Then I look at the hidden panel and get an idea. If all the stoves are connected by that passageway, shouldn't it lead to Jimmy's room? If so, we can talk in private and come up with a plan for tomorrow.

I slip into the passageway carrying the lamp and leave the panel cracked so as to be sure I can find my room again. Then I inch along the narrow passage, being careful to avoid brushing against the hot stoves as I pass. How many doors were between Jimmy's room and mine? I pause and close my eyes, visualizing the walk down the hall. Three doors—then Riley's desk—then two more doors, no three doors—and mine was the fourth. Seven doors. Jimmy's room should be the seventh panel.

When I reach it, I put my ear to the panel and listen before opening it, just in case. All is quiet. I turn the lantern down, push the panel open, and step into the dark room. It looks like the right room, but I only saw it briefly from the door, so it's hard to tell for sure. I creep toward the bed. There's someone sleeping, but the covers are pulled up over the head. Holding the lamp at a distance, I pinch the corner of the blanket with my other hand and gently pull it back. Jimmy lies on his side with his hair spread out on the pillow and his thumb stuck in his mouth. I'm not sure whether to laugh or cry, it's so cute.

As much as I want to discuss our plan, I can't bring myself to wake him. Instead, I stand and watch him for a long time. I'm not sure why. Maybe because I can picture him as a little boy, sleeping in his mother's lap. Or maybe because he looks so peaceful and I wish I could feel that way myself. I wonder if he's dreaming, and if so, what about. I remember watching him sleep in our tent in the cove, back when I still thought of him as ten feet tall and nothing but guts. And I remember him waking up and catching me and joking that he was going to start sleeping with his knife. That was the day he taught me to swim. We've sure been through a lot since then.

By the time I get back to my room, I'm tired again. I kill the lamp and crawl back into bed and close my eyes. I try to imagine myself sleeping as soundly as Jimmy. It doesn't work, but I do fall asleep with my thumb in my mouth.

CHAPTER 12
The Funeral

"Breakfast in ten minutes, sir."

Riley's voice through the door wakes me.

I toss the covers back and look at my leg. The scrape is crusted over with scab, and the flesh surrounding it is swollen. I sure hope it isn't infected. Ignoring the throbbing pain, I get up and step to the window and look out. The view is of the inland side of the castle where snow-dusted trees dot rolling hills of winter white. A road winds away through the trees, passing by some outbuildings and a stone and timber stable.

When I finally find the breakfast room, Jimmy is already seated at the table, pouring cream into a steaming mug.

"You's limpin' a little," he says.

"I know it. What are you drinking there?"

"Ain't totally sure, but it tastes great."

The breakfast room window overlooks a garden where an old man walks the rows of plants, stooping to inspect them and carefully dusting their leaves free of snow.

Riley enters with a steaming mug for me. "Good morning, sir. Your breakfast is just on its way."

I take the mug and thank him. Then I reach for the cream from Jimmy. "How'd you sleep?"

"Good, I guess," he says.

When I first walked in, I had planned to tell him about the secret passageway, but sitting here now it feels weird to admit that I watched him sleeping, so I don't say anything.

Next Riley brings a rack of toast with pads of butter and a dish of honey. Plates of sausages, poached eggs, and some kind of black potato cake follow. I watch the old man tend his plants out the window as I eat, and Jimmy watches, too. When Riley comes back to refill our teas, I thank him.

"Thank you, sir," he says, bowing slightly.

"But I didn't do anything except eat this great food."

"And I thank you for it, sir."

"You know," I say, "we'd be happy to work it off."

"Excuse me, sir?"

"Chores. Clean windows or mop floors or something."

"Very kind of you, sir, but everything is quite taken care of. Perhaps when his Lordship has time to see you he'll have some work for you, if that's what you're after. Until then, I'm happy to serve. Would you be staying on for the funeral then?"

"Funeral?" I ask.

"Yes. I'm sorry, sir. It appears as though the long wait has ended late last night. She suffers no more. We'll be gathering to see the departed off later this morning."

"Oh, we wouldn't dare interrupt something so personal."

"Quite the opposite, sir. While the preliminaries are a very personal time of mourning, of course, the passing itself is cause for celebration. It would be proper to attend. You must come."

I look at Jimmy. He smiles and shakes his head, honoring

his deal to leave the talking to me.

"Okay," I say. "Sure."

Riley smiles. "Very well. We meet at the steps at eleven."

"The steps?"

"Yes, sir. At the water's edge."

After breakfast we're not sure what to do until the funeral, so Jimmy and I wander around the castle. It's very homey, not at all pretentious. The walls are hung with tapestries and quilts, and the furnishings are big and comfortable. We find Junior in a room off the kitchen, eating with the deerhounds, all of them wet and dirty as if they've just come in from outside. He sees us and runs over and licks our hands. Then he returns and forces his way past the deerhounds and buries his face in the food.

"Made himself right comfortable, ain't he?" Jimmy says.

"He better not get too comfortable," I reply.

At the end of the great hall, we find a huge statue room. The high walls are lined with busts on shelves, and the floor is a maze of sculptures. It's all very strange because many of the faces look familiar. As if I'd known them. I wonder if some of them aren't famous people I might have seen likenesses of in educationals. Greek philosophers or something.

We stop to look at a sculpture of a topless woman. Both of her arms have been broken off, but the statue is still stunning. Jimmy caresses her cheek and I can't help but wonder if he sees shades of his mother in her. We carry on. Warriors and athletes, mothers with child, kings and their horses, it's an astounding collection. They must have been ancient long before the war.

Then I see it. At the end of the room, standing in the light of a tall window. I recognize the statue instantly. There's no other form like The David. It's much larger than I'd imagined from the images I've seen, and much more beautiful, too.

"Wow!" Jimmy steps up beside me.

"Makes you proud to be human, doesn't it?"

"Yeah," he says. "Must have taken a tribe to carve it?"

I shake my head. "Just one man."

"One man made this?"

I nod. "An Italian Renaissance man."

"Italian?"

"Yeah. It was a country on this side of the Atlantic."

The David is easily three times as tall as I am, and his face is so alive that it draws me to look in the direction of his stare to see what it is he's after, but I can't seem to pull my eyes away for even a moment. Chiseled muscles, striking features, lean body poised for a perfect throw. His left arm at his shoulder gripping the sling, his right hand at his side, holding . . .

"Jimmy, this is it. This is the hand!"

"I still cain't believe one man carved it."

"No. This is it. The clue. The David. 'In the right hand of David you shall find your key.' This must be it. The encryption key has to be hidden there somehow in his hand."

"In the statue?" Jimmy asks.

"This had to be brought here by Radcliffe. He had smaller things he'd salvaged around the lake house."

We stand on our tiptoes and inspect the statue's hand. It is gripping something, perhaps a stone for his sling, but it's all cut from the original block of marble and there doesn't appear to be anything added. Suddenly, I feel self-conscious, as if all the eyes of all the busts and statues behind us are watching.

I turn around and am startled by a strange man standing behind us. He's taller than I am, his shoulders filled out with muscle. And he's wearing a white tunic tied at the waist, giving him the appearance of one of the statues having come to life. His golden hair hangs to his shoulders, his eyes are piercing blue. He's older than we are, but still young. Maybe twenty-five or thirty.

"His hands always fascinate me too," he says, nodding to the David's hand that we had just been inspecting. "They seem so lifelike. If not a little large for the rest of his body, don't you think? But then, perhaps that's how they were."

I wonder how long he's been standing there and what he heard. I hold out my hand to shake, the way my father taught me too when meeting strangers. "Hi. I'm Aubrey."

Instead of shaking my hand, he catches my wrist and holds my hand up, inspecting it in the sunlight slanting in through the window. I feel awkward, caught in his strong grip as it dawns on me that it might not be their custom to shake.

"Amazing things, human hands are," the man says. "Don't you think so? You can use them to play a game, or to chisel a work of art, like this one here, or even to make a fist and strike down your brother. But the hand is indifferent, only doing the bidding of the mind." He pauses and looks me in the eye and

smiles. Then he says: "You've got good hands. Use them well."
He releases my hand and turns to Jimmy. "Let me see yours
now." Jimmy reluctantly holds out his hand, and the man looks
it over. "You have good hands as well," he says. "I'm assuming
you've come for the games?"

Jimmy looks at me, confused.

"Yes," I say, deciding to go along with it. "We have."

"Good for you. It's an honor many lesser men fear. You
don't look familiar to me, but perhaps I know your parents?"

"Both our parents are dead, sir."

He sighs. "Well, some of us get to go home sooner than
others, I guess. Which is why I've come to fetch you, actually.
I'd like your help with the catafalque."

"The cata-what?"

"The lowering."

"Oh, sure," I say, still having no idea what he means.

"Good," he says. "And please don't call me sir. Or His
Lordship. Or any of that fancy poppycock. I get enough of that
from Riley. Just call me Finn, and we'll get along fine. Now,
you said your name was Aubrey?"

"Yes, sir," I say, then quickly adding, "I mean, Finn."

"I'm very pleased to meet you, Aubrey," he says, bowing
slightly. "And what's your name, young man?"

"Jimmy."

"Aubrey and Jimmy. Good solid names. I'll cheer for you
in the games. Very well, then. Shall we go and do our duty?"

We follow him across the great hall, through a large pair of double doors and into a chamber room where a corpse lies in waiting, its body wrapped in a thin, white sheet and its head resting on a pillow. It's an old woman, her thin skin gray and sagging, but I can see the resemblance in her bone structure. She must be Finn's mother. The old man we saw tending the garden through the breakfast window earlier kneels beside the corpse, securing the sheet corners with pins.

"I brought some strong hands to help, Angus," Finn says.

Angus looks up without expression, nods to us, and turns back to his work.

"I promise he's not being rude," Finn says to us. "It's just that Angus doesn't speak. However, he hears just fine. Don't you, Angus?" Angus nods. "Be a couple of champs there, you two, and grab the head," Finn continues. "I'll take the other end, and perhaps Angus here can get the door."

Jimmy and I hesitate, making nervous starts toward the corpse, but not committing. Then I see that she's resting on a moveable board. Relieved that I don't have to actually touch the body, I grab a side of the board near her head, and Jimmy grabs the other. Then Finn snatches up the board at her feet, and we lift her from the platform and walk toward the door. She's surprisingly light.

As we exit the chamber and cross the great hall, Finn walks backwards, always keeping her feet pointed in the direction that we're heading. As he faces us over the corpse, he talks as if it were just another day and just another chore.

"I was sorry to see the snow," he says. "It's early this year.

Might delay the games by a few days, but don't worry, it'll melt. Have you any interest in joining the hunt tomorrow morning?"

"The hunt?" I ask.

"The men won't mind, I promise. We always celebrate a passing with a feast, and since you're here and helping today, I see no reason why you shouldn't enjoy the hunt tomorrow."

When we arrive at the end of the hall, Angus opens the same door Jimmy and I knocked on last night, and we carry the body outside. The castle exterior looks different in the light of day. Less frightening. The path has been cleared of snow, the steps sanded for traction. I can imagine in the summertime it's a gorgeous seaside spectacle of green lawns and flowers.

Several rough-looking men stand by the seawall, assembling a wooden crane-like contraption, wheeled out from a nearby stone shed. The water beyond the seawall is calm and dappled with dull silver as the sun tries to burn through high clouds in gray skies. Somewhere out there is the submarine, hovering beneath the gentle waves. I look to the edges of the seawall as our landmarks and try to triangulate where I think it should be. It's not as far out as I thought, but still an awfully long swim in the freezing black of night.

When we reach the last terrace, Finn steers us to the crane and lays the board in front of it. With all that timber scaffolding surrounding the corpse, it almost looks like the funeral pyre that I built in the cove, except the machine is connected with iron joints and iron hinges and the wear marks on the wood give it the appearance of something well used.

Finn thanks us and heads back into the castle, leaving us to watch as the men finish erecting the crane. I can't discern its purpose, though. With a long, weighted crossbeam hinged in the middle, it almost looks like photos of catapults I've seen, except I can't imagine hurling a dead body from a catapult.

The men eye us as they work, seemingly annoyed by our presence there. When their work on the crane is done, they return to the shed and wheel out a cast-stone firebox with an iron kettle suspended above it. While they load the box with wood and light a fire, one of them carries the kettle down the steps and scoops it full of seawater. With the kettle of sea water warming over the fire, the men drift off toward the shed and pass around a pouch, dipping something out and stuffing it into their lips and proceeding to spit on the ground while they visit.

People begin arriving in ones and twos. They drift down from the castle, carrying little pine wreaths woven with bright fabric bows. Each new visitor gazes a moment at the deceased and lays their wreath at the base of the machine. Then they mingle, discussing mundane things, mostly the weather.

"Is this how they go?"

"How what goes?" Jimmy asks.

"Funerals?"

"Pretty much so," he says. "But we usually had a day of silence. Then we'd tell stories about whoever died 'round the fire. What'd ya'll do?"

"We never had funerals."

"You didn't?"

"We just gathered at the platform and said goodbye when people left to retire."

After the last stragglers arrive, Finn comes out from the castle wearing a crown of pine branches on his head and an elaborately stitched cape. He carries an iron helmet attached to the end of a thick chain. Riley follows him, ringing a bell. The guests fall quiet as Finn descends the steps and approaches the machine. As I watch Finn move through the small crowd, it becomes clear to me that these must be his relatives. They have the same high cheek bones and wide-set eyes.

Finn bends over his mother's corpse, at least I assume it must be his mother, and caresses her gray and wrinkled cheek. Then he lifts the iron helmet on its chain and unclasps the sides and opens it like a clam shell on hinges. He slides the helmet over her head and closes and latches it again. Then he lifts the chain and hooks it to a rope running through a pulley on one end of the crane's main beam.

The corpse lying there wearing an iron helmet attached to the crane by a chain is an unsettling image, but the spectators seem bothered not at all, as if it were a common occurrence. I'm busy watching their faces when a ratcheting sound turns me back to the Finn at the contraption.

Finn is pulling on a rope fed through pulleys and raising the corpse off the ground by her head. It looks like a strange resurrection. The chain brings her to a seated position with her arms still crossed at her chest, either pinned by the loose sheet or locked that way in some kind of death rigor. Then the chain continues pulling her up, until she stands, hanging woodenly from the crane like some medieval puppet dancer as she twists on her tiptoes. When she's completely suspended, Finn ties off the rope and produces a knife from his tunic and bends down and slashes open her heels. No blood flows, but the flesh is flayed open to the yellow bone. I see Jimmy wince beside me. And he's no stranger to gore.

Several of the workers join Finn and help him push the crane toward the seawall. The crowd moves with it, following the dangling corpse like a prize and scooping up their wreaths as they go. Jimmy and I stay put and watch from the elevated steps. They stop the crane just short of the seawall edge and one of the workers chalks the wheels with wooden wedges. Then they swing the armature out over the water.

The second the dangling corpse's shadow hits the water, the sharks arrive. They rise to the surface in a boil of blue fins, their shadows gliding back and forth beneath the hanging body as if summoned by a dinner bell.

Jimmy and I turn to look at one another, our shared horror reflected in the other's eyes.

"You think?"

"I'll bet it was," Jimmy says.

I look at my scabbed-over calf. "But it wasn't a bite."

"No," Jimmy says. "But their skin is rough as sandpaper."

The thought of swimming past those sharks in the black of night makes me sick to my stomach. Almost as sick as watching what I know is about to happen.

Finn unties the rope and lowers the corpse slowly on its chain. The body turns left, then right, as if taking a moment to acknowledge each of the visitors through the iron eyeholes in the mask. Then her filleted heels hit the water and she sinks slowly from view until even the mask is submerged.

The sharks seem to hit the line all at once.

The chain pulls the rope taut, jerking back and forth in a froth of thrashing tails and white water. The crane strains, the timbers creak, the wheels slide a few inches against the chocks. A light breeze carries a spray of saltwater mist to my nose. I can't decide whether they're honoring the dead by returning her to the sea, or simply feeding their pet sharks.

It's horrific, but not so much so when I think about what I saw done to my father in Eden, or to Jimmy's family in the cove. This woman was old, and she obviously died of natural causes with her son at her bedside. And if this is their way of disposing of the corpse, then who am I to judge? There are many questions I'd like to ask, however, but I won't risk giving away the fact that we're not from around here, since nobody seems to suspect yet that we came from off the island.

The strain on the chain softens and the thrashing withers to an occasional tail breaking the water. Finn returns to the pulley and wrenches the chain up from the depths. Nothing remains except the head inside the iron helmet and a stump of vertebral column protruding where her neck had been. Finn undoes the clasps, opens the helmet, and removes his mother's head and holds it cradled in his hands. He seems to be smiling and crying at the same time.

The people walk up to him one by one and gaze into the lifeless eyes of the severed head, before tossing their wreaths into the water. When all the wreaths are tossed and floating, Finn carries the head to the firebox, kisses it once on the lips, and drops it into the boiling kettle of water.

Then he turns to address the crowd:

"Thank you all very much indeed for coming. The feast shall be tomorrow evening, here as usual. And, of course, you're each invited. Anyone who wishes to join the hunt should meet us at the stables half an hour prior to sunrise."

Finn strides off into the castle with his cape billowing out behind him. The crowd drifts away. And we're left alone with the boiling head and a few workers tending to the fire. I step closer and look into the pot. Hair swirls in the steaming water, and the severed head slowly turns to face me, an air bubble escaping her gaping mouth and rising to the surface like a silent cry for help. Then the head turns, and the face is gone.

The castle is deserted when we return. No sign of Finn, Riley, or Angus anywhere. We find Junior slumbering in front of the fireplace with the deerhounds, as if he'd always been among them. I slump down on the sofa to think.

"I'm glad now that the professor threw him out," Jimmy says, kneeling in front of the fire and scratching Junior's ears.

"You don't think he did that on purpose?" I ask.

"I know he sure didn't wanna be scoopin' his poop."

"Still," I say, "Junior could've drowned."

"That's pro'ly what he was hopin' for."

"You never did like the professor, did you?"

"I dun' like nobody who has anythin' to do with the Park Service. And I never will."

"Then let's remember why we're here," I say. "We need to find that encryption key and stop the drones. Let's go take a closer look at the David."

Later, after our search yields nothing new, I lie in bed and wonder where the encryption key could be. The only thing I can think is that it must somehow be hidden inside the marble in the David's right hand—perhaps in some kind of memory chip, or etched on a piece of inserted metal. But Jimmy and I didn't discover any obvious patch marks in the marble.

It's late and I can't sleep again. I'm tempted to creep down the passageway to Jimmy's room, but I can't think of anything to say if he's awake. Instead, I think about Hannah back at the Foundation. I wonder how she's getting along with Red. I wonder if she worries about me. Then my thoughts turn to the island and these strange people. How long have they been here? How is Radcliffe connected to them? I wonder about this hunt tomorrow and these games that Lord Finn thinks we've come for. There must be a decent size population spread around the island since he didn't seem to question where we came from.

I lie in bed and think about all kinds of things, which is fine with me as long as I'm not thinking about sharks.

CHAPTER 13
The Hunt

Just a hint of blue dawn rims the eastern horizon.

Wearing borrowed wool coats, our bellies filled with eggs and hot tea, and our ears filled with wishes of good luck from Riley, Jimmy and I join the men at the stables.

The horses stand in a row, stomping the cold ground and snorting smoke from their black muzzles, while the men work at cinching saddles and looping metal bits into their mouths. I've never seen a horse in the flesh before, and I stand a safe distance away and smell the manure and leather and hay.

Finn comes down from the castle, leading the deerhounds on a leash. Junior takes up the rear, trotting along untethered. Finn smiles at us as he passes, apparently pleased that we took him up on his invitation. He hands the hounds off to one of the men and walks the row of horses, inspecting them. Then he takes the leash back and mounts the lead horse and ties the leash to its saddle horn. The men wait for his nod, then mount their horses and sit atop them, looking down on Jimmy and me.

Two horses remain unseated.

Jimmy steps forward, places his foot in the stirrup, and swings into the saddle as if he'd done it a hundred times before. I approach my horse more cautiously. Just as I get my foot in the stirrup, the horse sidesteps away, and I have to hop along to keep from falling. The men laugh. It takes me three tries to get up. When I finally do, Jimmy has to reach over a hand to keep me from sliding off the other side.

"Grip with yer knees," he whispers.

"You've done this before?"

He shakes his head no.

Is there anything he can't do, I wonder.

Finn sets his horse moving down the snow-covered road with the deerhounds prancing along at his side. The other men fall in behind him. Jimmy and I take up the rear, our horses fortunately needing little direction from us. Junior runs back and forth along the line, visibly excited to be on an adventure.

We leave the castle road where it turns east, cutting due north instead and slugging across a snowy field toward the hills rising in the distance. The snow has frozen over in the night, and the horses' hooves crunch through it with high steps that kick up little showers of crystal powder. The deerhounds lope through the deep snow with their long legs, and Junior is smart enough to trail behind in the path already trampled.

As we climb to higher ground, the snow thins, and soon we enter a narrow gorge surrounded by rocky ridges and follow a stream upward. I try to do what Jimmy told me and grip with my knees. But when Finn holds his hand up, the procession comes to a halt, and I fall forward and nearly slide off my horse. I regain my balance in the saddle and follow everyone's gaze up to where the ridgeline is backlit by the rising sun. There stands the silhouette of a stag, its horns reaching like branches into the pink morning sky. We hold our ground and watch for a while. I smell the wet grass beneath the melting snow. The only sound is clinking tack, the horses' deep breathing, and the soft trickle of water running down the stream.

Then I blink and the stag is gone.

When we reach the ridge where the stag had stood, a world of highland beauty opens up before us. Hills of heather, their summits blown free of snow. Gorgeous outcroppings of rock standing like sentinels in the treeless land. Glens and valleys, shaded purple with deep drifts of snow. Pink light hovers over it all, making the scene appear like something from a dream that might slip away any moment. But there's no sign anywhere of the stag.

The sky fades from pink to orange and then to blue as we ride the morning into afternoon. We cross numerous valleys and crest countless hills, each time scanning the horizon for any sight of the stag. The deerhounds are surprisingly quiet. Never once do I hear them bark. The men are quiet, too. They mostly communicate with hand gestures and nods, leaving Jimmy and me to silently puzzle out what they mean, not daring to even talk amongst ourselves as we ride along behind them.

Then we crest a high hill, and Finn holds up his hand to stop us again, easing his horse backwards and pushing us down off the top of the hill. He dismounts and signals for us to do the same, and we creep to the summit on foot, keeping low and quiet. Sure enough, the stag stands just on the other side, in a wide glen, browsing among the exposed plants.

"Lord, I tell ya," one of the men whispers, "he's got ten points if he's got a single one."

Finn disappears downhill and returns a few moments later, leading the deerhounds. He sits them where only their heads crest the summit and faces them toward the stag. Their black eyes burn with hunger for the chase, flashing red as coals when their swollen tongues slide out to lick their chops. Their tails wag, their wiry coats bristle, their taut muscles shiver with fever. Still, they make no sound. Finn releases the buckle and slides the leash free from their collars, but the deerhounds sit quivering on their haunches, showing remarkable breeding for restraint. Junior, on the other hand, crouches beside them with his head on his paws, looking quite bored with it all.

The stag ceases its browsing and lifts its nose into the air, appearing to smell the breeze. Then it turns its head toward our hill and stands perfectly still, watching. "Kill!"

Before the echo of Finn's call can return, the deerhounds take off like arrows shot from a bow. They bound down the hill with long strides, heading straight for the startled stag. Junior scrambles after them. The stag jumps three feet off the ground, changes direction in midair, and lands running and leaping away across the snowy glen in a streak of brown fur and antlers.

And the chase is on.

The men swing back into their saddles and gallop off after the chasing hounds. It takes me a few tries to mount my horse, and thankfully Jimmy hangs back until we can set off together after the riders. I expect the hounds to bark, but they don't.

The chase is silent and must be followed by sight. Our horses seem to have done this before, following Finn's lead on their own, and with no effort from me besides holding on for sweet life with my knees. We quickly rejoin the group.

We gallop across glades, leap over rocky knolls, climb steep bluffs, and stop to scan the horizon for the dogs. When Finn or one of the men spots them again, usually scrambling over some distant hill, we kick the horses into pursuit and race on, trying to keep them in sight by keeping to high ground. All afternoon we chase them through the highlands with hardly a moment's rest, save the briefest of pauses to pass a canteen and look again for the lost dogs. A few times I catch a gray streak amidst the bounding deerhounds, telling me Junior is keeping up pretty well.

After riding hard for thirty minutes or so in the direction of our last sighting of the dogs, Finn halts the group and cocks his head, listening. A distant baying carries to us on the breeze.

"He's gone at bay," Finn says, flashing the group a grin.

"No rush now," one of the others says. "Those hounds'll keep him bailed up for a week if we leave them to it."

"Quite right," Finn says. "But we'd starve to death and so would they. Besides, we've got a feast to prepare for."

He starts us moving at a quick canter toward a distant river gulch and the sound of the baying hounds.

"What's he mean by bailed up?" I ask Jimmy.

"Hell if I know," he says. "But I'd guess by the sound of it those dogs got 'em pinned down somewheres."

We follow the ridgeline down as far as we can and search for a path to descend into the gulch. It doesn't look possible to me, but before I know what's happening, Finn guides his horse over the edge and the rest follow, including mine. The descent is frightening, the ground steep and rocky. I close my eyes, lean back, and squeeze with my knees, trying not to imagine how far I'd fall or how many rocks I'd bounce off of before I stopped. But I don't fall, and the horses all make it safely to the bottom of the gulch, and we take off following a widening brook down toward the ever-increasing howling of the hounds.

As we follow the gulch lower, tiny streams and trickling waterfalls join the brook until it widens into a shallow river, forcing us into a single-file line along its bank. Then we come upon a blind bend with a steep cliff ahead, and when we reach it and turn, the gulch opens into a kind of valley where the river spills into a shallow lake. Five meters off shore, the stag stands in water to its chest, using its antlers to defend against the dogs swimming circles around it. Several of the deerhounds stand in shallower water, catching their breath. Junior lies on the shore, soaking wet and panting. Jimmy dismounts to check on him.

Finn removes a rope from his saddle and drives his horse out into the lake and lassos the stag, catching it around the base of its antlers. Then he ties the rope off to his saddle horn and backs his horse from the lake and drags the stag, head-bent and bucking, into shallower water. The deerhounds leap all around it, yowling. The stag shakes its lassoed head and bellows.

Another rider drives his horse into the water from the side

and slips another noose over the stag's antlers and backs out farther up the shore, pulling the stag's thrashing points still, locked now between the two opposing ropes.

"Aubrey," Finn calls. "Come here."

"Me?"

"Yes, you."

I kick my horse in its side like I've seen the others do, but it doesn't budge.

Finn laughs. "I meant on foot, kid."

I dismount my horse and wade into the water and look up at Finn in his saddle. He unsheathes a long knife and hands it down to me. "Guests do the honors."

The stag stands trembling just a few meters away, pulling against the ropes, lungs heaving, eyes wide, nostrils dilated.

"Don't worry," Finn says. "He knows it's already done. If he does come at you, we'll pull his points there to the side."

I wade out to the stag, holding the heavy knife in front of me. The blade wobbles as my hands shake. When I get close, the stag rears back against the taught ropes and bleats with fear, its sweat-drenched muscles quivering with panic. The rider on the shore tightens his rope, pulling the stag's head to the side and exposing its muscular neck for the knife.

I look back. All the men sit on their horses watching me, waiting. Jimmy stands on the shore watching, too. I turn back to the stag and bring the knife point to its neck and prepare to thrust it in. The stag turns its amber eye to me, and I can see my face clearly reflected on its glassy surface. Its pupil dilates, the lens focusing on its final vision. Its golden lashes flicker.

No one says a word as I trudge back to shore. Jimmy takes the knife from my trembling hand, wades out past me, and slashes the stag's throat. I hear its gurgling bellow and turn to see blood gushing from the gash. The stag lurches left and right against the ropes, then slumps forward, its head dropping as its neck goes limp, its antlers clacking against the shallow bottom, its open mouth hanging in the water for a moment, giving it the appearance of bowing for one final drink. Then its amber eyes go blank, and it falls over sideways with a splash.

I sit alone on a rock and watch them field-dress it. Within minutes, they've strung it up by its horns in the only tree beside the lake. The tree is small and not very healthy, and the branch bows heavily with its weight. They slit the stag open, tie off its rectum, remove its organs, and pull the intestines free. They let the tired deerhounds eat the castaway parts, with the exception of the bladder, which Jimmy pinches closed and carries several meters away and tosses into a bush. When they finish gutting it, the deer hangs considerably lighter from the limb.

Next, they cut a ring around its neck and legs and loosen the hide. One of the men bunches the hide at its neck and ties it to a rope. Then he ties the other end of the rope to his saddle horn and backs his horse from the stag. The rope goes taut, the hide stretches, the branch bends, and with a wet, ripping sound that makes me want to puke, the entire hide peels off until the stag is hanging free of its skin, swaying pink and naked like a giant newborn fawn from the tree. The man loops in the bloody hide, unties it, and stuffs it into a saddle bag. The other men let down the stag and quarter the body and load the pieces into meat bags that they hang over the backs of their saddles. Only the head remains un-mutilated.

Jimmy comes over and sits beside me. "You all right?"

"Yeah, I'm okay. They're laughing at me, aren't they?"

"No, they ain't."

"Yes, they are."

"Maybe a little. But it ain't no big deal. It's a hard thin' to do when you ain't done it before."

"But I killed rabbits. And other things."

"It's different though, ain't it? When they's big."

"Yeah. It looked at me and it knew."

"Whataya mean it looked at you?"

"Like it knew what I was about to do. In an intelligent way. Like it was judging me or something."

"Let's jus' forget it and get on back."

We mount up with the others and ride back up the gulch and out onto the highlands, heading into the long light of late afternoon, back the way we came, although in a more direct route. The deerhounds trudge along beside us, their energy long spent. One of them has a bloody gash in its side, presumably from the stag's horns. Junior is too tired to keep up, and Jimmy scoops him into his saddle and carries him in his arms. I lag behind and feel less part of the group than when we left. Which is kind of hard to imagine.

The stag's severed head is tied to the rear of Finn's saddle, antlers up and facing back. And the entire way home it seems to stare at me with lifeless eyes, its frozen expression mocking me for foolishly thinking it makes any difference whose hand it is that moves the knife when the deed is already done.

"Dead is dead," it seems to say. "Your day will come."

CHAPTER 14
The Feast

The boiled human skull is the guest of honor.

It grins at us from the table's head in the great hall.

It's hard to believe I helped carry her corpse out just this morning. But despite death joining us for dinner, the mood is jovial as the guests laugh and tell stories, drinking wine poured from jugs and passing great platters heaped with food.

When the venison comes my way, I pass it on to Jimmy without taking any for my plate. Not because I have any trouble eating meat now, and not because I suddenly think hunting is cruel, but because I don't feel worthy of consuming the stag's flesh when I was too weak to take its life.

Finn sits at the head of the long table next to the skull. I notice that every time he takes food for himself, he places some on her plate, too. It's strange to see that lipless and bony grin disappearing behind a mound of uneaten food. But Finn seems remarkably celebratory, recounting the story of our stag hunt for those at the table who weren't present. Kindly, he leaves the part about my failure completely out in the retelling. As I watch the guests hang on his every word, it's clear that they really love him. I think I'm beginning to also. He has a cool kind of calm, as if nothing were ever any big deal to him, and his wide smile is an almost constant counterweight to his blue, twinkling eyes.

"Tell us a poem!" someone shouts.

"Yes," another chimes in. "Time for a poem."

The guests fall quiet by ones and twos until the only sound left is the splash of pouring wine as Riley refills glasses. Finn sighs unconvincingly, putting on a show of reluctance when his eyes clearly give away his pride in being asked. He stands and pushes his chair in, leaning against its high back. Then he reaches down and places a hand gently on the skull. "I'd like to dedicate this to Lady Awen, my dearly departed daughter."

His daughter? Did I hear him right? There's no way. That woman was twice Finn's age if she was a day. At least she was twice his apparent age. Then it hits me—what if Finn's like Radcliffe? What if he's had the serum? Could he be hundreds of years old too? Was he installed here to guard the encryption key hidden in the David? My head swirls with questions, but before I can even begin to sort through them, Finn sweeps his arms out theatrically and bursts into song:

"In the dawn of Earth's distant past, the gods gave birth to a lowly beast. Naked and cold in darkness vast, one grew bold and joined the feast.

"It's fair to say she raised a stir—how dare a lowly woman dine with gods. Fierce they fought over who would eat her, but not before one fell in love.

"Concealed in his cloak they snuck away, he pledged her his heart and began to weep. While in his arms she begged to stay, and on an island he made safe her keep."

Here Finn pauses to gulp his wine, grinning mischievously.

The crowd sits riveted, looking on and waiting, even though I get the feeling they've heard this many times. He continues:

"On the island god and woman together lay, safely hidden beneath his cloak of fog. Then there came at last a fateful day, when shame sent away the god.

"For inside the woman a child grew, from the seed of Mannan an immortal son. Half god, half man, a deadly duo—a gift of love by a woman's courage won.

"But the jealous gods had other plans, they opened hell above and sent beasts to kill. But preserved by sacrifices made of man, Mannan's cloak of fog protects the island still."

Finn finishes the song with a bow. The guests leap to their feet with wild applause. Jimmy glares a silent warning at me not to challenge anything in Finn's story, but he doesn't need to worry because I learned my lesson with the pig people. Besides, I'm still too hung up on the old woman being Finn's daughter to think much about the poetic mythology he just delivered.

Now that the poem is over, everyone reclaims their seats and commences another course of drinking and eating, this one more conversational than the last, either due to the elevated mood after Finn's performance or to the wine.

A woman turns to me. "Finn tells us you two are here for the games?"

"Yes, that's right." I nod.

"Did you travel far?" she asks. "I haven't seen you before. Wait. Let me guess. You must have come from Ayre in the north. You have that look."

"Yes," I say. "You guessed right."

"Does the heather still bloom purple there in the spring?"

I nod and smile, looking for a way out of the conversation. Fortunately, Jimmy jumps in.

"Tell us about the games?" he asks. "If you dun' mind."

"Have you never been?" She looks surprised.

"No," we say in unison.

"Well," she leans in closer, her tone conspiratorial, "I'll give you a tip then. But you mustn't tell, or they'll give away my seat. The one to watch out for this year is Bree."

"And why should we watch out for him?"

"Not him," she says. "Her. She was last year's runner-up, and I've heard talk around that she's been training ever since. Someone said they saw her running the eastern hills, carrying a goat on her back. But I happen to think that's exaggerated."

I want to ask her more about these games, but at the same time I don't want to give away the fact that we don't know anything at all. "Why would running hills help?"

"Stamina, of course," she says. "That and everyone knows she has a ball tied to a post in her uncle's pen that she swats at in-between doing chores. Strictly forbidden, but she does."

"A ball on a post?"

"Yes. To toughen up her hands."

Before I can get more out of her about these games, we're interrupted by Riley ringing his bell. Finn is standing at the head of the table, holding his daughter's skull in his hand and an auger drill in the other. He looks at his guests and says, "It would please me greatly if you would be so kind as to observe a moment of silence while I formally install Lady Awen in her place of honor among the Clan of MacFinn."

He lays the skull sideways on the table. Riley appears at his side and holds the skull in place while Finn sets the auger at its temple and rotates the handle, drilling a hole into the bone. When the drill is clean through, he backs it out and turns the skull and performs the same operation on the other side. Then he holds the skull up to the massive starlit window in the far wall and closes one eye and sights a line through the skull, as if he were some ancient astronomer contemplating the heavens through a telescope made of bone. He nods to Riley, apparently satisfied with their work. Riley steps over to the wall and pulls a gold, braided rope, and the tapestries covering the walls of the long hall part like curtains, revealing many hundreds of hanging skulls grinning down from recessed racks. Adult skulls, child skulls, baby skulls, even a few deerhound skulls. My skin crawls to think that they've been hiding there all during dinner, silently waiting behind their curtains.

Riley sets a stepladder against a corner of the wall, and Finn gracefully climbs up it, carrying his daughter's skull. He pauses to look down on the guests. "As you can see, we're quickly running out of space here. And as I have no intentions of remodeling again anytime soon, you Clan MacFinn folks had better just slow down with your dying already."

The guests break their silence with a laugh.

Finn reaches to the highest row, slides out the wooden

dowel that holds the skulls, and slips his daughter's skull onto the rack. When she's tucked away with the others, he climbs down, dusts his hands together, places them on his hips, and looks up at the wall. "Not a bad-looking family, if you ask me," he says. "I just look forward to the day when we're all together again." Then he nods to Riley, and Riley pulls the rope and the tapestries slide closed, covering the wall of skulls.

The guests raise up their glasses to toast. "Today for Lady Awen," one of them calls. "Tomorrow for us!"

Jimmy and I raise our glasses, too, although the wine is beginning to go to my head. I've tried to take only sips during dinner, mostly because it tastes horrid, but they seem to drink no other liquid here with dinner. Even so, I'm afraid I've had more than I should already, because the designs woven into the wall tapestries begin to swirl together in fantastic images of living color, and I can almost hear the chattering of all those grinning skulls hiding behind them.

The guests leave the tables now and spill into the center of the hall, carrying their goblets and jugs, and the party takes on a less formal feel. Candles are blown out, the lamps lowered. Several men grab the tables and slide them against the far wall. Angus wheels in a cart filled with wood and builds up the fire. Riley drags in deerskin bean bags, and people begin to sprawl on them in pairs. Finn disappears and comes back carrying a grand harp that he sits down with beside the fire and begins to play. The music is beautiful in the open acoustics of the great hall and even more beautiful yet when he begins to sing again.

Jimmy flops on a beanbag and closes his eyes, either entranced by the music or feeling the wine himself. Taking advantage of the distraction, I wander off by myself to explore.

The laughing and music fades in the hall behind me as I enter the dark statue room. No candles or lamps burn here, and it takes a long time for my eyes to adjust to the small amount of moonlight coming in through the tall windows. I dance my way nimbly betwixt the shadowy figures, as if trespassing into the distant past. Silent warriors stretch to strike me down; frozen mothers nurse their cradled infant sons; ivory angels rise up on outspread wings; busts follow me with shadowy stares.

By the time I reach the David, the music has faded to just a distant melody, soft like something I might have heard in a dream. The yellow, quarter moon hangs in the window, directly in the path of the David's stare. But the moonlight seems to have softened his gaze to a look of longing, as if the moon were his lover circling forever out of reach in the sky.

"What is it you hold in your right hand?" I whisper, half expecting him to turn to look at me when I do. But he stands as still as the stone he's carved from, and only the shadows of his eyes move to follow the rising moon.

I lie down on the cold, stone floor and rest my head in my hands and look up at the statue. It's so tall anyway, that lying on the ground it seems to be a god—a god who could easily reach up and pluck the moon from the sky like fruit if he really wanted to. I think about Finn's song telling of a god who fell in love with a woman and gave her a child. It doesn't seem so farfetched when you're looking at the David. I wonder about the skulls. About his old daughter. And while I can't believe in an immortal son of the gods, I can believe in the science of Radcliffe's serum. But how did Finn get it? And when?

My thoughts turn to Hannah and Red. I hope they're okay. I need to solve the riddle of this encryption key and get back to them. 'In the right hand of David you shall find your key.' It's an odd riddle for Radcliffe to leave, and it seems strange that all this could have been here without the professor or anyone else knowing. I think about the professor killing time, waiting for us beneath the waves. We said fourteen days. It's our third night.

And what about these games that we're supposedly here for? So far all I have is an image of a girl running the hills with a goat on her back and swatting a ball tied to a post.

I close my eyes and try to picture my father's face. Every day it slips away just a little farther. I see his hands sitting across the breakfast table from me. I hear his voice reading me stories. But I can't make out the features of his face. I wonder, for the first time, why we didn't take photos down in Holocene II. We had the technology. I guess we just didn't bother because we all assumed we'd spend an eternity together in Eden. But what a load of crap that turned out to be. I can remember my father hugging me before he walked through the door to Eden. I can still smell the tobacco in his hair. But I just can't see his face. I hope he heard me when I told him that I loved him. I hope he knew that I heard him when he told me.

When I wake, my arms are asleep, and I have to stand and

shake the feeling back into them. The room is dark, the David now just a black shadow looming above me. The music has gone away with the moon. I thread my way carefully through the statues and into the great hall where the only light is from the fire, now burned nearly to coals. Several people lie passed out on beanbags; several others lie on the floor. I creep through the room on tiptoes, looking for Jimmy, but he isn't there.

When I get to the upstairs hall, I stop at Jimmy's door. My hand rests on the handle, but I just can't turn it. I don't know why I can't. Now that we're around all these new people, things just seem different from when it was just him and me.

My room is empty, which surprises me with all of Finn's family crashed out in the great hall. But I'm grateful for it as I crawl beneath the covers and fall fast asleep.

CHAPTER 15
The Guests Arrive

In the morning, I can hardly walk.

My shark-scraped calf has begun to heal, but my legs are as stiff as boards from riding that mad horse all over the highlands yesterday. I hobble to the window and look out.

I must have slept late because the sun is up over the hills, shining on a caravan of horse-drawn wagons stretching as far down the road as my high window will let me see. Most of the snow has melted away, and the road is a muddy mess. Men walk beside the wagons, their boots covered in mud, while women huddle together in the seats, staying dry. I can see other wagons already in front of the castle. Men are busy unloading supplies and setting up tents in a grove of trees while their wives chase down children and direct the men with impatient gestures clear enough even to me.

I stop by Jimmy's room, but he isn't there. He isn't in the breakfast room either, although several of last night's dinner guests are. Riley pushes me into a seat and proceeds to fill me up with hot tea and leftovers from the feast. The guests make light conversation about what a splendid evening it was and about the upcoming games, but I get no better sense of things from eavesdropping on them. When they address me, it's all I can do to sit and nod without wincing from the pain in my ass. I'll be happy if I never ride another horse ever again.

When I've had all the food and company I can stand, I

politely excuse myself and head outside to look for Jimmy.

The drive is alive with excitement. Wagons are backed up waiting to unload, sweaty horses stamp and blow, people shout directions, kids scramble about, playing at wooden swords. Tents under construction fall and are pulled up again. One catches a draft of wind and goes cartwheeling through the trees while men scramble after it. And through the center of it all, Finn walks as fresh and as calm as could be, stopping to lend a hand wherever one's needed, answering questions, and greeting everyone with his charming smile. I get the impression he loves having company.

Jimmy doesn't appear to be anywhere amidst the madness of the camp construction, so I head toward the backside of the castle, hoping to find him there. But I don't get far when I'm stopped by Finn and asked to lend a hand offloading heavy sacks of grain for the horses, which I begrudgingly agree to do. Fortunately, the heavy lifting seems to loosen my stiff legs.

As I walk back from dropping a load at the stables, I see Jimmy beneath an oak tree with a raven-haired girl about our own age. She's tutoring him as he practices a swatting motion, squatting and whipping his open hand through the air, then looking at his palm. He says something. She laughs. He smiles. If a female version of Jimmy were possible, she'd be it. Tall and athletic, her outfit as rugged as the proud features of her olive-skinned face. I immediately dislike her. My heart quickens. My jaw clenches. My eyes narrow. And I don't enjoy the feeling at all. I wonder if this is how Jimmy felt when he saw me together with Hannah. I drop my gaze to the ground and head back up to the wagon for another load.

When I heft the bag of grain onto my shoulder, someone

behind me strips it away. I turn and see Jimmy grinning at me, the bag cradled in his arm.

"One at a time'll take us all day," he says. "Give me another'n."

I throw another bag at him. "Thought you were busy."

"Busy? I've been up since dawn waitin' on you."

"Who was that?" I nod toward the tree.

"Oh, that's Bree. The one the lady was tellin' us about at dinner last night. Remember?"

"Yeah, I remember," I say, shouldering another bag. "The girl who carries goats. I'm still confused about these games."

"Ain't you seen the court?"

"What court?"

"The ball court," he says. "Bree already showed me ever-thin'. Let's finish loadin' these sacks, and then I'll show you."

By the time the wagon is emptied, another one is waiting to be offloaded behind it, so we spend the next hour humping grain and hay to the stables, where the resident horses are none too pleased with all their new companions. We're both dripping with sweat when we finally sneak away.

Jimmy takes me to the south side of the castle where an expansive, open courtyard is enclosed by rock walls. In the center of the courtyard are tiers of stone bleachers surrounding a sunken, four-walled rectangular court, shaped like an enclosed alley. The court's walls are smooth concrete, and it looks like I'd imagine a deep swimming pool might look, except clever drains in the bottom carry away what little water remains from the melting snow. There appears to be no way in or out of the sunken court, except by being lowered from above. Of course, my mind races with crazy and horrific possibilities.

"What's it for?" I ask.

"It's a ball court," Jimmy says.

"Ball court?"

"Yeah. Handball. Bree says they call it hero's alley."

"Why hero?"

"I dunno. But she also said they's usin' a new ball this year. Somethin' called a goat-skinned alley cracker. 'Cause of the sound it makes against the wall."

"She sure told you a lot, didn't she?"

"Yeah. She's pretty smart."

"Really?"

"She said they mixed deer blood in with the concrete—is that what it's called, concrete?—to make it bounce better. See how it's kinda reddish?"

"I doubt that would help provide any bounce," I toss out.

"I dunno," he says. "But she said I'd make a good player 'cause of my long arms."

"You're not actually planning to play, are you?"

"Sure. Aren't you?"

"We didn't come here to play games, Jimmy."

"But that's why we told 'em we was here . . ."

"Yeah, but—"

"But what?"

"You can't possibly think you'd be any good. I mean, we don't even know how they play it, and we haven't practiced."

"Bree says practice is forbidden. There ain't even any other courts than this one. That lady was lyin' about her having a ball on a stake, too. And Bree says that goat is jus' a skin filled with water that she runs with sometimes."

"Sounds like you've got it all figured out, then."

"Well, I was thinkin' maybe I'd play, and while everyone's distracted by the games, you could figure out what's goin' on with the encrypto key."

"Encryption key."

"Yeah."

"What makes you think I'm not going to play?" I ask.

"I dunno. Are you?"

"No."

"Then what's it matter."

"What's what matter?"

"Why I figured it?"

"You don't make any sense," I say, turning to walk away.

For the rest of the morning, I avoid Jimmy and keep myself busy by helping with the wagons. By afternoon a full on camp has taken shape outside the castle. Tents everywhere, lanterns hanging overhead from ropes strung between trees, several outhouses patched together from gray-weathered wood over deep holes dug in the ground. The people who were here last night are clearly Finn's closest relatives, all bearing a striking resemblance to him, but the people setting up in the camp look to be from different parts of the island. Many with red hair and fair skin; others, like Bree, with dark hair and dark skin. An atmosphere of celebration hangs in the air.

It's clear who will be participating in the games and who will be spectating. Groups of athletic young men and woman gather together and eye one another with contempt. Flexing or spitting or just swinging at invisible balls. Bree is the loner in the bunch, and I notice that she stays clear of the others. Except from Jimmy, who I spot introducing her to Junior. Ugh.

The adults, on the other hand, sneak glances at the young

athletes, their longing looks filled with curious appreciation. I spot them nudging one another and appearing to comment on players' appearances. Several of them scratch notes on wrinkled parchments as if setting odds. They seem to pay a great deal of attention to Bree. I, however, do my best to ignore her.

By evening fall, the camp has settled down as everyone rests from their long journeys, and I head inside to find a bath. Riley, despite looking exhausted, brings me to a bathing room and fills an old oak barrel with steaming water. As I soak away several days' worth of grime, along with the aches and pains from my scabbed-over, shark-scraped calf and horse-bruised thighs, Riley busies himself with draining barrels and preparing them for other guests. He hums while he works.

"Riley, may I ask you a question?"

"Yes, of course, sir."

"How come you call me sir when I'm so much younger than you are?"

"Yes. I'm sorry, sir. Please forgive me. I'm afraid that I come from a long line of proud housemen, and the habit has been bred into me. Was that your question?"

"No. My question is about Finn."

"I'll be happy to answer anything Lord Finn wouldn't mind obliging you with an answer to himself."

"Well, it's just that last night he referred to—well, to the deceased woman—he said she was his daughter."

Riley nods. "Yes. I'm afraid she was the last of them, too, since he hasn't taken a new wife since Marta. Despite all my encouragements for him to find one. A solitary life is a sad life, I say. But he assures me he's seen off all the children and wives he can bear to part with. Although I can't imagine it's any easier seeing off your grandchildren and great grandchild."

"Well, that's my real question. Just how old is Finn?"

"How old? Well, I'm afraid you'll need to ask Lord Finn that yourself. And be sure to catch him in good spirits when you do. He sometimes doesn't like to talk about his condition." Riley lifts my pile of clothes to his nose and sniffs them. "Dear Lord. How can you stand to smell yourself in these? I'll fetch you a fresh outfit straight away, sir. Straight away."

Alone now in my bath, I sink beneath the water and hold my breath, listening to my heartbeats. They come at about one beat per second. That's sixty a minute, or 3,600 beats per hour. That makes 86,000-and-something beats per day. I wonder if a heart gets only a certain amount of beats. I wonder how many beats my heart will have now that I've been injected with Dr. Radcliffe's serum. I try willing it to stop. Or even to slow down. But it won't. It just keeps on beating with a rhythm of its own.

I skip dinner and stay in my room, alone. Nobody seems to notice I'm gone, anyway. I crack the window and lie on the bed, listening to the festivities outside in the camp. People sing songs and laugh at jokes. Someone plays a set of pipes. But exhaustion overwhelms me, and the chatter and music outside carries me away to a restless sleep filled with strange dreams.

I dream I'm flying over the ocean, my speed drawing up a wake of mist as I race across the moonlit waves. I can turn on a dime with just the twitch of a toe. I can rise and fall by simply moving my head. Soon, I come upon a massive ship silhouetted against the night sky, a ship like the one that slaughtered Jimmy's family in the cove. As I approach the ship, in the strange, inexplicable illogic of dreams, I can suddenly see clearly, as if it were midday and not midnight. The ship's decks drip with blood; dead people hang like fileted deer from its riggings, their entrails spilling out and swaying beneath them as the ship rocks on the waves. I circle the ship closer and see the Park Service crest on its side. And I know before I even look that all the dead people wear Jimmy's face.

My pillow is soaked with sweat when I wake. The room is dark; outside the window is quiet. It's cold. I search for a match and strike the lamp lit, carrying it with me into the secret passageway and down to Jimmy's room. I need to talk to him, to apologize for being a jerk, to make sure he's all right. I open the panel and step inside, expecting to find him sleeping as I did before. But his bed is empty and the covers undisturbed.

I walk to his window and look out. The camp is sleeping, the shadows of tents glowing in the dying light of abandoned fires. I know Jimmy must be out there somewhere, probably with Bree. But I can't understand why that makes me worry.

CHAPTER 16
The Games Begin

Crack!

An explosive sound wakes me.

Then another. And another.

The castle is deserted when I descend the steps to the hall, still rubbing sleep from my tired eyes, so I slug back some tea in the breakfast room and head outside to investigate.

The camp is mostly deserted too, and only a few stragglers remain, lined up at the outhouses and reeking of last night's wine. When I get inside the courtyard, however, I discover the people there crowded into the bleachers, their heads swiveling in unison as they follow the ball in the court below.

I force my way through to get a view.

Two kids battle it out in the court, taking turns swatting a small ball with their open hands, bouncing it off the forward wall in a way that is difficult for the defender to return. When a particularly forceful blow is made, especially if it's a serve, the ball cracks against the concrete with an explosive sound. This must be what Jimmy meant by "goat-skinned alley cracker."

The game ends with the players shaking hands. Someone lowers a rope ladder into the court, and they climb out, then two other boys descend. As the new players drop off the ladder and turn, I see that one of them is Jimmy. I didn't recognize him from behind, wearing borrowed shorts and no shirt. The other kid is much shorter than Jimmy is, but he looks springy and strong. Jimmy looks nervous. Finn, who sits at center court in the front row of bleachers, looking like he's having the time of his life, tosses down the ball with a bounce to start the game. The short kid snatches it before Jimmy can and lines up to serve. Jimmy crouches behind him with his hands on his thighs.

Crack! The ball flies right past Jimmy and bounces once, then again off the rear wall. But before it hits the ground for a second time, Jimmy catches it on the rebound and sends it whipping to the front wall again. *Crack!* So it goes for several minutes, back and forth, until Jimmy wins the round when Shorty misses a ball and lets it double bounce. Now it's Jimmy's chance to serve. He bounces the ball once in front of him, and, with a lightning quick swat, sends it blazing off the front wall with a *Crack!* that makes everyone in the bleachers flinch. He aces it right past Shorty.

"He's a natural."

I turn to see Bree standing beside me.

"Hi-dy," she says. "You must be Jimmy's friend Aubrey." She smiles and sticks out her hand. When I shake it, her palm is calloused to point of feeling like wood.

"And you must be Bree."

"Jimmy told me that I'd like you right away," she says.

"Is that so? Why?

"Why do I like you, or why did he say I would?

"Why'd he say you would, I guess."

"He said you were the smartest person he knows."

"He said that?"

"Yeah. My uncle taught me to read, but the only book he has is an ancient text about a boy who was raised in a jungle by apes. He keeps it locked up, though. I'm only allowed to read it on my birthday. Jimmy said you've read all kinds of books."

I shrug, as if it's no big deal to me. "Yeah, I've read a few. In fact, I have several hundred books in my slate on the su . . ." I catch myself before I say submarine.

Bree's eyes bulge.

"Several hundred? No way. I can't even imagine."

Crack! We both turn and look as Jimmy aces another one past Shorty.

"He's going to advance for sure," Bree says.

"How's it work?" I ask.

"The tournament? Single elimination. Finn split everybody up this morning. But I don't have to qualify," she holds up a red sash. "I get a bye because I was a finalist last year."

"What are the rules to the game?"

"Simple, really. Server earns points when she wins a volley. Player returning the serve only wins the right to serve. Ball can't bounce twice. Can't go into the bleachers, either. Gotta use your hands. No feet. First player to fifteen points wins."

"Sounds easy enough."

"Simple?—yes. Easy?—no." She holds out her calloused palms for me to see. "Three days of play, and that ball isn't exactly soft. Some kids leave up out of here bleeding. One guy bruised his bone so bad last year, it still hasn't healed." She nods to the court, where Jimmy is shaking hands with Shorty. "Looks like he's won his first round. I knew he would. Let's go congratulate him."

Jimmy climbs up the ladder, dripping with sweat, his hot breath steaming in the cool morning air. He sees us working our way toward him and flashes a big smile. When he manages to break through the crowd in the bleachers, he rushes past me and hugs Bree. She looks surprised, her arms pinned stiffly at her side. I get the feeling she's not a big hugger.

"Isn't it a little early to be celebrating already," I jab, hating myself for saying it the moment it leaves my lips.

Jimmy releases Bree. "But I won."

"But it's just a qualifier. Right?"

"I guess," he says. "But I dun' care. I feel great." He turns back to Bree. "No way I coulda done it without yer help."

Bree shrugs. "Like I said, you're a natural. I just hope I don't end up playing you myself. Then I'm sure I'll wish that I'd never helped you at all. Let's go get something to eat."

"You two go ahead," I say, not even sure if I was included in the invitation. "I've got business to attend to that's more important than silly ball games."

Bree laughs. "Is that so? What business?"

Jimmy looks at me and frowns, getting the message. "You want help? I dun' have another match 'til this afternoon."

"No. You two go ahead. I'll be fine by myself."

"Are ya sure?"

"I'm sure."

As Jimmy and Bree head off, I wander around to the other side of the castle, wishing I had gone with them instead.

The sun is fully up now, the snow melted from everywhere except the shadows, and I stand at the seawall and look out on the water where I know the submarine is floating just beneath the surface. At least I hope it's still there. No way would the professor abandon us. Would he? I wish I could just swim out there right now and head home, forget about ever having come here. But then I remember the sharks. and a chill runs up my spine. We'll have to find another way out to the submarine when it's time to leave—there's no way I'm swimming now that I know what's down there. If I could only puzzle out this riddle and locate the encryption key, Jimmy and I could get out of here, and things would be back to normal.

Inside, the kitchen is abuzz with workers preparing lunch for the crowd. But otherwise, the castle is deserted, everyone being outside in the courtyard watching the games. I head to the statue room and stand before the David, mumbling the encryption key clue to myself: "'Where man rises from the sea, in the right hand of David you shall find your key.'"

I drag a wooden chair over from the corner and stand on it to inspect the David's right hand. It's fascinating how lifelike it is. The detail. The veins seem to pulse with blood beneath the white-marble skin, and I'm almost surprised when the stone is cold to my touch instead of warm. The hand is connected to the statue not only at the wrist, but also where it rests against his thigh. And while he's definitely holding something, it's just a lump cut from the same stone as the statue. The encryption key must be hidden inside the marble somehow.

Then, from the height of the chair, I spot a worktable and a toolbox behind a partition where someone has been working with plaster to restore a bust with a missing nose. My mind begins to run with possibilities. I think about Hannah and Red waiting alone at the Foundation. I think about my people down in Holocene II, living trapped underground by a lie. I think about the drones silently patrolling the skies, about those seal hunters I saw cut to shreds on Dr. Radcliffe's command-center monitors. I think about Jimmy passing me by to hug Bree.

The next thing I know I'm standing at the worktable with a hammer and a chisel in my hands.

"Do I really want to do this?" I ask myself. "Do I really have any other choice?"

I climb up on the chair again and place the chisel against the marble where the hand connects to the thigh. I raise the hammer then hesitate, the hammer's head trembling in my grip. I think about the thousands of years that this statue has stood, about all that it has survived. I think about the man that carved it, and about the story of David that inspired him. I remember reading about the myth. About a young king who struck down a giant with nothing but a sling. But then I think about Jimmy's family being slaughtered in that cove. I think about my father walking into Eden only to have his head cut open and his brain consigned to Radcliffe's sick experiments. And suddenly, I'm overwhelmed with a feeling that the man who carved the David would understand. That I'm on the right side of history. That if this statue truly holds the encryption key hidden in its hand, then how much nobler would it be to stop an army of drones and free an entire society, than to stop only one giant with a slung stone. It must be forgivable to desecrate the David if it saves humankind from an evil that's far worse than anything before in our long history: the wholesale slaughter of people for the simple sin of being born human.

A spray of marble chips hits my face when the hammer drives the chisel into the stone. It's softer than it looks. Three solid whacks and a crack appears. Caught up in the excitement of possibly going home, I hammer harder and faster. Another crack. More marble dust drifting to the ground. Soon, the hand breaks free from the statue's thigh and a stress crack appears in its wrist. I move the chisel and continue hammering. The soft stone gives a little with every strike. Sweat rises on my brow.

My arm aches. I steady the chisel and level a flurry of blows on its head. Now the hand is hanging by a small piece of stone. I drop the hammer and chisel to the ground and wrap my hands around the marble and wrench. The David's giant hand breaks free. It's heavy and cold in my palms. Sweat drips down my back. My lungs heave. As the ringing in my ears from all the hammering fades, a heavy silence consumes the room. Then someone clears his throat behind me.

I turn. Finn stands in the doorway looking at me. A crowd of people peek past him from the hall. Finn strides across the room and yanks me off the chair by my belt and wrestles with me to free the statue's marble hand from my grip.

"No!" I scream, kicking and fighting. "I won't let you have it. I won't. I'm taking it with me."

As I struggle with Finn, I'm suddenly pinned from behind by someone strong. Finn strips the hand free from my fingers and looks at it, shaking his head.

"Get him out of here," he says.

Before I can even protest, I'm being half-carried, half-dragged, backwards from the room. The last thing I see is Finn standing with the marble hand cradled in his palms, like one might hold an injured bird, and the David looming above him, standing proud and indifferent, despite its amputated hand.

They carry me upstairs, screaming all the way, and lock me in my room. I immediately rush to the secret panel, but it's locked too, and I hear someone scurrying away inside the wall, probably Riley. I head for the window, but it doesn't open wide enough to let me out and even if it did, I'd surely break my legs.

I see groups of people standing around their tents talking and pointing toward the castle. I know they're talking about me, but I don't care. I had to do something. We've got to get that key and get out of here. Now I need to figure out how to escape this room, get that hand back, grab Jimmy, and go.

CHAPTER 17
Bad News, Worse News

It's long past dark when the knock comes at my door.

Getting up from where I lie on the bed, I move to open it, only to remember that I can't because I'm locked inside.

"It's locked," I call out, turning to flop back on the bed.

A key turns in the lock, the door swings open, and Jimmy steps in. I bounce up, thinking that we can make a run for it, but the door closes and the key turns in the lock again.

"Riley let you in?"

Jimmy nods and hands me a sandwich wrapped in a cloth. "I brought ya some dinner. Got a flask of warm tea here too if you's thirsty."

"Thanks," I say, unwrapping the sandwich and tearing into it, realizing I haven't eaten anything all day.

Jimmy walks to the window and looks out. The window is black against the night sky, and I can see Jimmy's reflection in the lamplight on the glass. He looks sad for some reason. I talk at his back in between bites.

"We have to find that marble hand and get away from here now. Maybe you could see if it's still in the statue room. Or did Finn take it somewhere? And there's a secret passageway for feeding the stoves, but they've locked me out. If you try from your room, you might be able to open it for me. Let me show you where the panel is."

Jimmy turns around. "I dun' wanna leave, Aubrey."

"What do you mean, you don't want to leave?"

"I mean, I'm happy here."

"What? Come on . . ."

"I am," he says. "For the first time since . . . well, ya know, since the cove . . . I feel like I fit somewhere."

"You're talking crazy."

"I'm crazy?" he asks, stepping closer and pointing at me. "That's what they's all sayin' 'bout you. Said you lost it in there and tore up that statue."

"You know that isn't true," I say, upset that I even need to defend myself to him.

"But you did."

"Did what?"

"You broke up that statue."

"Yes, I did. I was trying to find the encryption key, Jimmy. Remember? The whole reason we came to this stupid island in the first place. We didn't come for games and girls."

"Is that what this is about? You's bein' jealous?"

"I'm not jealous of stupid Bree."

"Who said anythin' about Bree? I meant yer jealous of me. That I did so well today in the games."

"Why would I give piss about some stupid game? And why do you even care about a game, either?"

"Because it's fun," he says. "And because it feels good to be good at somethin'."

"Well, whatever. I'm not jealous of anything, Jimmy. I just wanna get the damn encryption key and go home. What is this sandwich, anyway? Deer meat. Ugh." I toss it aside.

Jimmy sits beside me on the bed. "That's jus' it," he says. "It ain't home back there, Aubrey. And it ain't home for you no more'n it's home for me. You cain't tell me it is."

"My people are trapped underground, Jimmy."

"Yeah, I know it. But you coulda let 'em up when we was back there votin' and ya didn't."

"You can't be serious," I say. "You're really thinking about staying here? On the island?"

He nods. "I wish you'd think about it too."

"And just leave Hannah back there alone?"

"She dun' like me anyhow."

"But the drones, Jimmy. Think about the drones."

Jimmy jumps up from the bed and turns to face me, his gray eyes flashing with anger. "I do think 'bout 'em. Every darn day, Aubrey. Ya think I forgot that they killed my family?"

"Well, we have a chance to stop them with this key."

"That's great," he heaves a sigh. "But it's too late for my family. And it's safe here. There ain't no drones here."

"What about the serum? Have you thought about that?"

"What serum?" he asks.

"The longevity serum, remember? What will you do living here with people who don't have it, Jimmy? You wanna end up like Finn? Feeding your own daughters to sharks?"

"I dun' understand what yer talkin' 'bout."

"The serum!" I shout.

"Are you sure you ain't feelin' funny?"

"The serum! Back at the lake. Remember?"

"I remember you bein' upset 'cause Hannah snuck it while we was gettin' the boat, but what's that got to do with me?"

"You took it, too. That same night. In the shelter."

"No, I didn't," he says.

"You didn't?"

"No way."

"But Hannah showed me the syringe."

He shakes his head. "I dunno what she showed you, but I didn't let nobody put no needle in me."

Then it hits me like a wave of cold water. Hannah showed me an empty syringe all right, but it could easily have been the one she'd used to inject herself with. She lied. But why? So she could keep the third syringe of serum to study in her lab? Does it even matter why? Suddenly, leaving her back there doesn't sound so bad. But then the true horror of the situation sinks in, and my face flushes with blood. Jimmy hasn't had the serum, which means he'll die, and I won't. The thought terrifies me.

I leap to my feet and pace the small room.

"We've got to get back, Jimmy! We've got to get you that serum. Don't you see what's happening here? Finn is somehow connected to Dr. Radcliffe. He's old, he has to be. You saw the skulls. I mean, how old was his daughter? And we can't trust Hannah, either. She lied about the serum. She sent that damn antimatter along. And now you're going to die on me, Jimmy!"

I grab him by the shirt. "You're going to die!"

"Whataya mean I'm gonna die?" He looks frightened.

"Not now. But in seventy or eighty years, you will."

"Maybe they was right about you losin' yer head."

I pull him to me and hug him tight. "I don't want you to die, Jimmy! Not without me."

"Maybe get some rest tonight," he says, hugging me back uncertainly. "We'll talk some more tomorrow, okay?"

"Tell me you'll go back with me."

"I can't tell ya that right now."

I release him and turn away. "Fine. Just leave me alone, Jimmy. I'll figure a way out of here without you."

"Aubrey, listen to—"

"I said get out!"

Jimmy drops his head and walks to the door. He raises his hand to knock, but stops and turns back first. "They ain't bad people here, Aubrey. I told Finn you's under some stress. Told him ya never meant no harm to nothin'. He said they'll let you out tomorrow when you's cooled down some."

"Gee, thanks for vouching for me. Now get out!"

Jimmy knocks on the door. A few moments later the door opens and I hear Riley say: "Is everything all right?"

"Yeah," Jimmy says, slipping past him into the hall. "He'll be fine tomorrow." Then the door closes and the key turns in the lock.

I'll be fine tomorrow? Screw you!

Alone again, I spend hours looking out the window at the

camp. People gather around their fires, telling stories or playing music, just as they did the night before. But everything seems somehow different to me now. Like the world is a party and I wasn't invited. Why does everything I think I know always turn out to be wrong? I can't trust Hannah now. At all. I don't know where Jimmy's coming from anymore. I'm not even sure this encryption-key treasure hunt isn't just some big joke Radcliffe is playing on us from beyond his watery grave. And I can't see how Finn is connected to the Foundation, either. He's so very different from Radcliffe. And he seems to love his people.

But what's killing me most is the thought of Jimmy getting old and dying without me. No way can I let that happen. Ever. There's no doubt that I have to convince him to come back with me now. I just hope that Hannah still has that serum.

Late in the night I hear the door creak open and then shut again. I sit up in the dark, wondering who's in my room. Then Junior jumps onto the bed and licks my face. I know Jimmy let him in to comfort me. I scratch Junior's ears, and he lies down beside me and falls right to sleep. How great it must feel to be a dog—or, as in his case, a fox—and to not have to worry all the time. To eat and sleep and play and love and just always be in the moment. Seems to me the human brain comes with a curse. Maybe Jimmy was right not to take the serum.

I keep telling myself that I don't need to have it all figured out right now. Tomorrow's a new day. Isn't that what people say? Just for tonight I'll try to be like Junior and sleep without dreams. I can always worry about tomorrow, tomorrow.

CHAPTER 18
Outside Looking In

The door is unlocked when I wake.

I peek my head out, but the hall is empty.

Downstairs, I find Riley setting up the breakfast room, preparing for the day. He nods and says good morning, but mentions nothing about yesterday. After a quiet meal by myself of toast and eggs and tea, I wander outside. The camp is just waking up. A man stretching outside his tent yawns and waves at me. Another darts for the outhouse.

Inside the courtyard, the empty bleachers are littered with scraps of paper from yesterday's betting. I sit and watch the pool of shadow disappear in the court below as the sun climbs in the sky, its warmth drawing a mist off the damp concrete.

"Beautiful, isn't it?"

I'm startled by the voice and look up to see Bree sitting in the shade across from me.

"I like to come and see it like this," she says. "In the morning. When it's just a blank slate, and anything is possible."

"Why does it mean so much to you? Winning, I mean."

"It's a huge honor," she says. "The greatest honor on the island. We grow up idolizing past winners."

"But why such an honor?" I ask. "Isn't it just a game?"

"Just a game?" She shakes her head. "You guys must really

have grown up isolated. After the fall harvest, we all gather here to pick the strongest athlete among us. The person who will be the island's protector through the winter."

"Then why would you help Jimmy?"

"Because I only want to win if I'm truly the best. You look like you're feeling better today," she adds, changing the subject.

"What's that supposed to mean?"

"Nothing. Just that Jimmy was worried about you."

"What do you care, anyway? All you care about is a stupid game. You don't even know anything about me or Jimmy."

"Maybe not," she says. "But I know Jimmy was wrong."

"Wrong about what?"

"Wrong about me liking you."

She stands and walks away.

I sit for a long time by myself, just thinking about things. Eventually, people begin wandering in and taking seats. They avoid me, sitting as far away as possible until the bleachers are fairly crowded, leaving a wide, empty space on either side of me. I get up and walk out, brushing past Jimmy on his way into the courtyard.

"Good luck," I mumble.

He stops and turns. "Ya really mean it?"

I look at him, his face genuine and kind, his brows lifted, waiting for my reply, hoping I'm still on his side. He does look happy for the first time since the cove. It's impossible to stay mad at him. "Yeah, I mean it," I say. "Good luck in there."

His eyes sparkle with excitement. "Thanks, Aubrey."

I can hear the balls cracking against the wall all day. When nobody is around inside, I try the statue room door, but it's locked now. With everyone engrossed in the games, and Junior out running with the deerhounds, of which he quickly seems to be becoming one himself, I'm left by myself with nothing to do but think. Think and feel sad. I don't know what to do.

The room where Riley brought Jimmy and me that first night in the castle seems to be the only place I can't hear the cracking balls, so I sit and stare at the patterns of the rug, trying to make them fit together in my mind like puzzle pieces. Angus comes in a few times and adds wood to the fire, but he doesn't say a word, of course, because he's mute. Later, Riley brings in tea service and a platter of food and sets them on the table for me, smiling uncomfortably as he bows and takes his leave. But I'm not hungry, and I let the food sit uneaten.

I feel like a crazy person. Like I'm outside looking in. Like everyone is watching me from a distance, concerned but also afraid. I'm surrounded by people, but I've never felt so alone.

When I stand to leave, I catch my reflection in the window and realize that I look like a crazy person too. My hair is wild and unkempt, having been slept on several nights now without a bath, and my face is gaunt from hardly eating these last two days. I trudge upstairs, lie on my bed, and stare at the ceiling, watching a spider inch its way across it toward the far wall for who knows what spidery purpose.

Several hours later, the door opens, and Jimmy comes in. He flops onto the bed next to me and sighs. "Man, am I beat."

"What are you doing here?" I ask, sensing him looking at me, but not taking my eyes off the ceiling.

"I guess they needed my room for someone," he says. "So now we're bunkin' together."

"You mean they put us together so you can keep an eye on me?" After several minutes without an answer from Jimmy, I add: "How'd you do in the games today?"

Jimmy props himself up on his elbow and looks at me. "You really wanna know?"

"I asked, didn't I?"

"I did it," he says, smiling. "I made it into the finals for tomorrow. Check out my hand."

His palm is swollen, a puss-drenched piece of string threaded through an enormous blister.

"Bree used a needle to pull the string through. She said it'll help drain it overnight without tearin' the skin. Smart, huh?"

"Pretty smart," I say, hating to admit it.

"Will you come watch tomorrow?"

"Come on, Jimmy . . ."

"It'd mean a lot to me."

"We came here to get the encryption key, remember? Not to compete in their silly island games. Geez. I can't figure out if it's me who's gone crazy or everyone else."

"I know, I know," Jimmy says, rolling off his elbow onto his back. "You's right to be mad at me, too. How 'bout we make a deal? You watch the match tomorrow, then I'll help ya find that hand, and we can see if there's even anythin' inside."

"What do you mean: if there's anything inside?"

"I jus' dun' see how you hide anythin' in a marble statue."

"Well, how hard would it be to drill a hole in it and insert a chip or something and then seal it up again? Think about it?"

"Jus' come watch the games, and then I'll help you."

"Will you leave with me once we get the hand back?"

He takes a deep breath. "I cain't promise you that, Aubrey. But I ain't made up my mind yet, neither. But you's right about your people underground. They deserve to be set free. So after the tournament I'll help ya get that key. Then maybe we can send the professor back with it and both stay here."

There's no way I'm doing that, I think. But I decide to take the small victory and worry about convincing Jimmy to come back with me later. "Okay," I say. "I'll come tomorrow, but as soon as it's done, you've got to help me get the hand. Everyone here is watching me like I might hurt myself or something."

"Would you?"

"Would I hurt myself?"

"Yeah."

"Don't be stupid."

"Well, ya did it once before."

"You mean the river?"

"Yeah."

"That was different."

"Okay," he says.

"Hey, what did Finn say after he caught me?"

"What'd he say?"

"Yeah, what'd he say about me breaking off the hand? I mean, did he seem to know that something might be hidden in it? Did he appear to know about the encryption key?"

"I dun' think so," Jimmy says. "When I got there, he was jus' looking at the statue. shakin' his head. He asked me, 'What in hell's got into that kid?' He has Angus workin' on fixin' it now, but that ain't gonna be easy the way you tore it up."

"I hope Angus doesn't work too hard," I say. "Because I'm going to get my hands on it and smash it to pieces anyway."

A long time passes with us lying side by side, looking up at the ceiling. Then Jimmy says, "Ya want me to take the floor?"

"No, we can share the bed. It isn't like we haven't spooned before. To keep warm on the mountain. Remember?"

"Yeah," he says. "I remember. Seems so long ago."

"You ever wish you could go back?"

"Go back where? Why?"

"I don't know. Just go back and do things differently."

"Sometimes I do. Mostly when I think about my family."

"Yeah, me too," I say. "Me too."

CHAPTER 19
The Champion and the Truth

I'm not sure who's more nervous, Jimmy or me.

He's shadowboxing with Bree to warm up for his first match of the day, against a real monster they call "Ralph the Mouth," apparently because he gets in his opponents' faces and yells every time he scores a point. Ralph might be a few years older than us, but he's twice as big—although a cold look from Finn shuts his mouth in a hurry as he descends the ladder into the court. Jimmy scrambles down after him.

Finn tosses the ball in, and Jimmy jumps and snatches it before it even bounces. So he's up to serve. Jimmy winds up, bounces the ball, and aces a hook right past Ralph.

"Go, Jimmy!" I shout. The crowd cheers, too.

"They like him," Bree says, squeezing in beside me.

"He's easy to like," I reply. "Sorry about the other day."

"No worries. I'm glad you're here for Jimmy."

Jimmy runs Ralph all over the court. He's so exhausted from chasing Jimmy's balls, he doesn't even mouth off when he finally scores a point. But Jimmy quickly wins back the serve and finishes him off, to wild cheers from the audience. Finn reaches Jimmy a hand and helps him up the ladder. Papers fly as people line up to place bets on the next match.

I turn to ask Bree how many matches there are before the final, but she's gone. When I look back, she's scaling down the ladder and dropping into the court for her first matchup.

Jimmy joins me in the bleachers, unable to contain a huge smile, his bare chest still heaving from the match. I notice that his palm is bleeding. "You all right?"

"Never felt better," he says.

We watch as Bree battles a red-headed boy, finally winning fifteen to twelve. Both of them are so spent when the game is over that they have to be hauled up the ladder by the crowd.

"Let's go eat," Bree says when we go to congratulate her.

"Shouldn't we stay and watch?" Jimmy asks. "Get an idea how the winner plays in case we end up goin' against 'em."

"Nah," Bree says. "You know Quinn's gonna win, and if you play him this afternoon, just push to his left. He's weak there. I'm beat and so are you. We need energy."

Jimmy agrees, and we gather in Bree's tent and sit down for a meal of cold meat and cheese, a hunk of dry bread, and some warm tea. She doesn't say anything about what a jerk I was to her yesterday, and I even catch her smiling at me a few times. She actually seems kind of cool.

"Make me a promise," Bree says, looking at Jimmy with a very serious expression. "Aubrey, you're a witness. If we play each other in the final, you have to do your best to beat me."

"But Bree," he protests, "this means more—"

"I said promise me, Jimmy. I don't want to win it that way. I want to earn it. Winning isn't winning when you cheat."

After hesitating, he nods. "Okay, I promise."

We sit quietly eating, the sound of our chewing interrupted only by the distant cracking of the ball. After a while, Bree asks, "So where'd you two come from again? It's hard to believe you know so little about the games, since it's all most people on the island can even talk about."

"We come from a long ways away," Jimmy says.

"It can't be that far," she says. "The island isn't that big."

"We're not from—"

"We're from Ayre, in the north." I cut Jimmy off.

"Figures," Bree says, biting off a hunk of bread.

The handball players compete all morning into afternoon, eliminating competitors match by match until Bree advances to the championship by winning her semi-final round against a small but fierce girl named Cordelia. The crowd cheers Bree as she climbs from the court, but boos Cordelia when she refuses Bree's offered hand. Nobody likes a poor sport, I guess.

Jimmy's up next against Quinn. If he wins, it will be him and Bree fighting it out for the title. There's a brief pause in the excitement, and I watch as Bree hugs Jimmy and wishes him luck, holding up her left hand to remind him of Quinn's weak spot. Then she works her way through the crowd toward me as Jimmy climbs down into the court. Quinn follows him. He's an odd kid. He's a year or so younger than we are, and he looks completely harmless, his thin shoulders slumped, his pale face void of any expression. But once the ball's in play, he turns into a madman, scoring four quick points against Jimmy.

Bree sits beside me and drains her canteen. "Looks like it'll be Jimmy 'n me after all," she says, wiping her mouth with the back of her hand.

"He has to beat this Quinn kid first."

"He will," she says. "He will."

I know she's right. Quinn has a massive serve, but Jimmy plays it smart, letting the ball slow down and bounce off the back wall, then returning it to Quinn's left. They battle it out for nearly forty minutes, with long, exhausting volleys, until

Jimmy hits a short pop low and scores the winning point. Quinn's face shows its first expression as he sadly shakes Jimmy's hand. They climb up and head for their canteens.

Finn stands and thanks all the competitors, announcing a brief break before the championship match. Then he gathers Jimmy and Bree and walks them toward the castle, presumably to have a talk. The crowd disperses as people run to outhouses or jog to their tents to freshen up. I hang back and watch as workers descend into the court and scour the ground for scraps of paper or bits of trash that might have fallen in.

Before long, the crowd is packed back into the bleachers and buzzing with excitement as they wait impatiently for the athletes to return. They cheer when Finn leads Jimmy and Bree back into the courtyard, each of them now wearing a red sash tied at their waist. Finn sees them to the ladder, shakes their hands, bows, and returns to his seat as they climb down into the court. Jimmy looks up and scans the bleachers and locks eyes with me and smiles. I give him thumbs up.

Finn removes the ball from his pocket and holds it up, as if truing its shape against the high winter sun; then he lobs it into the court. Bree nabs it, but Jimmy hardly seems to move. I see Bree glare at him, as if reminding him of his promise. She lines up and serves a rocket to his right and scores. The crowd goes wild. Jimmy backs up for the second serve and returns it, starting a long volley that he ultimately wins. Back and forth, they trade serves for a long time, but hardly scoring at all. I notice Jimmy is favoring his right leg, probably from his old wound that I stitched shut in the cove. But true to her word, Bree shows him no slack and works the ball hard toward his right side. Her hand is a pistol, firing serves with blinding speed and returning them with deafening cracks. Jimmy has a difficult time winning the serve, and when he does the score is 11 to 6. But Jimmy isn't licked yet. He switches things up and serves with his left hand. Bree scrambles to modify her game, but not before Jimmy's evened the score.

As Bree lines up to serve, Finn calls down: "Eleven all."

Jimmy sends back a hook, and Bree dives for it but misses, falling and scraping her knee. Jimmy helps her up and pauses to make sure she's okay before serving. Three aces and it's game point, 14 to 11. The crowd falls quiet, anticipating Jimmy's win. But Jimmy serves a soft one, and Bree easily streaks it past him to the corner wall. She eyes him suspiciously as she sets up her serve. She scores. I get the feeling Jimmy's letting her win. I think she does too, because her next serve blasts straight at Jimmy's head, forcing him to duck and giving her the point.

"Thirteen serving fourteen," Finn calls.

But this time Jimmy manages to send back her serve and they volley for several minutes before Bree collapses trying to rush to the forward wall for a short ball. Jimmy lines up the serve from his left again.

"Game point serving thirteen."

Jimmy sends a clean serve hard against the wall, and Bree easily returns it. Jimmy slaps the ball back, soft and short, and I'm certain it won't even make the front wall. But it does. It hits the corner where the wall intersects the ground and rolls out across the court, coming to rest at Bree's feet.

The crowd goes wild, leaping to their feet screaming: "Roller! Roller! Roller!"

I don't even think Jimmy realizes that it was a legal shot, because he looks confused when Bree walks up and shakes his hand. Then she hurriedly climbs the ladder and exits the court. The crowd descends on Jimmy, dropping from the bleachers and rushing to congratulate him. Slapping his back, crowding him, touching him. The court fills with rowdy fans, and they hoist Jimmy in the air on a hundred hands and pass him across the court and lift him up like a prize to Finn, who pulls him onto the bleachers and hugs him. Jimmy is suddenly a star.

I try to make my way over to congratulate him, but there's no chance. The crowd is just too thick. Bree appears at my shoulder. "We'll be lucky to even get a chance to say goodbye," she says, looking sad. "They'll be celebrating him all night."

"You played really well," I say, realizing too late that it's probably little consolation to hear.

"Thanks," she says, graciously. "But Jimmy was the better player. Maybe next year it will finally be me."

While the crowd sweeps Jimmy away to the castle, Bree and I wander around the quiet camp, alone except for a few mothers nursing crying babies. We sit on the back of an empty wagon and swing our legs, watching the late afternoon dissolve into evening. I can tell she's down about losing, and I figure we both could use some company.

"So tell me about this book you read on your birthday."

"Half a book," she says.

"Only half?"

"Yeah, the last part is missing, so I just make up my own endings every time."

"At least it's always different then."

She smiles. We kick our legs. I try to whistle a tune. After a while I turn to Bree. "Hey, do you know how old Finn is?"

"Finn? I don't know for sure. Nobody really knows. He's

old, though. Some people say he's immortal. That he's older than the island, even. But I don't think so. A couple years ago, Brent and me—he won that year—we were snooping around some, and we found a room from the original castle, before they rebuilt. It's kind of a basement. Anyway, there were lots of kid's drawings down there on the walls that made it look like beings came from the sky. Brent said Finn was an alien."

I can't help but laugh. "An alien?"

"I'm not sure I believe that," she says, "but who knows?"

I'm a little worried with Jimmy being so lavishly celebrated that he'll forget his deal to help me get the David's hand back. I'm even more worried that he'll really want to stay on now that he's the island hero.

"Hey, Bree. Do you think you could show me that room?"

"The basement?"

"Yeah."

"Sure," she says, hopping off the wagon.

She fetches a lantern from her tent and leads me to the deserted north side of the castle, down a flight of stone stairs winding around a circular tower. The ancient wooden door at the base of the stairs appears to be locked, but Bree wiggles the rusted iron latch and shimmies it open.

"Not very good security," I say.

Bree shrugs. I hold the lantern while she lifts the glass and strikes it lit. Then I hand it back and follow her inside.

The room is dank and musty. The lamp casts a dim glow on stacks of old barrels and piles of antlered deer skulls tangled like bleached branches in the corners. I eye them, wondering if one of them belonged to the stag we killed.

Bree walks me to the back of the room and opens another

door onto a narrow passageway.

"You can see that this was the wall of the original castle," she says, pointing out the worn, hand-laid stones. Then she stops at yet another door, this one half-rotted. She puts her shoulder to it and forces the door open on creaking leather hinges, dried and brittle with age.

Inside is a small room that was once partitioned into two, except the wall between them has largely crumbled. Bree steps over the tumbled stones and leads me to the far wall.

She holds up the lantern—

Faded but detectable, black charcoal drawings adorn the wall like ancient cave paintings from a people long gone. I can see right away why Bree joked about aliens, because the most prominent image is a drone lifting off into the sky while a mother and son stand below and wave goodbye.

"Is that what I think it is?"

"What?" Bree asks.

I take the lamp from Bree and hold it closer, inspecting the drawing. Sure enough, a Park Service crest is clearly visible on the side of the drone. I move the lamp around and see that the valknut symbol is reproduced in other places on the walls, too. Then my eye spots something on a lower stone, beneath the waving figures. I set the lamp down and drop to my knees. It's a signature, scrawled by a child's uncertain hand—DAVID.

"Who's David?" I ask, pointing.

"Why, that's Finn," Bree says, seemingly surprised that I don't know. "His name's David Robert MacFinn. But since he's the head of Clan MacFinn, everyone just calls him Finn."

An image of Finn's face pops into my head—his sharp nose, his crystal blue eyes. I've seen those eyes before. I try to recall Finn's song the other night: "Inside the woman a child grew, _something, something_, an immortal son . . ."

Bree finishes it for me. "Half god, half man, a deadly duo. A gift of love by a woman's courage won."

The truth springs into my consciousness with the clarity of a cold, clear morning. The drawing. The drone. The signature.

"Finn is Dr. Radcliffe's illegitimate son."

"Whose son?" Bree asks.

It's the only explanation. It explains the island being off limits to the drones. It explains the secrecy. The myth. Didn't the professor tell us Radcliffe spent a lot of time here in the early years? I'd bet my head Radcliffe had an affair with Finn's mother. And I'd bet he injected his son with the serum, too, before he left him to spawn a clan of descendants, most of whose skulls now hang on the wall. But most importantly, it means that the encryption key I've been looking for isn't in the statue's hand at all. It's in his hand, David MacFinn's.

"'Where man rises from the sea, in the right hand of David you shall find your key.'"

"I don't know that one," Bree says.

I turn and hug her. "You're amazing, Bree. You have no idea what you've done for me."

She pats my back uncomfortably. "Okay, easy there, tiger."

All night the castle rings with the sounds of celebration. The wine flows, the music plays, the guests dance. A royal feast is prepared, even bigger than the last. There are so many dinner guests they won't all fit in the great hall, and the statue room is opened so people can eat amongst the marble figures, including the David with its still missing hand. But I pass it by with little interest now, because I know we were looking for the key in the wrong David. All I can think is that Dr. Radcliffe must have inserted a chip in his son's hand. Or perhaps the code is some algorithm from his fingerprint, if fingerprints don't change as we age. Anyway, I don't know how it's hidden in his hand, and I have even less ideas about how to get at it.

I try to corner Jimmy to tell him what I've learned, but he's overwhelmed with attention, and I can't even get close. He sits next to Finn at the head of the big table, receiving a long line of people presenting him with gifts. Precious stones and feathers and even a gray rabbit-fur coat that Jimmy slips on, making him look ridiculous. But Jimmy's loving it. And who wouldn't? He's suddenly the island's favorite son. And he's not even from here.

The guests raise their glasses to toast. "Today for Jimmy," someone calls. "Tomorrow for us!"

I refuse to wait in line to talk with my friend, so I grab Junior from the study, where I find him asleep in front of the fire, and carry him upstairs to my room and shut out the sound of the festivities and lie on the bed and think.

"What am I going to do, Junior?"

A warm lick on my forearm is the only answer I get.

Maybe with Jimmy's newfound fame, he can convince Finn to come back with us so that Hannah might use her equipment in the lab to find the encryption key hidden in his hand. Which reminds me, she had better have that longevity serum for Jimmy. I force myself to forget her betrayal, to focus instead on getting us home. I'm more than a little worried that Jimmy really won't want to leave the island now. But we'll see. Maybe he'll be bored with it all tomorrow when things settle down. Just maybe.

Part Three

CHAPTER 20
My Sacrifice

Junior's whining wakes me.

I get up and open the door to let him out. He races down the hall, probably to go outside and pee. It's early, the window in my room touched with gray. I wash my face in the basin and run my wet fingers through my hair. Then I step into the cold privy to do my own morning business.

I stop at Jimmy's door and peek in, but he hasn't been to bed. Downstairs it doesn't look like anyone else made it to bed either. People lie passed out everywhere—beanbags, chairs, couches. The main door is open, and a cold draft blows through the hall. Riley must be passed out somewhere himself.

I step outside and close the door behind me.

The cold morning air bites my lungs and stings my cheeks, waking me with a quick shiver. There's a fog socked in over the water. A black crow pecks at the grass. Noticing movement at the water's edge, I cross the terrace for a better look. As I cut through the fog toward the seawall, the wooden frame of the shark crane comes into view.

"You're up early."

I whip around to see Bree sitting on the steps behind me.

"You scared me," I say, clutching my chest. "I didn't see you there."

She holds out her canteen. I take it and sit down beside her and swig warm tea, laced with a bite of something bitter.

"Who died?" I ask, handing her canteen back and nodding toward the crane.

"Nobody's died yet," she says.

"What do you mean 'yet'?"

"They're getting ready for the oblation."

"The what?"

"The sacrifice," she says. "You know, from the games."

The way she says it, with a sad look in her hazel eyes, fills me with sudden horror over what she means. Is that why she's out here so early sipping spiked tea?

"Don't tell me they sacrifice the loser to the sharks," I say, my voice filled with terror for her.

"No," she says, shaking her head.

I sigh with relief. "Good"

"They sacrifice the winner."

"What?"

"The winner gets to join Clan MacFinn on the skull rack."

"Please say you're playing some kind of sick game."

She looks at me. "You didn't know?"

"No, I didn't know."

"Does Jimmy know?" she asks.

"Of course not," I say, still thinking this must be a joke. "This is ridiculous. Nobody's sacrificing anyone."

Bree's face goes white and she shakes her head. "It isn't a joke," she says. "They'll sacrifice him at noon."

"I don't believe it."

"That doesn't mean it isn't true," she replies.

"You wanted to win yourself," I say, determined to out her for pulling my leg. "Why would you do that?"

"Yes," she says. "I wanted to be the sacrifice. It's an honor to protect the island. We dream of it growing up. How do you not know this? I though you said you came from Ayre?"

As I realize she's not kidding, my pulse quickens, and it's suddenly hard to breathe. "We've got to stop it."

"You can't stop it," she says. "Nobody can. The winner has to go willingly. If he doesn't they feed him to the sharks anyway, but without any honors. Then the runner-up gets to go. That'd be me, but I don't want to win that way."

A loud clanking draws my attention to the crane where the men work in the fog, attaching the crossbeam to the murder machine. I leap to my feet. "Where's Jimmy?"

"Shh . . .," Bree holds a finger to her lips and nods toward the men. "Keep it down. Jimmy will be in bed with Finn until they bring him down."

"What do you mean: 'in bed with Finn'? What's this, some kind of sick sex thing on top of killing him? You people are royally screwed up here."

Bree shushes me again. "Calm down now. It doesn't have anything to do with sex. Lying next to the young champion is supposed to keep Lord Finn young. Something about the purity of youthful body heat. But that hardly matters. Are you serious that Jimmy doesn't know what he was playing for?"

My mind races away from me, searching for solutions. Create a distraction. Escape. Maybe we can fight our way free. Then I remember the men hunting that stag. How skilled they were at the chase, how easy it was for them to rope it.

"There has to be a way to stop it, Bree."

She shakes her head. "I've never seen it stopped before."

"Come on, Bree," I plead with her. "Please think. There has to be a way. There has to be."

She stares at the crane and the workmen there moving like ghosts in the fog. "There is a story they tell sometimes," she says, after a pause. "A popular player arrived late, his father had been dying or something. Anyway, he challenged the winner by claiming to be the more worthy sacrifice. They let them have a match to decide. But only because he had a red sash from being a finalist the year before."

"You have a red sash," I say, pointing to the sash still tied at her waist.

"Yes, but I've already lost to Jimmy," she says.

"I haven't."

"You mean you want to . . ."

Sound seems to fade away until all I can hear is my own heartbeat. I take a deep breath. I feel as though I'm hovering above, watching myself standing on the edge of an irreversible decision. I feel curiously detached. The sun rises behind the castle, sending ladders of golden light angling through the fog, and we seem to be floating on the very light itself. My course is clear. My future certain. "That's what I'll do."

"You mean challenge Jimmy?"

"Yes."

"But if you win, they'll sacrifice you."

"I know it. But I owe him. How much time do we have?"

"Maybe four hours," she says, looking at the rising sun.

I grab Bree by the shoulders. "Listen, I need you to coach me quick. Teach me everything you taught Jimmy. Teach me everything you didn't. Then I need to get in there and challenge this before Jimmy realizes what's happening."

Three and half hours later, I storm into the castle, dripping with sweat and feeling more alive and more determined than I ever have before. I push through the mob of people gathered in the great hall, wave off Riley's good morning, and force my way to the front of the crowd just as Finn is walking Jimmy downstairs, still half asleep and wearing that ridiculous coat.

"I challenge the winner!" I shout.

The people nearest me fall silent. Finn stops on the stairs.

I say it again: "I'm challenging the winner."

A wave of whispers passes through the crowd, silencing their chatter until all I can hear is my own labored breathing.

"You don't have a bye," Finn says.

"Yes, I do." I wave the red sash.

"Where did you get that?" he asks.

"Bree gave it to me."

"Well, then," he says, "it isn't yours to use."

"Nothing in the rules says I can't."

I'm just making stuff up now, but a murmur runs through the crowd and some people nod.

"And, besides," I add, sensing hesitation on Finn's face, "I'm the more worthy for the ritual. I should have played, but I was locked in my room, if you remember."

Jimmy stands next to Finn. looking down on me, his gray eyes burning with anger. I can't blame him for hating me. He doesn't even know where they were taking him yet. From his point of view, I must be a jealous prick.

Finn shakes his head. "Sorry, kid. You can't use someone else's bye. You're too late besides."

"If you're sure you have the best, what are you afraid of?"

"You can't possibly think—"

"I wanna play him," Jimmy says, cutting Finn short.

Another murmur of excitement runs like a wave across the

crowd. Jimmy stands frozen on the stairs, glaring at me. Finn looks between us, his mind working behind his blue eyes. Then he shrugs. "Fine, then. Let's have ourselves a little match."

I can feel Jimmy's contempt as he brushes past me.

The crowd pours into the courtyard and swarms to the bleachers. Jimmy wriggles out of his fur coat and hands it to Finn, then he throws me a look that cuts to the bone as he descends the ladder into the court. I strip off my shirt and toss it to the ground. I catch sight of Bree in the crowd but find no comfort in her expression. I climb down to the court, watching as the ladder is hauled up, trapping me here with my choice.

Jimmy spits on the ground. "Ya jus' couldn't stand to see me be more popular than you's, could ya?"

I want to grab him and shake him, tell him everything that I know. But I can't. If he learns what's really on the line, he'll fight even harder to beat me—sacrificing himself to save me, just as I'm sacrificing myself to save him. I know he would.

I hear the ball hit the court. and the next thing I know it's in Jimmy's hand. He lines up to serve, keeping his eyes locked on mine as he aces the ball right past me. I'm still hearing the ring of its crack against the front wall when he snatches up the dead ball and prepares to serve again. Pay attention, Aubrey, I tell myself. Remember what Bree said: watch his hand and anticipate where the ball will go; don't watch the ball itself.

His second serve is less fierce. and I manage to smack the ball with my palm and send it back to the front wall, but Jimmy catches it before the bounce and taps a soft return, forcing me to run forward to reach it. Too late.

"Two serving zero."

I notice Jimmy's serving with his left hand, his right one

red and raw. Try and return it to his right, I tell myself. But he aces it past me.

"Three serving zero."

Then another kill shot.

"Four serving zero."

And another.

"Five, zero."

On his sixth serve, I manage to get behind the ball and send it back, bouncing low toward his right. Jimmy stretches, but misses. Finally, my chance to serve.

"Zero serving five."

I bounce the ball in front of me and level a monster swipe at it. I miss the ball entirely. The crowd laughs. Jimmy shakes his head and smirks as he scoops up the ball.

"Five, zero."

I return his serve, finally seeming to get the hang of it a little, and we volley for several shots until Jimmy beats me. The next volley is longer still, but by the time I win back the serve, it's eight to zero. The thought of Jimmy being clamped into that iron mask and lowered to the sharks makes my blood boil. I funnel my panic into a laser beam focus with only one goal—winning. I try to forget about what happens after. I send a serve to Jimmy's right, acing it past him. I'm not sure who's more surprised by it, him or me. I keep the serve for several points, winning the next four volleys, but losing the serve to him on the fifth. Now it's my five to his eight as he sets up a serve.

My body is getting loose.

My mind is getting focused.

Soon, I'm not thinking about anything, not even winning. I'm just alive in the moment, anticipating the ball and guiding it to the wall in ways that make Jimmy run the court. We spend nearly an hour fighting out long volleys, trading off points, trading off serves. I notice Jimmy is resting longer between his serves. And he's limping more than ever, favoring his right leg and the old wound in his thigh from that day in the cove. I can still see the wide scar from my rough stitch job.

I remember swimming him to shore and dragging him into that cave and worrying sick that he was going to die on me. Who could have known we'd end up here? Halfway around the world, fighting over who will be sacrificed by trying to best one another at handball. Jimmy's serve blazes past my ear, and I run after it, scooping it off the rear wall, but my shot falls short.

Focus, I tell myself. Focus.

"Twelve serving ten," Finn calls from above.

If Jimmy scores three more points, it's over. He's shark meat, and I'm doomed to live a thousand years without my best friend. I can't stand the thought of it.

I return his serve, and we volley back and forth, our breath heavy, our hands slapping the ball, the ball cracking loudly off the concrete wall. Then Jimmy hits a high ball, and I leap off the court to return it. But something happens while I'm suspended above him. Everything seems to slow down. Or maybe it just seems like slow motion because my mind speeds up, calculating a million possibilities in a fraction of a second. I see the ball in midair, I see my arm cocked to smack it. I see Jimmy beneath me, his right leg stretched out as he tries to move out of my way. Then I do something that would make me sick with guilt on any other day. I change the direction of my swing and drive the ball into Jimmy's thigh, aiming for the center of the white scar. The ball connects with an audible thud, and Jimmy falls to ground shrieking and holding his leg.

The crowd gasps and leans over the court to see if Jimmy's okay. He pulls it together, pushing himself up off the ground. It's his serve now, and he limps over to collect the ball, carrying it back while looking down. When he lines up to serve, he looks at me and breaks my heart. His eyes are gray pools of light, his brow pinched with confusion. He looks at me like he doesn't recognize me at all. As if I remind him of someone he used to know, but he just can't place who.

"Thirteen serving ten," calls Finn.

Jimmy serves, but the energy is gone out of his game. We volley a few turns but he seems to hardly try, limping after the ball without enthusiasm. I can't tell whether it's because of heartache over what I appear to have become, or the pain in his leg, but he no longer seems to care. I want to grab him and hug him and apologize. I grab the ball instead and line up a serve.

The next five points are the easiest and hardest points of the game. Every time Finn calls down the score, I'm one point closer to saving Jimmy's life. Every time Finn calls down the score, I'm one point closer to losing my own.

"Game point serving twelve."

The crowd is quiet. Nobody cheering me, nobody enjoying the game. I suck it up and wipe away a tear with the back of my hand. Then I serve the final ball. Jimmy makes a show of going for it, but the moment it's passed, he drops his head and walks to the ladder and climbs from the court. The crowd parts to let him through. They stare down at me—judging me, loathing me, shaming me. Maybe they should.

"I didn't have a choice!" I shout.

Nobody listens. Several of the rough men from our hunt

climb down the ladder and grab me. They carry me to the ledge and hand me up to others waiting to take me away.

"You don't understand. I didn't have a choice!"

My instinct is to struggle, to fight for my life and run. But I remember Bree telling me that the champion has to go willingly to his sacrifice or they kill him and the runner up. Which means they'll kill Jimmy if I fight. I relax and let them take me.

Someone ties my hands behind my back. Then someone else ties my ankles together. Now any chance of escaping my fate is gone for good. As I'm picked up and carried toward the seawall and the waiting crane, I don't see any sign of Jimmy. Oh, well. It's better that he doesn't know until it's over.

I do catch a quick glimpse of Bree, but I immediately wish I hadn't because the horror of what's about to happen to me is clearly reflected on her face.

CHAPTER 21
A Message from the Gods

Oh God, if you exist, what have I done?

The world shrinks into two small windows of faraway blue as Finn clamps the iron mask on my head.

I smell the saltwater, I hear the clinking chain.

Finn's blond hair appears in the mask's eyeholes, his head bent as he traces something with his finger on my bare chest. Then I feel the prick of his knife, the cutting sting as he drags its blade across my flesh, followed by the warmth of my own blood. He's carving something in my chest. Perhaps a message for me to carry into the afterlife. I struggle against my bonds, but then, remembering that this only works if I'm a willing sacrifice, I clench my teeth and promise myself I won't scream.

The crowd surrounding me is silent, but I can feel them watching. Finn works for several minutes, and by the time he's finished I don't even mind the pain any longer. In fact, I wish he'd continue. Anything except what I know is coming next.

Finn's head disappears from the eyeholes, and I glimpse the blue water beyond. I see the shadow of the crane's boom swing over the waves, bringing the shadows of the sharks up from the depths. They cruise their vicious circles like angels of death swimming in a watery sky. A fin breaks the surface. I hear the rattle of the chain as the rope pulls it up. I feel the tug of the iron helmet on my neck. Warm piss runs down my leg. Please, I pray, to anything, just let my neck break before I'm eaten. Just let me die and join my mom and dad.

My mind leaves my body and floats over an ocean of time, retracing my short life. The journey here in the submarine, the adventures at the lake. I'm on the mountain with Jimmy now. We're sitting on the glacier, looking at the rising moon. I can see the glint of wonder in his eye, his long lashes visible even in the moonlight. It's funny what images stick with you. Suddenly, I'm in the cove, learning to swim. I hear Jimmy laughing. He calls me buddy for the first time, and I recall how good it felt. Now, I'm standing at the shore after my trip down from the wrecked train, and I'm seeing Jimmy again for the first time, crouched on that rock, the orange sun oozing into the waves as if setting only for him. Now, I'm back underground, my father is rushing to the closing elevator, his words making it just in time: "I love you, Son." Three simple words—I love you. I only said them once in my life. I said them to my father on his last day alive. I should have said them more. I should have said them to—

Something grabs my legs.

I brace for the pain.

The pressure eases on my neck as I'm lifted and my soul seems to slide back into my body.

"Put him down!" a distant voice yells. "Put him down, I said. Do it now!"

Jimmy? Is that you, Jimmy?

"You lost your chance," I hear Finn say.

"Jus' put him down and let me explain."

My feet hit the ground and Jimmy's strong hands hold me up. Everything is white and blurry outside the eyeholes now.

"You's got this all wrong," Jimmy says. "You dun' need to kill nobody to be safe. There ain't no gods out there tryin' to destroy you here. We can explain ever-thin'."

An angry growl rises from the crowd.

"Throw him to the sharks!" someone shouts. "Yeah, string him up, too," another says. "Double, double!" they chant.

"Somebody restrain him," Finn calls.

"Wait! Wait!" Jimmy yells as he struggles with someone beside me. "Wait! I'll prove it. Jus' give me a chance."

"Prove what?" Finn asks. "That you're delusional?"

"Jus' hear me out," Jimmy says. "You give me three stones and nothin' more. Then let me in the water and I'll call up an iron shark like you've never seen."

"What do you mean, an iron shark?" Finn asks.

My legs buckle, but Jimmy's hands jump to hold me up.

"Let me show ya," he says. "We're not from here, Aubrey and me ain't. We came from far away to bring you a message."

"He's got a message from the gods!" someone shouts.

"A message from the gods!" others chant back.

Then I hear Finn's voice again: "Are you claiming to have a message from the gods?"

"Sure," Jimmy answers. "From the gods."

"Fine," Finn says. "You go call up your iron shark. But if

you're telling the truth, you shouldn't need any stones to do it. The gods will protect you. So go ahead. Dive in." He laughs, obviously thinking Jimmy won't do it. The crowd laughs, too.

Jimmy's hands leave me, and the next thing I hear is a loud splash. Without Jimmy supporting me, it's a struggle to stay on my feet. But refusing to surrender to exhaustion, I stiffen my legs and straighten my spine. Then I press my head forward in the mask for a better view. Jimmy swims amongst the sharks, his head down, his strong arms stroking confidently, propelling him elegantly through the dangerous water. As he breaks past the thickest of the sharks, several fins turn to follow him out to deeper water. But he swims without panic or fear.

A strange sense of calm comes over me. As if my life is in the hands of something bigger. Some fate that I can't change and shouldn't bother trying to change even if I could. Not even with a wish. I doubt Jimmy will be able to locate the submarine in time, especially when he's surrounded by sharks. And if he does find it, I have no idea how he'll raise it with no stones, or why the professor wouldn't be sleeping, or perhaps catatonic in one of his moods. I just wish Jimmy didn't have to die too.

Once he's far from shore, but still short of the submarine by my estimate, Jimmy dives, surrounded by circling fins. A tail splashes. A minute passes. Then Jimmy pops up, treading water farther away. My eyes focus on nothing but him, wishing I could at least say goodbye with a look. Jimmy sucks in a deep breath and dives again. The fins disappear beneath the waves with him. Time creeps past. Two minutes—three—maybe four minutes now. The crowd starts to murmur. A dog yips somewhere behind me. Or maybe a fox.

The crowd's murmuring increases as the seconds pass:

"Nobody can hold his breath that long," a boy says.

"He's gone for sure," a man's voice chimes in.

"The sharks got him for a snack," a woman adds.

"Let's lower the other one now, too," another calls.

I hear the clattering chain, rising on its pulley again. The mask is caught up, pulling against my neck. I rise to my tiptoes, ready to die. Oh, well, I think, at least we'll be together.

Then Jimmy's head appears, bobbing on the waves. Sharks rise with him—fins circling, tails thrashing. Jimmy punches at the water, defending himself. Do I really have to watch him get eaten before I die? Must fate truly torture me before I slip to the other side? Why? It doesn't seem right.

Suddenly, the fins scatter, the sharks disappear, and the patch of water surrounding Jimmy goes calm. Jimmy faces me, treading water, and although he's much too far away for me to make out his eyes, I swear I see him smile. Then he rises from the water with his arms outstretched like some long departed sea god returned to embrace the world. He rises until his waist clears the water. Then his thighs, his knees, his feet. Next, the black, protruding submarine sail rises beneath him, lifting him above the waves, and the Park Service crest faces us, glinting in the sunlight. When he stops rising, Jimmy stands six feet above the water on the highest part of the surfaced submarine.

The crowd behind me gasps.

Someone screams.

Several quiet seconds pass, and then I hear the rattle of the chain, the opening of the clasps.

The mask is pulled from my head.

My head lolls forward, my chin rests on my chest.

I see my belly and legs covered in my own blood and I'm suddenly dizzy, feeling faint. I try to look up again, but my neck won't budge. Even the effort is too much. My world spins, my legs collapse, and I fall backwards, caught in strong, but no longer enemy, arms.

I close my eyes and surrender to oblivion's sweet relief.

CHAPTER 22
No Turning Back

"Tell me about my sister again."

Finn sits on the edge of his chair beside my bed, his arms propped on his knees, his chin resting in his palms. Jimmy sits beside him. I elbow myself up, wincing when the bandage pulls against my wounded chest where Riley patched me up.

"Half-sister," I say. "And she's only about sixteen to your six hundred."

"But what's she like?" he asks.

"She ain't none too nice," Jimmy says.

I cast Jimmy a disapproving glance before answering Finn: "She's got red hair. And freckles. She's smart as they come, too. Although we sure do have some talking to do when I get back."

"And this serum that keeps me from aging," he says, "You have it in your blood also?"

"I do," I answer. "And Hannah does. Jimmy doesn't have it yet, but he will once we return. Won't you, Jimmy?" Jimmy tips his chin and looks down instead of nodding yes, and I can't help but wonder if it's because he still doesn't want the serum, or if it's because he isn't coming back with me.

Finn stands and walks to the window. He holds up his right hand, inspecting it in the light. "This key you talk about. You're certain that it's in my hand?"

"That's what the clue says. And you yourself said that you remembered being pricked the last time you saw your father."

"And his name was Radcliffe?"

"Yes," I reply, "Dr. Robert Radcliffe."

"I do remember him doing something to my arm or hand that hurt me. I tried not to cry, and he told me I was strong. But that could have been this serum you talk about. And besides, my memory is worthless. I thought he was a god."

"Well, who wouldn't have? You didn't know any better. Him flying in and out of here in some machine like nobody in these parts had ever seen or even dreamed. And the gifts. I'm assuming he brought all those statues here."

Finn nods. "They came on ships, offloaded by cranes that seemed to work themselves by some magic of the gods. Gifts for my mother in between his visits. Then while he was away, she got sick. I must have been seven, or maybe eight. He came one last time. I remember him holding her skull and crying. I have it still. My mother's skull. It's the first one in our family wall." Finn turns from the window and I see that he has tears in his eyes. "I really messed up badly."

"What do you mean?" I ask.

His voice quivers, "The games. The sacrifices. All those kids. Hundreds of them." He covers his face with his hands and weeps. "Oh, sweet Mother, I really messed up."

"But how could you have known?" I ask, wanting to ease his grief. "If that's what the adults taught you, that the gods demanded sacrifices to protect the island, how could you have known any different? I was taught lies. I was told none of this was even up here. And I believed it, too, until I saw for myself. You couldn't have known, Finn."

Finn drops his hands, but his eyes are still filled with tears. I can see the pain in his expression, the self-judgment written there. It must be torture.

"I could have known," he says. "I should have. The truth is, I had suspicions over the years. Deep down, I did. But the people believed the stories. And the rituals made them feel safe. I'm not an evil man. I know that I'm not. But I have a strange feeling I'll pay somehow for what I've done."

I don't know what to say to that, so I don't say anything. Jimmy and I share a look as Finn stares at the floor. When he speaks again, his voice is soft, as if he's speaking to himself.

"I used to climb to the highest point on the island—on clear days, in the early years, when I was young. I remember looking across the water to distant lands and wondering. I knew there were answers out there somewhere. But I never found the courage to leave the island. I just never did. I chose to remain ignorant and believe the old myths. I failed my people."

"You would have been hunted by drones anyway," I say. "So you were stuck here. It just wasn't the gods and the sharks that kept you protected. It was your father's mercy, something he seemed to have little of for anyone else." I lean forward, not wanting to take advantage of his regret, but not wanting to miss an opportunity either. "Now's your chance to change all that. Come back with us, Finn. Let Hannah X-ray your right hand. The code hidden inside you has the power to save countless lives. If that's not some kind of amends, I don't know what is."

"What about my people here?" he asks.

"We'll bring you back to the island after. We can do the round trip in less than two months. Can't we, Jimmy?"

Jimmy nods.

Finn paces the room, shaking his head.

"I'm not at all certain they'd make it here without me," he

says. "I'm not even sure they'd let me leave, to be honest. Even though they call me Lord, they're possessive of me, too."

"We can sneak away then," I suggest.

"Never work," he says. "There'll be chaos here for sure. And who knows what sacrifices they'd make without me here to deny them. I won't let another innocent islander die."

I sit up and swing my legs over the edge of the bed. The pain brings tears to my eyes, so now both Finn and I are crying, although for vastly different reasons.

"You have to come back with us," I say. "If you don't, you'll be responsible for killing many more people out there. In the world."

"That's not fair!"

He stops pacing and faces me.

"It might not be fair, but it's the truth," I say, locking eyes with him and holding his stare. In my peripheral vision, I notice Jimmy shifting uncomfortably in his chair. After a long silence, in which Finn seems torn, I ask: "Are you afraid?"

"I'm not afraid of anything," he says.

"Are you sure? Six hundred years and you've never even left the island. I had already been on adventures far from my home, and I was afraid to leave and set out for here."

"I said I'm not afraid."

"So you just plan to take the encryption key to your grave, whenever that is? Locked forever in your hand. Think about how many people you'll be responsible for killing, Finn. The number makes that skull rack down there seem like nothing."

Finn's face flushes red, his lips twitch. He looks like he's about to say something, but instead he storms to the door and jerks it open. He stops and looks back, his blue eyes burning.

"You'll have my answer in the morning, before you leave."

The door slams behind him.

I ease back onto the bed.

"That could have gone better."

"He'll do what's right," Jimmy says.

"You think so?"

"Yeah."

I turn my head and look at Jimmy, slouched in his chair, a bloody bandage on his ankle. "Did it hurt?"

"What?" he asks.

"The bite," I say.

"Nah. It jus' caught me with a little tooth while I's kickin'. I never even felt it at the time."

"What I wanna know is how you knocked on the sub loud enough for the professor to hear without any stones."

"Submarine," he corrects, with a sly smile. "I dove and got one off the bottom and used it to pound on the side."

"Pretty deep, though," I say.

"I've dove deeper."

"But the sharks?"

"I jus' ignored 'em."

"Jimmy, I don't know how to thank you."

"Thank me? You's the one saved my life."

I take a deep breath. "If I told myself the truth, I think I'd have traded places with you as soon as they put that helmet on my head. I was scared, Jimmy. Really scared."

"You was brave," he says. "Besides, it was my fault. My ego was wrapped up in winnin' those games. I shoulda listened to ya. I shoulda kept focused on findin' that encryption key."

"Does this mean you're coming back with me?"

Jimmy smiles, his eyes welling up. "If you still want me."

"Will you take the serum?"

"Does it really mean that much to you?" he asks.

"Yes," I say, my eyes welling up now too. "It does."

"Then I'll take it."

We look at one another for a solid minute or two, not even bothering to dry our eyes. Finally, I break the emotional silence: "Well, let's quit blubbering like a couple of babies and go roust up some food. Help me get up, will you? Maybe old Riley down there can whip us together some shark-fin soup."

The next morning, Finn is nowhere to be found.

Most of the guests who came for the games have stuck around, quietly gathering in groups on the terraces, as if they're not quite ready yet to let yesterday's excitement go. Some sit and repeat quiet prayers, others kneel, facing the Park Service crest on the submarine's sail, bowing their foreheads to touch the grass. The workmen disassemble the crane, apparently on Finn's orders, and light a bonfire from its timbers. Jimmy and I sit together on the castle steps, with Junior lying at our feet, and watch the black smoke rising into the gray, morning sky.

I haven't been on the submarine yet, but Jimmy's been back and forth a few times, testing out a raft that Finn had his workers make to float us past the sharks. Jimmy ran a line from the raft to the submarine's deck so we can pull ourselves out. Of course, the professor hasn't shown his face yet, still recoiling from the light, and, I suspect, more than just a little fearful of the islanders, who Jimmy said he referred to several times as savages.

The door behind us opens, and we both turn, hoping to see Finn. Instead, Bree steps out and sits between us on the steps, offering us a swig from her canteen of spiked tea. In a way, we both owe our lives to her: Jimmy for her teaching me a crash course in handball, me for her chasing down Jimmy and telling him what they were doing to me after I'd beaten him.

"I want to thank you two," she says.

"What for?" I ask.

"Giving me my life back. All I ever dreamed about before was winning the games to honor my family, so I never planned a life for myself. But now that Finn says they're over, I've got many years ahead to think about. It's like being reborn."

I hand her my reading slate that I had Jimmy retrieve from the submarine. "Here's something to keep you busy then."

"What's this?" she asks, looking it over.

"A gift," I say. "It's got about five hundred books in it. Let me show you. This button turns it on. Here's the library. Look. And the professor says the battery should be good for about five years. I thought maybe you could copy your favorites down on paper in that time, so they'll never be lost."

Bree throws her arms around my neck. "You're the best," she says. "Thank you, thank you, thank you." Then she turns and hugs Jimmy. "And you too, Jimmy. I'm gonna miss you."

None of us knows what else to say, so Bree sits between us, exploring her new electronic library while Jimmy and I watch as the strange scene plays out in front of the castle. Groups of people sitting on the lawns softly chanting and bowing toward the submarine. The workers standing around the burning crane, spitting their chew juice into the flames. The raft rocking in the waves, tied off to the seawall with a line.

After what seems like an eternity, the door opens again. But again, it's not Finn. Instead, Riley stands in the doorway and shakes his head. I stand and face him. "He's not coming?"

"I'm afraid not, sir," he replies. "But he wanted me to wish you safe travels. And to give you this."

Riley holds out the David's broken hand.

"But that's not—"

"I think you'll find it's what you need," Riley cuts me off.

I take it from his hands. It's much lighter than I remember it being, and it's not cold like marble should be. Jimmy steps up beside me and looks at it. "Thought ya said that wasn't it?"

"Let's just go," I say.

"Ya sure?"

"I'm sure."

Before we go, Riley reaches into his pocket and presents Jimmy the championship game ball. "Lord Finn wanted you to have this, sir." Then he bows and retreats back into the castle.

Jimmy slips the ball into his pocket, and we all walk down to the seawall steps with Junior following behind us. Jimmy steadies the raft as I step aboard. Then he turns and hugs Bree. When they part, he unties the shoreline and steps onto the raft.

"Come on, Junior," he calls. Junior stays put, sitting on the seawall steps. "Come on, boy. Hop aboard." Junior whimpers, turning his head to look back at the castle. Jimmy turns to me and frowns. "I think he wants to stay."

"Maybe he'll be happier here," I say.

Jimmy looks out toward the submarine, then back to the castle. When his eyes settle on Junior again, he looks sad.

"Come on, boy," he calls. "Hop on."

Junior whimpers again but doesn't move.

Jimmy steps off the raft and scoops Junior up and hugs him. Junior licks his face, his front paws hanging over Jimmy's shoulders, his rear legs hanging like a doll from Jimmy's arms.

"I'll keep an eye on him for you," Bree says.

After their long embrace, Jimmy sets Junior down again, steps onto the raft, and picks up the waterside line and pulls us toward the submarine. He doesn't look back. But I do.

Bree stands on the seawall steps watching us go. Junior sits at her feet watching, too. I think he might jump in and swim after us, but he doesn't. As they shrink into the distance, Junior yips twice, as if saying goodbye. Bree reaches down to pet him. I look at Jimmy and see that his eyes are wet. Or maybe it's just the cold wind coming off the water. But I doubt it.

We climb aboard the submarine and set the raft adrift.

"No turning back now, I guess."

"No," Jimmy mumbles. "No turnin' back."

Jimmy pauses at the hatch, as if he might look back, but he takes a deep breath and descends into the submarine without once turning around. I pause for one last look. The fire burns. The people mingle on the lawns, watching. Bree sits now on the steps, her arm around Junior, sitting next to her. Then I see Finn step from the castle door into the morning light. We stand looking at one another across the water. His tunic parts as he lifts his arm to wave goodbye, and even from this distance I can see the bloody, bandaged stump where his hand had been.

I hold his plaster-encased hand up for him to see, cradled in my palms with care, a small sign of our thanks for what he's parted with, then I carry it with me down into the submarine.

CHAPTER 23
What Have You Done?

"The fools went willingly to the sharks?"

"To appease their gods and protect the island," I answer.

"Nothing surprises me about people," the professor says, shaking his head. "I've been on this crazy Earth too long."

"I'm just glad you heard Jimmy's signal and surfaced."

"Yes," he replies. "As luck would have it, I had just woken from a dead sleep."

"You really had no idea that Radcliffe had a son?"

The professor shakes his head. "Of course, I didn't. But he always was a secretive man. I'm not surprised."

When we leave the Irish Sea and are once again in the deep Atlantic, the professor brings us down to a comfortable depth and sets our course for home. After our week on the island, I feel cramped and claustrophobic on the submarine. I wander around, looking for something to distract me, since I no longer have my reading slate. I open the submarine's specimen freezer and look at the hand, both fascinated and sickened by what's inside the plaster mold. I can't imagine hacking off my own hand. But I'm grateful for Finn's sacrifice.

"Hungry?" Jimmy asks, appearing in the doorway.

I shut the freezer. "Sure. Let's see what odd mix of spices you've cooked up this time."

A strange depression settles over our journey. All three of us make half-hearted attempts at conversation with each other, but nothing seems to stick. The professor focuses on getting us home, constantly monitoring our speed and depth, taking short naps at the controls but never really sleeping. Without Junior around to keep him company, Jimmy spends hours in his bunk, bouncing the ball that Finn gave him against the wall. I know he already misses the island and the excitement of the games. And Bree, too. Although, I'm sure he misses Junior the most. I begin to feel bad for having pressured him to come back with me. And I have plenty of time to feel bad because the painful scabs on my chest keep me awake at night.

In the middle of the second night, I stretch the wrong way in my bunk, and the scabs crack and ooze blood. I get up and take a warm shower to loosen them. It helps, although I have to grit my teeth to suffer the stinging pain. After my shower, I stand in front of the tiny bathroom mirror and look at my chest and the permanent reminder of how close I came to death. Not to mention a symbol of how I'm connected to this mess.

I remember when I first met Jimmy's family, that night around their campfire when he convinced them to take me in. He told me about the Park Service for the first time that night. And I remember when I asked him who the Park Service was, he said that they were me because their crest was on my zipsuit. And now I've got that same emblem carved on my chest.

The afternoon of our third day at sea, I ask the professor to surface so I can go topside and breathe some fresh air.

"Better to stay submerged," he says.

"Come on," I beg. "Please. Just for a couple of hours."

He shakes his head. "I said no."

I'm not happy with his answer, so I enlist Jimmy's help to persuade him. We sit in the control room, throwing Jimmy's ball back and forth over the professor's head, while loudly talking about how great it would be to go outside. He finally relents and blows the water from the ballasts, bringing us up. We open the hatch and climb out into the fresh air and blue sky of late afternoon.

"This is more like it," I say.

We sit across from one another on the deck and bounce the ball back and forth, playing catch. A cool breeze tickles my hair; the sun warms my cheeks. A long time passes without a word between us, just the sound of the bouncing ball and the water sliding by. As the sun drops toward the horizon, it looks like an orange halo around Jimmy's head.

"I can hardly see the ball with that sun in my eyes."

"Here we jus' started playin'," Jimmy says, "and yer makin' excuses already."

"Very funny," I say. "How's your leg?"

He looks at the bandage on his ankle. "Gettin' better."

"Not the shark bite," I correct. "I meant your scar there on your thigh. Where I hit you with the ball."

"It's all right," he says. "It still aches a little."

"I'm really sorry."

"Sorry? Ya done it to save my life. And I'm glad for it, too. But jus' so ya know, you never coulda beat me playin' fair."

"Oh, you don't think so?"

"I know so," he says, laughing. "Plus, you was fresh."

"If you say so," I laugh. A few bounces later, I add, "Maybe we can build a court when we get back and have a little re-match."

"Maybe we will," Jimmy says, bouncing the ball back.

The sun finally gives up the sky and drops into the ocean.

Jimmy sits silhouetted against it, reminding me of the first time I saw him crouched on that coral rock. We've been through a lot together. More than a lot. We've seen our parents die. We've nearly died ourselves. We've burned Eden, overthrown Dr. Radcliffe, and travelled across the sea to solve a mystery. All we have left to do now is get back and stop the drones and free my people. Then it's nothing but peaceful days ahead.

Jimmy must be thinking the same thing, because he asks, "What are ya gonna do when we get back?"

"Get that encryption key and stop the drones."

"I meant after that," he says.

"Well, I haven't thought about it much, really. I guess once my people are free, they can figure out what to do."

"But are you gonna stay on, at the lake or wherever?"

"What are you going to do?" I ask, answering his question with a question.

"I'd like to go find somewhere peaceful in the woods," he says. "Some place quiet to make a home, ya know? There's lots of land out there, and a man could make an easy livin' if there ain't no drones to worry about no more."

"That sounds nice."

"Yeah," he says. "I jus' wish I had Junior to share it with. But I think he finally found his home on the island."

"He sure did think he was a deerhound, didn't he?"

Jimmy laughs. "It was somethin', him keepin' up with 'em on that hunt. I ain't too manly to say I miss him already. It was nice always havin' him around for company."

"Maybe I'll come keep you company instead?"

"Come where?" he asks.

"Your home in the woods," I say. "If I'm invited—?"

"What about Hannah?"

"I don't know," I sigh, bouncing the ball back. "I've sure got some things to sort out with her."

"Maybe cut her some slack," he suggests.

"Yeah, maybe. As long as she has that serum for you."

Jimmy nods, but doesn't say anything. We bounce the ball for a while without talking. The last crescent of orange sun slips beneath the waves, and the cloudless western sky holds little of its light. Jimmy and the ball fade to just shadows.

"We better quit before your ball goes overboard."

"Okay," Jimmy says. "but let's not go in jus' yet. It's nice out here. I feel good for the first time in a long time."

"Me too," I say. "I feel happy."

We lie on our backs and watch the stars appear as the sky fades from blue toward black. I guess they're always there, the stars, burning in timeless space. It's just that you can't see them when something brighter gets in the way. It's peaceful lying next to Jimmy—the smell of cool saltwater air, the splash of the submarine cutting through the gentle waves. I think about how lucky I am to have met Jimmy and to have him as my friend. I'll never know how, of all the places in this world I might have ended up, I ended up with him. It reminds me of something the professor said about a cosmic destiny playing out again and again. If that means I get to lie here like this for all time, looking up at the stars with my best friend, then count me in. Then. Now. Forever.

A burst of white light flashes in the sky.

Light so bright that I shut my eyes to protect them and can see the red blood vessels in my eyelids.

When the initial flash fades, we both bolt upright and look

toward the northeast, where a fireball glows on the horizon. I'd almost think it was the sunrise if the sun hadn't just set in the west. The fireball slowly burns out, as if being extinguished by the waves, but the eastern sky glows with an aurora of orange light that spreads its wavering fingers like an electric dome over the dark ocean behind us.

"It's beautiful," Jimmy says. "What is it?"

"I have no idea."

But the second I say it, I do have an idea. A terrible idea. An idea that makes me leap to my feet and race for the hatch. I rush down the ladder, run along the passageway, and throw open the torpedo room door—

It's gone. The antimatter is gone.

Before I know what I'm even doing, I've got ahold of the professor's hair with both hands and I'm slamming his head against the submarine controls as Jimmy tries to pull me away.

"What have you done!" I shout, slamming his head again. "What have you done, you sick bastard! Tell me!"

Jimmy successfully tears me away from the professor and pushes me against the wall and holds me there.

"Hey, now," he says. "Settle down. What's goin' on here?"

"The antimatter's gone."

"The what?"

"Ask him," I say, pointing.

Jimmy turns to the professor. "What's he talkin' 'bout?"

"I should never have let you go up," the professor says, almost mumbling to himself. "Stupid, stupid, stupid."

"Tell him what you did, you bastard. Tell him!" I scream it so loud the professor startles and looks up at us again. He's never seemed more pathetic than now, with his hair a mess and a bruise already purpling on his forehead.

Jimmy releases me and turns to the professor, his curiosity overcoming his desire to restrain me. "What'd ya do?"

"It doesn't even matter now," the professor says, turning to face the controls again. "Let's just get back."

"I'll tell you what he did," I say. "He left that antimatter back there in the water. Just offshore. At the Isle of Man. Then he set it to detonate when we were safe away."

"Detonate?" Jimmy asks. "Like a bomb?"

"Like much more than a bomb. The energy released by that much antimatter? I can't—I mean—poof! I'm guessing the island isn't even there any longer. Is it, Professor?"

Jimmy looks confused. "Not even there?"

"Tell him, Professor."

"We thought it was an intelligent thing to do," he answers, finally. "The containment device was failing. It couldn't be kept any longer at the Foundation. So why not use it?"

He flinches as I step toward him.

"You said we," I say.

"Excuse me?"

"Just a second ago," I reply. "You said: 'We thought it was an intelligent thing to do.'"

"Yes," he says. "We did."

"Who's we?"

"Myself and Hannah, of course."

"You mean you and Hannah planned this?"

He laughs nervously, shifting in his chair. "I'm just an old man. I don't make those kinds of decisions."

"But there was people there," Jimmy says. "Lots of 'em."

"I know," the professor replies. "That's why the island had

to be destroyed. Don't you see?"

"You bastard!"

I grab him by the neck and lift him off his chair and squeeze with everything I have. I'm going to kill him, and it's surprisingly easy. His face turns red, then blue. His eyes bulge, panic in his stare, his quivering lips turning pale.

Jimmy lays a hand on my shoulder. "That's enough now," he says. "We ain't like him."

I drop the professor, and he falls to the floor, clutching his neck and gasping for air.

When he's recovered enough to speak, he looks up at me with tears in his eyes and says: "You didn't really think we would abandon the cause just because a couple of teenagers decided that they like humans after all, did you?"

I shake my head, disgusted. "You knew before we even left what we'd find on that island, didn't you?"

The professor smirks, showing a side of himself I haven't seen before. Something evil. "Of course I did. Every one of us knew what a philandering fool Radcliffe was. And his guilty conscience put the entire mission at risk. Protect the island. Ha! Love made Robert soft. He never should have let those people live. And to breed like they did? You saw yourself how they'd multiplied already. Imagine what they'd do if they made it to the mainland. Ever seen a goldfish get a bigger bowl? Well, of course you haven't, but you get the idea. We had no choice. They were far too numerous already to take out with drones." When he finishes his speech, he stares up at us from the floor.

"So why even bring Jimmy and me along if you planned to blow the island up anyway?" I demand.

"To get the encryption key," he says. "And you did it. Just

like we knew you would."

"How do you even know the key's in there?"

"David's hand is in there, isn't it?"

"Yeah. So?"

"The key is sequenced from his DNA. Silly old Radcliffe was even sentimental in his safeguards."

"You knew it was him, and you didn't tell us?"

The professor shrugs a shoulder. "We didn't know he'd be calling himself Finn. Or that the David was there to confuse things. But Hannah said you'd get it. And she was right."

"And Hannah knew all this then?" I ask.

"I think I've said enough."

"If she knew, she's just as evil as you are."

"I'm proud of Hannah," he says.

"For what?" I ask. "Sending us in blind to nearly get killed? For murdering her own brother?"

"That's one way to put it," he says. "But I'd say for having the courage to rise above sentimentality and do what's right."

"Right for who?"

"For the planet, of course."

"You make me sick."

"Believe me," he says, half sitting up, "I make me sick too. I am human after all, you know."

The entire time we're talking, Jimmy stands looking down at the professor with his head cocked to the side and a strange look in his eyes. As if he's still trying to process something said a long time ago. I can almost see the questions running through his mind. When he finally speaks, he asks the professor, "What about Bree? What about Junior?"

"They're gone," the professor says.

"Whataya mean they're gone?"

I reach for Jimmy's shoulder to console him, but he pulls away and steps closer to the professor, glaring down at him.

"I asked you somethin'," he says.

"And I answered," the professor replies. "They're gone. Got it? Incinerated. Vaporized. Dead. As if they'd never been. But don't worry yourself, kid—they didn't feel a thing."

Jimmy steps up and kicks the professor's teeth in with the heel of his bare foot. The professor's eyes go cross with pain, and he falls back and lies on his side, moaning with his mangled mouth open and blood gushing out. Jimmy raises his foot to stomp him again, but I grab his arms and hold him back.

"You were right, Jimmy," I say, my voice feeble now that the initial anger is subsiding. "We're nothing like them. Besides, we need his help to get us back. We'll deal with him later."

"What about Hannah?" Jimmy asks.

"Her too."

The sun rises, just like any other day.

The cloud of debris in the eastern sky paints the sunrise in beautiful shades of purple and orange. It looks as though we've sailed straight out from heaven. It feels as though we've sailed straight into hell. I try to imagine what it looks like now, back there, with the island gone. You could probably sail right over it and never even know there'd been an island there. It turns me ill to think of all those people dead. Just like that. It makes me so sick that my mind won't even let me quite believe it yet.

We couldn't get another word out of the professor last night after his confession, and I have no idea how much of this was Hannah's idea and how much of it was his. But I plan to make damn sure they both answer for it when we return.

I can't imagine feeling more betrayed. I guess I never knew Hannah at all. Not the real Hannah anyway. The manipulation, the lies, the outright evil of sending Jimmy and me onto that island to possibly lose our lives. And all for what? They never really planned on stopping the drones—they just want control of them again. And they don't want to free my people from Holocene II—they used this trip to deliver a bomb that wiped out the few people who were living peacefully on the surface.

It's clear to see what happened now, looking back. I think about all those hours Hannah spent alone with the professor—in the command center and in the scientists' apartments. The whole time she must have been planning this with him right behind our backs. Then the last minute show she acted out on the dock the day we left. The fake emotions.

"Someone needs to be here for the people," she said. And the professor rushing us off like he did. What lies! Nothing has prepared me to accept what I now know Hannah is: a lying murderer who used me.

I feel hatred.

I feel rage.

I feel sad.

But mostly, I just feel over my head.

A dark speck catches my eye, black against the sun on the eastern horizon. I squint to get a better view through the glare. I could almost swear I see the silhouette of a warship plying the waters on its silent hunt for humans to slaughter.

When I return inside to the submarine control room, I find Jimmy right where I left him—guarding the professor with his knife. His eyes are focused like a laser beam on the back of the professor's head, and I see so much rage twitching beneath his determined features that I'm nervous to even rouse him from his vigil. I set aside my fear and lay a hand on Jimmy's shoulder.

"Why don't you go rest," I suggest. "I'll watch him."

I expect Jimmy to protest, but he rises and hands me the knife and heads off toward the bunkroom without a word.

A long time passes as I stand watch over the professor. He consults his charts and works the controls, easy and calm, as if nothing had transpired between us at all. I look at his head of wild, white hair and wonder what disease infects a brain that could do what he and Hannah have done. What genetic trait or youthful trauma turns a man or woman's self-righteous desire to do good into the megalomania of a mass murderer?

Maybe humans are the problem. Some humans, anyway. At least a person can see a shark's teeth. They don't hide their intentions. And they don't kill because they can kill, they kill because they need to survive. And what's a drone except an extension of the human brain? A mechanical hand of sorts. I'm reminded of something Finn said to us about the hand being indifferent as it does the bidding of the mind. I was once afraid of drones. A few days ago, I was afraid of sharks. But the only thing that I'm afraid of now is the 1,400 grams of gray matter firing inside two human skulls. The professor's. And Hannah's.

I have no idea what we'll discover when we finally get back to the Foundation, but it worries me more than a little that the professor seems happy to take us there. Their scheme to send Jimmy and me blind onto the Isle of Man was so well thought out that I can't imagine they planned nothing for our return.

As if reading my thoughts, the professor turns and flashes me a bloody, toothless grin. He doesn't say anything, but when he turns away again, I tighten my grip on Jimmy's knife.

THE END *of* BOOK TWO

About the Author

Ryan Winfield is the *New York Times* best-selling author of *Jane's Melody*, *South of Bixby Bridge*, and *The Park Service* trilogy.

For more information go to:
www.RyanWinfield.com

Made in the USA
Lexington, KY
17 September 2018